ERICA DRAGO IN
HEART OF THE ASSASSIN

Donna Tellum

ISBN # 978-0-615-89721-9

Printed In the United States of America

ACKNOWLEDGMENTS

Thanks to those who have helped take *Heart of the Assassin* from a germ of an idea to finished book. To Tom for the confidence in me. My brilliant editor, Weston, first readers, Monica, Cynthia and Kennetha. Their input in the writing of this book, is greatly appreciated. To all my friends and family who have supported me throughout this incredible journey. Thank you Kiff Scholl, for your outstanding cover design. None of this would have been possible without all of your love and support.

ERICA DRAGO IN
HEART OF THE ASSASSIN

1

Circling Her Prey

CONGRESSMAN WILTON BENNETT, the handsome and wickedly charming head of the Foreign Energies Committee, had a reputation for never being late to a meeting. His impeccable record on the Hill is that of legend. One of the most respected legislators from both sides of the aisle, a crusader for family values his popularity amongst both parties, unprecedented. His future had all the earmarks of political greatness. However, after tonight, Wilton Bennett would be known as the late congressman.

Erica Drago prepared herself in a hotel room that overlooked the Potomac River. She slipped on a little, black dress that accentuated every curve of her slender athletic body. Applying her makeup in the mirror, Erica's bright blue, vibrant eyes stared back at her. These eyes hid a pain that would never be comforted, a hurt that could never be soothed. Her complexion, pale and angelic as smooth as bone china had a radiant glow. Red lipstick highlighted her generous mouth. Erica looked at herself in the mirror and smiled with such radiance that a simple look would halt the advance of a thousand armies. She pulled her dark, shoulder-length hair back with both hands and skillfully fitted a red-haired wig over her dark brown locks. The transformation completed. Tonight Erica would be Samantha Kendall, a Political Science teacher at a small college in the Midwest who had established a casual acquaintanceship with the congressman.

The Crown Plaza Ballroom a bustle of activity; red, white and blue bunting hung from the ceiling encircling the plush carpeted gold, columned room reserved for this political fundraiser. Waiters in starched white shirts, black bowties, and crisply pressed black slacks glided around the massive space offering glasses of champagne and hors d'oeuvres to the smartly dressed dignitaries from silver serving trays.

Congressman Bennett, dressed in a perfectly tailored navy blue suit, accented exquisitely with a red and blue striped power tie, chatted with a group of older women constituents, each hanging on his every word. Bennett charmingly excused himself when he heard his cellphone ring and trotted off to a nearby cloakroom to give him some privacy.

"How are you this evening, Mr. Ratko?" Bennett said as he answered the call.

"I've been expecting a call from you," replied the voice on the other end of the line.

"Yes. I've been a bit busy the last few days, but . . ." Bennett stopped and peered over his shoulder to be confident his conversation could not be overheard. "I received confirmation of the deposit into my Cayman Island account. Tomorrow morning I will make the necessary arrangements. Global Energies will be the only company allowed to make a bid on the government contract. Congratulations, Mr. Ratko, you've just secured a five-billion-dollar deal."

Bennett clicked off his cellphone and slid back into the ballroom, smiling and nodding at well-wishers as he lifted a glass of champagne from the tray of a passing waiter.

Erica sauntered into the banquet room in her little black dress, wearing a simple string of pearls around her graceful neck. She caught sight of Wilton Bennett across the vast room and swam through the dense crowd like a shark circling its prey.

Erica smiled and said as she approached Bennett. "You look dashing, Congressman."

"Ah, Miss Kendall."

"Please, Congressman, call me Samantha."

"Well then, you must call me Wil."

"Wil," she repeated in a very seductive, breathy voice, making the congressman a little aroused. "I must tell you, my time in Washington will be a great help to my poli-sci lectures next semester. Experiencing the workings of government first hand is so much more valuable than studying it in books." Erica couldn't be sexier if she tried. She sold charm, and Bennett was buying.

"I always make time for anyone willing to learn about the ins and outs of Washington."

"Well, Congressman, I couldn't be more willing."

"Please, call me Wil," Bennett stated again as he leaned closer and filled his nostrils with her intoxicating scent. "And what are you wearing? You smell good enough to eat."

"It's called Midnight Desire, Wil." Erica wet her lips as she hung on to the "L" in his name.

"And it's working quite well. Let's say we go back to your room at midnight and have a little desire of our own."

"Aren't you the naughty little congressman, but I don't think that would be a good idea."

Bennett noticeably disappointed, frowned.

"The thing is, hotels are so cliché and thin walled, wouldn't you say? It would be so much more discreet if we knew someone with an apartment in D.C. where we could engage in a real uninterrupted conversation about those 'ins and outs' of politics." She bit her lower lip.

"Well, Samantha, it just so happens that I do know someone with an apartment."

Bennett pulled out a pen and a business card, wrote down an address, and handed the card to Erica.

"Say, eleven thirty?" An evil glint flashed behind his dark eyes.

"Perfect. Can't wait," Erica whispered with a smile as she licked her lips.

Erica drove a rental car through the narrow roads, circling a dark, residential neighborhood in the Georgetown area. A low-lying fog cast a pall over the tree-lined streets. Erica drove by the congressman's townhouse twice before parking a block away. She took a quick survey of the quiet neighborhood, pulled out a laptop, and began to type. On the screen appeared a schematic of the neighborhood's power grid. Erica typed in an access code, and in an instant, a graphic of a power switch appeared on the screen. She clicked on it, and just that quick the block plunged into an unholy, pitch-black darkness. She closed the laptop and exited her car into the ominously quiet street.

Erica had changed into a simple, white blouse and a plaid, schoolgirl skirt. She pulled a tan London Fog trench coat from the backseat and put it on along with a floppy, large-brimmed hat. She walked up to Bennett's brownstone and took a 360-degree survey before she proceeded further. The street deathly quiet for at this hour most of the neighborhood would be asleep.

Erica knocked loudly on the front door. She heard the sound of a man's footsteps as they approached. A latch pulled back with a metallic click. The door opened a quarter of the way, and Bennett's head appeared from behind it. Seeing Erica, he invited her in with a wave. Bennett had removed his coat, and his tie loosened, a brandy clutched in his hand, a broad smile on his face.

"I've been ringing your doorbell for a couple of minutes. I thought you stood me up."

"Sorry. That's so weird, but the power went out, and I've been running around lighting candles."

Erica entered the house and walked into the living room. Candles illuminated the perfectly neat living space, complete with a floor-to-ceiling bookshelf on the far wall. The decor exuded masculinity and power. A red leather couch and love seat in the center of the room gave the space an almost erotic feel. Next to the couch, an expensive Tiffany lamp rested on a small oak table. So this is the place where Bennett preys on young, innocent girls, Erica thought to herself as she turned to the congressman.

"Aren't you going to take my coat?" she asked.

"Oh, I'm so sorry, yes. Let me get that."

Erica unbuttoned her coat and Bennett froze, as she revealed her little schoolgirl outfit. Erica held out her coat and hat to Bennett. Leering, he seized the items from her.

"You changed," he said as he threw her coat and hat on the nearest chair.

"You said you wanted to teach me about the ins and outs of Washington, so I came prepared for class," Erica cooed.

"Can I get you a drink first?"

"A drink would be lovely," she expressed as she set her purse on the lamp table behind her next to the love seat. Bennett strolled to the far end of the room, where a mahogany wet bar fully stocked with only top-shelf alcoholic beverages stood.

"What's your poison?"

"Scotch. Neat. I'm just going to have so many wonderful stories to tell the faculty when I get back to school."

Bennett crossed the room with two drinks in his hands and stopped, centering himself in front of Erica.

"You can cut the act. I know what's going on," he alleged as he offered her the scotch.

Erica, slightly thrown off her game, held her breath.

"I've done some inquiring, and I know you're not who you say you are. I've found you out," Bennett proclaimed confidently.

Erica steeled herself; her mind raced. Where did I mess up? What does he know? A trapped feeling overcame her. She could feel the blood rushing through her veins. Suddenly the temperature in the room seemed to increase exponentially. Then in a split second, she took a deep breath, remembering her training. She took the drink and downed it, then presented her empty glass to Bennett.

As Bennett strolled back to the bar, Erica calmly reached behind her and put her hand directly into her open purse without looking, slipped her hand in and wrapped her fingers around a small automatic pistol.

Erica thought to herself that all her planning had gone to shit. I can't believe I'm going to have to shoot this fucker now and abandon my perfect plan. She slowly started to remove the gun from her purse.

Bennett returned to where Erica had been standing and centered himself again in front of her.

"Just what do you think you've found out, Wil?"

Bennett stared at Erica intensely, waiting for her to crack, to come clean. He took a sip of his bourbon, smiled slightly, and offered Erica her glass.

"You're not a Political Science teacher. I'm not sure if you've even taken a Political Science class. I know what you're after," Bennett remarked knowingly.

Erica had taken the gun out of the purse, concealing it behind her back.

"Is that so?"

"You're a reporter. You must think I'm stupid."

Erica carefully slid the gun back into her purse.

"You're wrong there. I don't think you're stupid at all. You're a very intelligent man, and I'm the stupid one for thinking I could pull one over on you. Yes, I'm a reporter." Erica accepted the drink from Bennett, took a sip, then turned to the table behind her and set her glass down.

"You want to get the inside scoop on the energy deal with China, right?

Erica nodded. "Yes, you're right, again. But how do you suppose I could get to you if I were just another reporter looking for an exclusive?"

"That's where you're wrong. You're not just another reporter."

Erica smiled. Her eyes searched the floor.

"Just how did you think you'd get the information anyway?" Bennett inquired.

Sheepishly, Erica explained, "Men tend to reveal a lot of things after a night of hot sex with a woman who knows what she's doing."

"And you know what you're doing?"

"Know it. I wrote the book."

An oily smile curled Bennett's lip as he eyeballed Erica's ample cleavage. Erica reached out and took a firm grip of Bennett's tie. She pulled him into her and planted a wet kiss square on his lips, sliding her hand down the front of his pants, eliciting a low moan from deep within him.

"You did write the book, didn't you?" he said with a glint in his eye.

"Every chapter," Erica confessed seductively.

Erica took the drink from Bennett's hand and set the glass on the table next to her purse. With his hands free, Bennett hurriedly explored Erica's body, squeezing her ample breasts and stroking her taut ass.

It's almost like he doesn't know where to start, thought Erica. "Easy there cowboy! No need to rush."

Erica gave Bennett a gentle shove, and he backed away from her. She seductively turned to the table where she had set her purse and their drinks. Pulling out a small, plastic vile, she wiggled it in front of Bennett's face.

"It's always better when I gets a little high," she quipped in a playful tone.

"I'm fine with the bourbon,' Bennett uttered, not taking his eyes off her for a second.

Erica unhooked her bra and seductively slid the straps down her shoulders. She held the bra cups over her breast as she teased Bennett with anticipation.

"Oh my god, you're killing me," Bennett blurted with a certain amount of foreshadowing of things to come.

Erica let the bra drop to the floor, revealing her spectacular mounds. Sensually, she ran her fingers around her areolas until her nipples stood at attention. The glow of the candlelight reflecting off Erica's creamy, naked flesh brought Bennett to a point where he just couldn't take it anymore. He hurriedly pulled off his pants, nearly falling down in the process, his eyes still fixed on her.

Erica took the vile and deposited some of the cocaine on her left breast. She held her breast up with her hand and invited Bennett to try some. Bennett pounced up to her like a ravenous dog.

"My god, they're incredible."

Bennett cupped his hand under her breast and buried his face in her cleavage. He enthusiastically snorted the cocaine then began licking the remnants of the drug off her body. Erica cupped her hands on Bennett's cheeks and raised his head to eye level.

"Here's to the ins and outs of politics," Erica said with a wink.

"You're something else."

She placed her arms around Bennett's neck; he wrapped his arms around her waist sliding his left hand down and around her firm butt. Erica untied his tie and unbuttoned his shirt. He kissed her neck as he slid his hands up to her breasts. Bennett had a huge grin on his face, but suddenly the grin turned into a quizzical look. Something seemed odd. Bennett clutched at his chest, then gasped, struggling to breathe.

"I can't breathe for some reason."

"You're having what will look like a massive heart attack to the coroner," Erica replied coldly.

"Wha . . . What did you say?" Bennett choked, gasping for air.

"You are having a heart attack, dear!" Erica repeated as if she were ordering another drink.

"How do you know that?"

"Remember Tina Reynolds?"

"What the fuck does that little tramp have to do with anything? Call 9-1-1 goddamn it!"

"Before she disappeared, Tina met with her older half-sister, Claire Markert. You remember Claire?"

"Fuck you. Help me," Bennett demanded as he clutched his chest.

Weakening by the second, Bennett dropped to his knees.

"You and Tina started an affair a couple of months after she started interning at your office. You were extremely discreet, seeing that you're the poster child of family values and the front-runner as the next resident of the White House. Follow my drift?"

Erica bent down and picked up her bra.

"You couldn't be connected in any way with infidelity by rumor or innuendo, especially if there was a child involved. Tina wanted to keep the baby. You definitely couldn't have that," Erica stated as she put on her bra.

Bennett struggled to get to his feet.

"You're the anti-abortion guy. How would that look to your constituents if it got out you made your mistress get an abortion? So you did the next best thing."

Erica moved to him and with a shove of her foot, pushed him back to the floor.

"You had Tina and the baby murdered," Erica pronounced with absolute certainty.

Bennett's breathing became more labored, and he groaned in pain.

"Oh, does it hurt, you bastard? Did Tina suffer when you killed her, or did you have someone else do it for you like the fucking piece of shit coward you are?" Erica coldly uttered. "Tina disappeared, and Claire went to the authorities, but with your connections, her accusations fell on deaf ears. You even had your people contrive a phony psychiatric file indicating Claire had hallucinated the molestation by her since-dead stepfather. She spent the next six months in a mental institution."

Erica picked up her blouse from the floor and put it on. "Then came the stabbing. By the time Claire got out, she was out of her mind with grief, and she attacked you with a knife. Once the press got a hold of her mental records, conveniently provided by an unnamed source, they painted her to be basically, a bat-shit crazy woman who attacked you for your pro-life beliefs. Claire got arrested and sent to prison for attempted murder. You were free and clear," Erica said as she collected the drinking glasses and placed them in her purse.

"Who . . . are . . . you?" Bennett asked, struggling to speak.

"Your worst nightmare, you sick bastard." Erica spit the words out with the venom of a viper.

"Okay, what do you want from me?" Bennett blurted, hearing enough. "You want a confession? I'll confess; just call me a doctor, first." Bennett groaned as the pain in his chest increased.

"Okay, you're a doctor," she said, laughing.

"You bitch! You'll never get away with this." Bennett's voice had been reduced to only a strained whisper.

"I've already gotten away with it. I don't need a confession, asshole. The world will be better off when you're gone, and that will be in about thirty more seconds."

Erica went to the chair in the corner and picked up her coat and hat. Bennett groaned and attempted to drag himself to the lamp table where his cellphone rested. He managed to get himself up onto a wobbly knee. He steadied himself on the arm of the loveseat just a few steps away from the table and slowly rose to a standing position. As he took two steps toward the table, Erica stuck out her foot and tripped him, sending him crashing to the floor. Bennett struggled to push himself up, but he had barely enough energy to breath and collapsed, gasping for life-giving air.

Erica surveyed the apartment. Satisfied that she had collected all her belongings, she strutted to the front door, slipped on a pair of leather gloves, turned the doorknob, and opened the door. Bennett, eyes wide open, lay dead on the floor. Erica examined the apartment one last time; the glow of the candles gave Bennett's former living quarters an almost cathedral like feel. She twisted the lock on the knob and stepped into the cold, dark night, shutting the door behind her.

Erica strolled down the dark street of the quiet neighborhood. Only the sound of light traffic could be heard off in the distance. She stopped as she reached her car. Quickly got in, opened her laptop and typed in a code. In a matter of seconds the power to the neighborhood came back on and all returned to normal, no one the wiser.

2

I want Jason Brent dead!

THE FLAGS of several European nations, as well as the Stars and Stripes, snapped in the wind in front of a pricey, downtown Los Angeles office building. A huge chrome block set in granite let anyone know within a two-mile radius that this is the home of Global Energies International. The chrome monolith reflected the bright sun, blinding anyone who tried to look at it directly. The 110-story structure that stretched into the sky was a monument to the greed and opulence of today's society. To some, it's just an eyesore, but to others it's a symbol of a future society void of humanity.

A day just like any other with businessmen and women crowding the streets. An African American homeless man, who looked to be elderly but actually in his mid-thirties, hustled the morning pedestrian traffic for spare change, protectively holding onto his shopping trolley full of aluminum cans and various other broken and dirty items. He dressed in dirty jeans and a U.S. Army field jacket with the name Johnson above his left pocket. His hair, ratty and speckled with debris from god only knows what. The Global employees stepped around him without a trace of acknowledgement.

In his penthouse office, Zubin Ratko rocked back and forth in his massive, leather chair as he gazed out the window that overlooked the entire Hollywood basin, deep in thought. Zubin Ratko, the CEO of Global. An imposing man his shocking white hair, testimony to his sixty-eight years on this earth; even though he would look a decade younger if he had his mane colored. Fit and tanned, Ratko reeked of authority. When he walked into a room, he commanded attention. He elicited fear with just a look; even strong men have crumbled under his stare. Ratko ruled his empire with an iron hand where mistakes were punished severely. Global's golden rule, one strike and you're out. Zubin, always willing to take risks to get what he wanted, but these risks were calculated and the odds of success were constantly in his favor. His dark brown eyes hid something more sinister than just the determination of a ruthless businessman. Be it innocent children, mothers, or grandmothers, Zubin would not let anyone impede his efforts to reach his goals. In his mind he wasn't just above the law, he made the laws suit his needs.

Zubin spun his chair around to face David Edison, Zubin's right-hand man, ruggedly handsome and approximately forty years of age. David had been with Zubin long enough to know to sit patiently and allow his superior to mull over his next move. Dark haired with just a touch of gray at the temples and cold steely blue eyes, David carried himself with the confidence of a man who knew where all the bodies were buried . . . because he dug the cold dark graves.

"You've read this shit?" Ratko asked, waving a folded newspaper at Edison.

"I've read it," Edison responded without emotion.

"He's connected us with the rig explosion."

"It's only speculation," Edison interjected.

"This has to be perfect." Ratko leaned forward to emphasize his point. "Perfect."

"I understand."

"He's getting information from someone," Ratko insisted.

"I'm working on it."

"Get me results. If he connects us with that operation on the Serbian border, a deeper investigation will be imminent."

Edison shook his head in agreement. "We're taking an awful risk here."

"I don't care about the risk. The congressman's death is going to cost us billions. We can't afford to let Brent dig any deeper. This must look like an accident-no trace of foul play. Just one of those crazy things that can happen to anybody."

Edison flipped through some papers that he had on his lap.

"He's too young for a heart attack. He's in perfect health and works out religiously."

"Get someone who's not connected to us. And get it done quickly. Go outside the normal channels. I don't care what the cost."

"I've a name—comes from a reliable contact and highly recommended."

Zubin looked Edison straight in the eye. "I want Jason Brent dead!"

Jason Brent, an impressive looking man in his mid-thirties with a constant five-o'clock shadow and a dazzling smile, indeed handsome. He had an unmistakable air of worldliness and a childish playfulness that made him irresistible to women of all ages. Expressive dark eyes, broad shoulders, and a square jaw rounded out his movie-heartthrob looks. The kind of man who could attract women to him, as a Bloomingdale's 75 percent-off Manolo Blahniks sale can on a Tuesday afternoon.

He knocked on the door of the penthouse suite of the Saint Bonaventure Hotel. When the door opened, standing before him, the stunningly attractive Jennifer Carbone. Jennifer, a long-legged beauty with dark hair down to the middle of her back, had heaving breasts that could beckon a man at will. Dark brown eyes and a clear, bright face rounded out this classic beauty of the girl next door turned Miss America. Confident and completely sure of every move she made, Jennifer was Jason's editor and best friend with benefits.

She stayed single by choice. If asked why, she simply replied, "I don't need a man to complete me, not even Tom Cruise." Jennifer, talking on her cellphone, motioned Jason in and pointed to the fully stocked bar.

"I could use a drink," Jason mumbled.

He strode to the wet bar along the wall next to the windows. Outside of the hotel, the sun hung low on the horizon, painting the sky a pale shade of purple. He fixed himself a stiff drink. "You want one?"

"Please. Make it strong," Jennifer said in a hushed voice while covering the phone.

A moment later, she pressed a button on her phone with her thumb, ending the call, and tossed it gently on the overstuffed couch as she floated over to Jason. He handed her the drink as she exhaled the pent-up tension she had been holding onto.

"It's been one of those days," Jennifer remarked as she took a long draw on the drink, letting the liquid slide down her throat. "So, how's the Global Energies investigation coming?"

"Slower than I'd like. I don't have enough information to connect all the dots that make any sense yet."

"This story is huge, Jason, but it's dangerous. You could win a Pulitzer, but you could also wind up dead," she said as she slipped her arms around Jason's neck.

"Dead? Oh, Jennifer, you're always so damn melodramatic!" He laughed.

Jennifer planted a wet kiss on him and grabbed his firm ass. "I'm serious. There's a lot more here than meets the eye."

Jennifer took another sip of her cocktail.

"So you do care about me?" he quipped with a shit-eating grin.

"Of course I do. If anything ever happened to you, I'd be out of business."

"All I am is a meal ticket to you? A piece of meat?"

"A grade 'A' prime choice piece of meat to be accurate."

"I love it when you talk dirty."

"I think it's time we got down to business. I have some input for you."

"I got something to input you!" Jason wryly smiled and wrapped his arms around her slim waist.

They kissed passionately. Jennifer tried to push Jason away, but he held on tight.

"Jason! I need to talk to you."

"We can talk later," Jason said in a husky voice, running his hands down and cupping them over her well-toned butt.

Jason covered her mouth with his, groping and removing her blouse. Their lips separated, and Jason kissed the side of her neck, moving his lips up, caressing her ear with his tongue. A rush of hot blood surged through Jennifer's body, culminating between her thighs. She unbuttoned his shirt down to his waist. As she stroked Jason's chest, she could feel his heart pounding like a jackhammer. He pressed up against her, causing her to moan softly. Jason's lips continued to explore her neck. Sliding his tongue across her throat sent chills down her spine. She moaned louder. Jason's mouth roamed up the other side of her neck and gently bit her earlobe, causing her to let out a slight squeal. Jennifer didn't know how much more she could take. She wanted him now!

"Take me!"

Jason ripped her bra apart from the front, and her breasts bounced out like two ripe melons ready to eat. He threw the bra across the room and grabbed her left breast while kissing the right. He ran his hands through her long, dark hair and then grasped a handful, pulling her head back so her face looked right at him. He took a moment and then kissed her open mouth, driving his tongue deep into her throat. Jennifer responded by grabbing his throbbing member. Jason let out an audible gasp.

"That's for later," he said huskily.

He picked her up and carried her to the dining room table. He gently placed her in the center and backed off. Jennifer looked at him like, "Come on!" He slowly removed his undershirt and waved it over his head with a giant smile, then let it fly! His ripped abs resembled a steel washboard. He unbuckled his belt, slowly pulled it out through the loops. Just as he got to the end, he whipped it out with a snap. With a quick flick, Jason cracked the belt like a whip on the edge of the table, causing Jennifer to let out a scream! He moved to her and took her hands gently, then rapped the belt around her wrist, biting her nipple as he backed away again. Jennifer was about to explode!

"Come on! Fuck me now!"

"Patience, Jennifer. Patience."

He slid his pants off and tossed them over his shoulder nonchalantly. Jennifer's eyes locked on the mammoth bulge in Jason's boxer briefs.

"I want that input, now!"

"Hush."

Jason took hold of her foot and started to lick her toes. He kissed each one and then proceeded up her leg, kissing and caressing every inch. Jennifer couldn't contain herself any longer.

"Oh my god, Jason! Oh my god!" Jennifer screamed.

Jason reached up, grabbed her by the back of the knees, and pulled her down to the end of the table, leaving her legs hanging loosely.

"Yes! Taste me!"

Jason slid up a chair and sat down. He moved his head further up along the inside of her thighs, kissing his way to paradise. Jennifer let out a long, deep, guttural moan that reverberated off the walls of the room. Jason's tongue caressed her wet lips, savoring her nectar.

As he raised his head up, Jason whispered, "I love the way you taste. It's like sweet papaya dipped in honey."

He buried his head again into her Gates of Heaven. Jennifer squirmed with delight, wrapping her legs around Jason, clutching the sides of the table while thrusting her hips toward the ceiling. Jason could feel her body tense under him—he grasped the table with both hands tightly when Jennifer's entire body convulsed with an exquisite wave of pleasure. Jennifer let out a gratifying scream as she reached the peak of her climax.

Erica strolled through Rawlins Park the next morning—a clear, crisp winter day. The Washington Monument sparkling in the sun, could be seen off in the distance. She approached a park bench and sat. A quick scan of the area assured her that no one was around. Reaching under the bench, Erica retrieved a cellphone. She hit the call button, and a number automatically dialed.

"Most people don't know the name of the eighth dwarf," a man's voice said through the earpiece.

"Ronda," Erica responded.

"You come highly recommended. My name's David Edison."

"You have three minutes, Mr. Edison."

"I'll get right to the point. This must look like an accident, nothing suspicious. Name your price."

Erica constantly surveyed the area as she talked. "Two million, American. One million up front deposited today, and the second to be deposited when the job is complete. I don't meet employers in person. All contact will be either through the dead-drop location that I'm sending you or this cellphone. You'll get a numbered account to deposit the money momentarily."

"Your instructions will—"

Before David could finish his sentence, Erica disconnected the call. She then sent a text of her bank account number and the drop location to Edison. After taking a quick look around, Erica casually got up and walked along the park sidewalk, just like anyone else enjoying the sunny winter day.

Jason wore a towel strategically placed around his waist when he opened the hotel-room door just a crack to peek up and down the hallway. Clear, Jason gingerly bent down and retrieved the morning paper left at the foot of the door. The headline read: 'Chairman of the Foreign Trade Commission Found Dead.'

Jason shuffled back to the bedroom and found Jennifer sitting with her back up against the headboard as she talked on the hotel phone.

"I just ordered us some breakfast," she declared, hanging up the phone.

"Great! I'm always famished after a night of sexual gymnastics."

"The Russian judge gave you an 8.5," she said matter-of-factly.

"The Russians always score on the low side. How did you rate the performance?"

A wry smile claimed her face. "I'd have to say . . . ten and a half?

"Ten is the highest you can go dear." Jason remarked as he tossed the newspaper aside and flopped onto the bed.

"I'm a rule breaker; you know that."

Jason slid up the bed and stopped just inches from her pretty face. "I like it when you break the rules."

He kissed her deeply. As they broke, Jennifer slid down the bed. Jason positioned himself over her and looked down at her lustfully.

"Room service is bringing breakfast." Jennifer frowned.

"They take forever; we'll have plenty of time."

They kissed deeply. Jason whipped the bed covers off and onto the floor. He pulled off the towel wrapped around his waist, flung it over their heads, then looked down with pride. "You're right: ten and a half!"

Only the twinkling lights of the city illuminated the dark sky. Zubin Ratko sat at his desk, the phone pressed tightly to his ear.

"It's being taken care of as we speak," Ratko affirmed, his face showing extreme concern. "I completely understand."

Ratko listened to the caller as David Edison entered the office.

"As soon as I've got confirmation, I will let you know," Ratko said, as he pulled the phone away from his ear, the call abruptly terminated on the other end of the line.

"I'm getting undue pressure from our associate."

"I've taken care of our plumbing problem. The leak has been terminated," Edison reassured. "Walker will not be a concern for us any longer."

"Good. I'll let our people know. What is the situation regarding Brent?"

"I've made contact. It will look like an accident."

Ratko relaxed back in his massive desk chair and let out a long sigh, rubbing his hand over his eyes and forehead in an attempt to relieve the tension in his head.

Washington's Dulles International Airport crowded with travelers as usual. Erica dressed in a professionally styled navy-blue dress and dark, floppy hat she kept pulled down to conceal her face. She sat in the boarding area reading the story of Congressman Bennett's death in the local newspaper while waiting for her flight to be announced. Erica's chin and mouth were exposed from underneath the hat. Her hair, now blonde, covered her collar. She had become very adroit in keeping to herself, a necessity in her line of work as a contract killer. Indifferent to the movements of the other travelers, Erica focused on her newspaper as the public address system sparked to life. The dry, droning voice of the gate attendant crackled through boarding area speakers.

"All first class passengers for Flight 1701 to Los Angeles may begin boarding at this time at gate twenty-three."

Erica gathered her belongings and moved to the line to board. Just a few steps in front of her, a young girl about ten or eleven years old dressed in a pink skirt with a white blouse and traveling with her beleaguered father, a man about thirty with short-cropped, sandy-colored hair.

"How long before we get there, Daddy?"

"What's your hurry, honey?" he said in a warm, soft tone. "Life is not about getting to the destination; it's about enjoying the journey. Remember how I always tell you to take time to see the world, to see everything around you and enjoy it?"

Erica smiled a sad smile as she remembered her father on that winter day. She found him standing in an open field, staring at the snow-covered trees when she was about this girl's age. She had asked him if there was anything wrong, and he slowly looked down at her and replied, "No. I'm just taking a moment. I want you to remember something: no matter how crazy or insane life can be, you can always take time to see the world around you and just enjoy it." For the next twenty minutes, the two of them just stood there marveling at the site of the snow-covered trees and the wind blowing through them, a moment that she cherished for all these years.

Erica found her seat on the plane and settled in for the long flight, still thinking about her father's words that day. As the plane rumbled down the runway, Erica stared out the window and drifted back in time to her tenth birthday.

3

Istanbul

THE LIVING ROOM of Erica's house, filled with her young friends on her tenth birthday, watched as she opened her presents. Her mother, Andrea, a beautiful, dark-haired woman with green eyes entered the room with a cake lit up by candles. Even at ten, Erica resembled her mother's beauty in many ways, except for the heart-shaped birthmark on her neck just above her collarbone that her parents showed off at every opportunity.

"Mommy, we must wait for Daddy before I make my wish!" Erica pleaded.

From outside a car horn honked.

"There's your father now! Just in time."

Andrea set the cake on the table and rushed to the front door, followed closely by Erica. Her mother opened the front door to see her handsome husband's classically chiseled features and understanding eyes. Then, Goran Sekulic had turned back to retrieve something from his car.

Erica tried to brush by her mother to get to her father, but Andrea grabbed her forcibly and threw her to the floor, covering her completely with her body as the force from the exploding vehicle tore through the front of the house, raining debris down around them. The plane shook violently, startling Erika out of her reverie.

The Captain's voice crackled through the sound system. "Sorry about that, folks. We're experiencing a little turbulence, but we're about forty minutes out from LAX, so if you'll return to your seats and buckle up, we'll have you on the ground shortly."

Erica's mind drifted back to the smoke-filled house. The screams of children and adults she heard that day echoed once again in her brain. Goran, injured and dazed, dragged himself to his feet and stumbled up the front porch stairs, fighting his way through the smoke and debris to get to Erica and her mother. Goran rolled the body of his dead wife off Erica and cradled her in his arms.

"It's okay, baby. Daddy's got you." Erica remembered looking up at her father and him telling her, "You need to be strong."

The next few weeks were a blur as her father recovered from his injuries at a remote hospital. Fearing for her safety, he secretly relocated the both of them to a secluded village on the Serbian-Romanian border after his release from the hospital and resignation of his position as security chief to the prime minister.

Two years into their Romanian exile, her father began a rigorous training program for Erica. She studied five languages: English, French, Italian, Russian, and Spanish, learning them fluently. She not only studied liberal arts, but the martial arts, including an all-encompassing weapons program. Erica became proficient in handguns, assault rifles, explosives, and the silent killer, the crossbow. Erica took to her training like a duck takes to water.

"I can only protect you for so long, and at some point you will need to take care of yourself," her father avowed with the utmost importance. Igor Tepic, her father's chauffeur, had betrayed him the day of Erica's tenth birthday, setting him up for the attack from his second in command Mikael Vukuvic, who killed his beautiful wife. Goran reminded Erica over and over again that there may come a day when her father's enemies would find where they were hiding, and her life would be in extreme danger.

Erica knew she had to always be aware and have an exit strategy. In her mind, not just a matter of knowing what to do for protection, but these skills were necessary to accomplish the vow she made; she would find the people who killed her mother and exact justice if it took the rest of her life.

Jennifer sat, back against the headboard, munching on a slice of toast while Jason sipped a cup of coffee. He turned his head slightly, gazing at his lovely editor.

"You were hungry." Jason flashed his patented smile.

"No kidding. With you around, I don't have to worry about hitting the gym. You give me a workout. I need to compensate for the loss of calories," Jennifer quipped between bites.

She looked at Jason's plate balanced on his lap.

"You going to finish your bacon?"

Jason offered her his plate. Jennifer grabbed the strip of bacon and stuffed it in her mouth.

"I've never been so hungry in my life," Jennifer mumbled with a mouth full of food.

Her cheeks puffed out with toast and bacon, Jennifer stopped chewing. She sent a sideways glance at Jason, whose smile spread across his entire face. Jennifer couldn't control herself and began to laugh.

"Are you refueled, dear?" Jason asked.

"Yes, but no more gymnastics. I need to get dressed and make myself presentable for a meeting in . . ." Jennifer leaned over to get a look at the digital clock on the nightstand. Shit, an hour," Jennifer uttered in a panic.

She threw off the bed covers and trotted to the bathroom. Jason followed her with his eyes, enjoying the view of her tight body moving away from him.

"I hate Friday meetings," she said as she entered the bathroom.

"What did you want to talk to me about?"

"Global," Jennifer yelled from the bathroom.

Jason heard the shower water turn on. "These guys at Global know how to cover their tracks."

"What? I can't hear you."

Jason sat down his coffee cup and slipped out of bed. He casually walked into the bathroom.

"I said. These Global guys know how to cover their tracks."

"Oh."

Jennifer stuck her hand in the shower to test the water. Satisfied that it wasn't too hot, she got in with Jason close behind.

"I'll scrub your back," he said casually.

Jason soaped up a washcloth and started to slowly wash Jennifer's silky smooth back. She couldn't hold back her delight in the treatment. Jason took her by the shoulders and spun her around. Face to face as the steamy water gushed down on them, Jason kissed her long and hard. Jennifer, floated in a state of bliss for a moment, then shook off the thoughts of Jason making love to her again. She pushed him back.

"I have some information for you, and I've got to go to this meeting; so hold your horses, we can play later."

Jason kissed her again.

"Jason! Stop, I mean it." Jennifer's tone he recognized as the one she used when she was dead serious.

"I've got a name for you to contact: Paulina Gregory. Mid-level executive at Global, she's worth taking a look at as someone who can get you information."

"Have you heard from Peter?" Jason questioned. "He's not returning my calls."

"No. He hasn't returned any of mine, either. The last thing I knew, he was taking a much-needed vacation with his family."

Jason continued to soap Jennifer. Jennifer turned her back to Jason to let the water run on her face. Undeterred, Jason continued to soap. As his hands reached around to caress her ample breasts, Jennifer grabbed Jason's wrists.

"Stop!" Jennifer exclaimed.

"I was just . . ."

"I know what you were just . . . Listen to me! Peter's information has dried up. He got antsy, and he stopped returning my calls. From what I understand, this Paulina likes to have fun, and she likes her men fit, sophisticated, and handsome. You're up!"

"Sounds like my kind of girl."

"Well, you've got two out of three requirements anyway. So try your best," Jennifer responded sarcastically as she stepped out of the shower.

"Which one am I missing?"

"You figure it out?"

In a flash, Jennifer had wrapped a towel around her and out of the bathroom, leaving Jason standing in the shower contemplating her last statement. After a long deliberation, Jason couldn't for the life of him, come up with which one of the qualities he lacked.

"So which one am I missing?" he yelled from the shower.

Jennifer poked her head into the bathroom. "And you call yourself an investigative reporter. Ha!"

The flight attendant interrupted Erica, still lost in the thoughts of her past.

"Please bring your seat up, Ma'am. We're about to land. Thank you," the attendant requested in a faux-polite manner.

Erica's mind, still back in that small village where six years had gone by, remembered how she'd spent the day shopping.

As she rode her bicycle down the dirt path toward home, she noticed something odd. The smoke coming from the chimney caught her attention right away. The smoke, a distinctive blue color, caused Erica to stop her bike. She jumped off, leaving it on the side of the path, and ran into the woods out of sight. Her mind told her to run, but she, overcome by the urge to do something to help her father, stayed and observed the house. She remembered him telling her, "No matter what happens, you must promise me you will run. Don't try to save me." A single gunshot rang out from the house. Erica froze, her eyes fixed on the humble dwelling. Moments later, two men emerged from the house and into the cold air. Erica tried desperately to focus on the men, but could only make out their silhouettes from that distance. Her training kicked in, and she jumped back on her bicycle, frantically racing back to the village as she took one last glance at the house that had been her home.

Erica peddled furiously, tears streaming down her face. She could only imagine what awful thing had happened to her father. She rode into the small Romanian town of Orsova, completely ignoring greetings from the friendly locals.

Determined to get to the center of town as fast as she could, Erica nearly collided with a truck loaded with produce. She swerved, narrowly missing a group of young children crossing the street.

She slid her bike up to a large, old and weathered, granite building with an inscription over the entrance that read: 'Orsova Library.' Her bike fell to the ground as she rushed up the steps.

Erica ran past the front desk without stopping.

"Walk please!" the librarian commanded with a look of disapproval.

Erica slowed down to appease the old, crotchety woman. She headed to the rear of the library to the research section that seemed to be abandoned. She searched frantically for a certain book. As she held back her feelings and tried to stay focused, she began to remember her training. She stopped, gathered herself, and began breathing slow, deep breaths. After a moment, her composure regained, she walked down a long aisle and looked up. High above her, she spied what she had been looking for, a very large book about six inches thick titled: 'Grain Yields of The Soviet Union Post The Bolshevik Revolution.' The book had a very thick, padded-leather cover and about twenty inches by fifteen inches in width.

Erica lugged the book down and placed it on the floor. She looked around to see if anyone could observe her, then swung her backpack off her shoulders, unzipped the side pocket, and removed a pocketknife.

She opened the cover of the book and slipped the blade under the paper glued to the inside cover.

Carefully she slid the knife around the seam, loosening the glue, then pulled the paper back to reveal a hidden pocket. Inside she found a passport and other personal documents. She took the papers and put them in her backpack. She turned the book over and opened the back cover, repeating the procedure. Inside the back cover were several large bills in U.S. Currency. She stuffed the money in her pants' pocket, closed the book and returned it to the top shelf. She looked around as she zipped up her backpack, slung it over her shoulder, and anxiously walked out of the library.

Istanbul, the bustling port and Capitol of Turkey, was hot with temperatures in the mid-eighties on that June day. Erica arrived by train from Bulgaria and went directly to Istanbul University, located northwest of the city's downtown area. The one place a girl of her age could blend into the population without arousing much interest.

Erica obtained information at a very high price, that Igor Tepic, had escaped Serbia and sought refuge in Istanbul with his cousin Victor Bortak. Vlado Nikic, her father's aid lived somewhere in the United States and Milan Petkovic had successfully vanished. Erica immediately went to work to find Bortak, determined to convince him to tell her where Igor was hiding.

After three days of searching the seediest areas of the city, Erica hit pay dirt. Victor Bortak worked as a recruiter for a prostitution ring run by Igor. It seemed almost too easy that warm night when Victor approached her standing in front of a local seaport tavern. Victor, in his mid-forties, sported a large potbelly. A cigarette hung from his lips, his dark hair greasy. He had a scruffy beard and sweated profusely as he sidled up to Erica leaning against the dirty wall of the low-rent establishment.

"You are new here; I have not seen you before. You look Serbian," Victor said, blowing smoke from his cigarette into Erica's face.

Erica turned to leave, but in a quick move, much faster than Erica could have imagined, Victor shot up his arm and pressed his hand against the tavern wall, blocking Erica's exit.

"I just want to talk to you. Relax."

"What is it you want to talk about," a disgusted Erica responded in Serbian.

"Ah, I knew you were from my country. You need work?"

"It is possible, but what is it to you?"

"I can help you. You are a pretty little thing, and with your looks, you can make some easy money."

"Not interested." Erica tried to push Victor's arm away.

"Easy, little one. All you have to do is dance. You know how to dance don't you?'

Erica nodded a tentative "yes."

"My cousin owns a club—many pretty girls. They make a lot of money dancing."

Erica bit her lip pensively. "I will just have to dance?" Erica asked apprehensively.

Victor reached into his jacket pocket and pulled out a business card.

"Come to this location tonight. Take a look."

Erica took the card and looked at it. Victor smiled a yellow-toothed smile. He spotted another young, attractive girl coming out of the tavern. Victor strode toward her. Erica watched with disdain. Her "scared rabbit" demeanor quickly changed to one of a woman of confidence, a woman who had a plan, and the plan coming together nicely. I'll be there, you piece of shit, Erica thought to herself.

If the dive bar Erica encountered Victor in was the seediest part of town, the section of the city around the strip club his cousin owned ran a close second. The building sat a hundred yards, give or take, from a major causeway heading out of the city.

Angel's Nest vibrated as heavy trucks rolled along the road on their way to destinations across the country after picking up loads at the docks.

Several drunken men covered in their own vomit lay passed out next to trashcans in an alley that smelled of urine. Across the street from the club, a homeless man missing a leg covered himself with a large piece of cardboard to prepare himself for a night's sleep. How much sleep he expected to get in this noisy, filthy neighborhood, only god knew.

Erica cautiously entered the "Nest," as it had become known, and surveyed the interior. The small bar up against the right-hand wall had only six stools.

Across from the bar an area where patrons could stand along a wooden rail, with a shelf to place their drinks. This gave the patrons a perfect view of the dance floor, a large, raised platform with two chrome poles where the strippers did their acts. Tables and chairs surrounded the dance floor. The DJ, spun records in a booth stuck in a tight corner. One would have to shout to be heard over the loud, pounding music. Erica directed her attention to the bar and spotted Victor sitting on a stool at the far end. Victor had his attention directed at the dark-haired bartender, a buxom woman who had seen her share of troubles over the years that seemed to have aged her at least ten years. As Erica got closer, she could distinctly make out the outline of a scar on the woman's neck, right along her clavicle.

At the end of the bar, sipping a beer was a man, about twenty-five, tall with long, dark hair and a thick mustache. The tight, blue T-shirt with a faded beer logo on it drew Erica's attention to every muscle and nipple outlined under the fabric. Erica felt his icy stare as she tentatively walked to the end of the bar and stopped at the stool facing Victor's back.

The bartender saw Erica approach, her shoulders dropping an inch. The bartender nodded in the direction of Erica for Victor to turn around.

Victor glanced over his shoulder and saw the pensive Erica standing there. He smiled, but before he could speak, Erica, playing her part to the hilt, shied away and tried to leave. Victor grabbed her arm.

"Don't go, my Angel," Victor pleaded in a loud voice.

The bartender rolled her eyes. Shaking her head in disgust, she walked down to the other end of the bar.

"I don't think I should have come," a frightened Erica shouted over the music.

Victor put his hand up to his ear, indicating he didn't hear her. Erica moved closer to him.

"I should not have come."

"You don't want to go on living on the streets, do you?"

Erica shook her head "no" and stared at the floor.

"Then why not make a little money for a while. Then you can find a place to live. While you are working here, we give you a place to stay."

Erica looked up, torn as to what to do.

"What is your name, little one?"

"Erica."

"Good. Now come, I will show you around."

Victor slid off the bar stool and gently guided Erica to the rail across from the bar. He pointed to the two girls performing on the stage.

"You see, there is nothing to it. You just dance." Victor yelled in Erica's ear.

Erica nodded.

"You will be paid thirty lira for a shift. Each shift is three hours."

The music set ended, and the DJ asked the sparse collection of clientele to give the girls a round of applause.

The girls circled the dance floor, encouraging the audience to give them money. Several men sitting along the dance floor handed bills to the girls as they passed, whooping, whistling and trying to cop a feel of their naked bodies.

"You get to keep half of your tips," Victor pronounced, smiling broadly.

Victor took Erica by the arm and escorted her to the kitchen behind the bar. The two squeezed past the next girl in a hurry to get out on the floor and perform her routine. Erica followed Victor out through the back door of the establishment and into an alley. They turned left and walked down the alley about twenty yards and then turned right. Victor stopped and pointed to a small, motel-like structure. There were eight doors along the front of the building.

"This is where the girls who work for us stay. There are four girls to a room and it's free as long as you work for us."

"When I make enough money I can leave at any time?"

"You leave when you want just as long as you finish your shift. You will do three shifts each day, seven days a week. You can make lots of money."

Victor looked directly at Erica, smiling.

"You want to start tonight or tomorrow?"

Always close with at least two choices, Erica thought to herself. Victor is a salesman all right.

The two just stood there silent for more than a minute. I give you a lot of credit, Victor, Erica thought. First one who talks loses.

"I think I will start tomorrow."

"Fine, fine. You've made a good decision. Soon your pockets will be full on money," Victor said, smiling.

A smile barely showed on Erica's face as she sheepishly looked down at the ground.

"I hope I will be able to do this."

"Don't be scared."

Victor eyed Erica up and down lustfully.

"You've got what it takes, my Angel. Believe me."

Victor's glare made Erica's skin crawl, but she had gotten in and would just have to be patient before she could exact revenge on the man who betrayed her father.

4

My god what a mess

THE FOLLOWING EVENEING, Erica arrived at the club looking older than her age due to the heavy makeup and provocative clothing.

The Nest, a bit more populated this evening than the night before, and the music somehow seemed louder tonight. Erica scanned the bar area, Victor nowhere to be found. She approached the bartender.

"I'm Erica. I'm supposed to start work tonight," Erica yelled across the bar.

The bartender signaled for Erica to follow her. She led her to the kitchen behind the bar. Once in the kitchen, the sound of the loud music became muffled and one could speak in a more normal tone.

"Everyone calls me Sasha," the bartender said, extending her hand.

Erica shook Sasha's hand. "I'm Erica."

"Are you going to stay in the apartments?"

"No, I have a place to stay. So I will just be working my shifts."

"That's good; you don't want to live there. There is a ladies room in the corner." Shasha pointed to the back of the kitchen. "You can change in there before going on. Check with the DJ, and he'll schedule you a time."

"Is Victor here?"

"He'll be here later. You'll get paid after your shift."

Erica nodded.

"Good luck." Sasha smiled and returned to the bar.

Left alone, Erica, given the opportunity, cased the joint. The two windows in the kitchen covered with filth, made them opaque, not to mention, they had also been barred. The only window not barred the small window located in the lady's room at the back of the kitchen.

Erica darted out the kitchen door into the alley and trotted down to the apartments at the end. Lights could be seen coming through the windows of all the apartments. As Erica got closer to the building, she could hear women's voices coming from them. Erica carefully skulked up to one of the apartments. She tried the door and found the door locked. Erica stepped away and darted back to the Nest's kitchen.

Erica walked in the kitchen door and was greeted by D.J., the DJ.

"Are you Erica?" he asked, leering at her, not even concerned about what she had been doing out in the alley.

"Yes. I am," Erica muttered quietly.

"Well, you're on next. What name do you want to use?"

"Name?" Erica said inquisitively.

"You got a stage name?"

"No. I've never done this before."

"No problem. Just shake your tits and show them your ass—a lot. I'll introduce you as Chiffon."

"Oh, thank you. That never occurred to me," Erica remarked in a convincing manner. "You're a prince," she mumbled, walking away. "Prince as in P-R-I-C-K."

"Boombastic," by Shaggy, thumped through the bar, as Erica timidly took the stage, her face registering the look of a deer caught in headlights. She barely moved as the crowd started to get rowdy and began to boo.

This prompted her to start swaying her hips back and forth and running her hands up and down her chest. She grabbed the pole and swirled around, nearly slipping off and crashing to the stage floor.

She unhooked her bra, and the guys on the front row jumped up hollering, "Oh yeah, baby!"

"Take it off!" shouted the four drunken men close to the stage.

"New girl's going to get eaten alive," Sasha stated to the bouncer at the end of the bar.

Dimitri, the bouncer, the man Erica saw sitting at the end of the bar the first day she arrived at The Nest, had been observing her closely. His deep, emotionless eyes could take in every detail displayed before them in just a few seconds. Victor's man and his most trusted soldier. He followed Victor's orders to the letter.

"That scared little girl thing could be huge." Dimitri said. "If she learned how to use it."

Erica teasingly held her hands over the bra cups covering her breasts as she tried to keep tempo with the music.

The men in the bar got more agitated at Erica's poor performance and started throwing rolled-up paper napkins at the stage.

"Let's hear it for Chiffon," the D.J. announced over the P.A. system, eliciting a chorus of "boos" from the crowd.

Erica glanced toward the D.J., who signaled her to get off the stage. Erica took a little bow, rushed off the stage, and dashed directly to the kitchen.

As Erica burst through the kitchen door, Dimitri who casually leaned against the wall immediately met her.

"Just what are you doing here, little girl?" Dimitri inquired.

"I'm trying to make some money."

"Not like that, you won't."

"Who are you to tell me what to do?"

"My name is Dimitri. I run security. You should go home to where you came from. You don't belong here."

Erica told Dimitri. "It's none of your business. I do what I want."

A tall, redheaded girl emerged from the women's restroom dressed in a revealing American Indian costume, complete with headdress.

"Marka!" Dimitri called.

The woman stopped and turned to him.

"This is Chiffon. She needs some coaching. Help her out for me."

"I saw her performance," Marka admitted, smiling. "It's your first time, right?"

Erica nodded; her eyes searched the floor.

"Don't worry. I'll show you a few tricks after I'm done. You'll get the hang of it quickly," Marka said as she disappeared through the kitchen door. The crowd in the club erupted in catcalls and applause.

Dimitri moved close to Erica.

"Once you have enough money, you need to leave this place. Nothing good can come from this," Dimitri said as he turned and walked back into the club.

Erica finished her second shift, which went much better after her coaching session with Marka. On her break, she had another opportunity to check out the apartments. This time she saw a shift change in progress. Dimitri and a fat bouncer escorted three of the dancers to the apartments. Dimitri unlocked the door to one of the units, and after the girls entered the apartment, he locked the girls in, then trudged to a unit two doors down and unlocked that door.

Three girls came out, and the fat bouncer escorted them back to the club while Dimitri locked the door again. It became painfully obvious that these girls were prisoners.

After Erica's third shift, Victor arrived, very happy to see her in her skimpy outfit, accentuating her assets to the maximum. He stopped her at the door to the kitchen.

"You need to . . . you know, greet the customers. Make them feel comfortable. You can make many more tips," Victor leered at her.

Erica nodded in agreement and sauntered to one of the tables where several men were sitting, drinking, and whistling at the dancer on stage.

Erica made the most of her free reign to roam the club, checking out all the exits and where they led. In the far corner of the club, Erica discovered a staircase just past the men's restroom. The area dark and with the walls painted black it gave off a sinister feel. The floor had stickiness, due to several missing tiles. It smelled of stale beer and some unrecognizable funk. Erica made a point to keep an eye on the area. Every so often, one of the dancers would go up the stairs with one of the male customers.

It dawned on her. This is where Igor is running his prostitution business.

From what she observed, some of the girls going up the stairs were not dancers. They looked to be fourteen or fifteen years old. Igor was the lowest of the lowest form of pimp—prostituting under-aged girls.

Three days passed, and Igor still a no-show. Erica, by day three, became the most popular girl in the club. She garnished the most tips after her performances and became aware that some of the patrons were cornering Victor to set them up with her for a session upstairs.

Erica drifted through the club one night when a table of well-dressed men decided that they were not going to wait for Victor's approval to get Erica upstairs.

A big burly man wearing sunglasses in the dark club pulled Erica by the arm and into his lap as she passed the table. She tried to push herself away, but the man had already wrapped his arm around her waist.

"Come on, little one. Let's go upstairs, and I'll show you how a real man treats you."

The other men at the table laughed and cheered him on. Erica tried to slide off the man's lap, but his hold too tight. With her feet off the floor, she had very little leverage to extricate herself from the man's grasp. As she struggled, she heard a familiar voice.

"Take your hands off of her," Dimitri said calmly, his face close to the man's ear.

Jerking his head toward Dimitri, the man shouted, "Who are you?"

"Do what I told you."

"This girl is just a whore, just like the rest of the girls here."

The men at the table burst into laughter.

With his right hand, Dimitri placed his thumb on the base of the man's neck, just where the tendon extends from the neck to the shoulder, and pressed down hard.

The man immediately released Erica from his grip and winced with pain. As he tried not to cry out, Dimitri continued the pressure. The man could no longer stand the extreme pain and cried out in agony.

With his left hand, Dimitri gently assisted Erica to her feet, nodding to her to move away from the table. Once Erica had stepped away, Dimitri released his thumb, and the man fell into the lap of the man to his right, clutching his neck with his left hand.

"Pay your bill and get out," Dimitri ordered as he backed away from the table, giving the other patrons at the table a stare that could burn a hole through a steel door.

Dimitri signaled one of the cocktail waitresses to bring the bill to the offending table as he made his way to the end of the bar. Dimitri had just taken his position on his stool when Erica appeared at his side.

"Thank you for looking out for me," Erica said.

"It's just part of my job. This can be a very dangerous place. You should think about what I told you."

"I've thought about it, and I don't expect to be here much longer,' Erica confessed.

"That's good," Dimitri replied, keeping his eyes straight ahead, as he took a sip from his bottled beer.

Erica stood for a moment, expecting a "you're welcome," but when it didn't come she turned and left the bar.

Erica's fifth day of work finally paid off. Igor showed up along with two girls that looked to be about twelve years of age. Igor looked about fifty years old now, a broad man with dark hair and dark eyes. His pockmarked face, made him look sickly. Boisterous and pushy, he smelled of violence. Erica entertained on the dance floor that night. Igor noticed her right away. Erica always had the ability to stand out, and she was in true form that night.

After she finished her set, Victor intercepted her on her way to the kitchen. He brought her to the bar to introduce her to Igor. Igor like what he saw, immediately attracted to her, but there was something about her, that triggered some sense of familiarity, but he couldn't put his finger on what it could be. Erica's heavy makeup made her look five years older than her actual age, and the last time Igor had seen her, she had just turned nine. Igor never paid much attention to Goran's family, so Erica willingly took the chance that Igor wouldn't immediately recognize her. What he did recognize? He had a moneymaker in Erica, especially if he put her to work upstairs.

Erica had conned her way into the university dorm when she arrived in Istanbul. When alone, she sewed lengths of piano wire into her bras. Erica was ready, and now it became just a matter of circumstance coinciding perfectly for her to go into action.

Erica arrived at the club just as she had on the first day. Igor had been sniffing around her night after night, and this night, he would put Erica to work upstairs. Igor couldn't ignore the requests from the customers any longer. As far as he was concerned, he was losing money. Erica came out of the lady's room when a smiling Igor met her.

"You don't need to go on right now. I switched you with one of the other girls."

"What is going on?"

"I want to talk to you. You could be making much more money than you are."

"I am making enough money for me."

"You could be my best girl."

Igor took a long look at Erica. That familiar something about her still haunted him.

"Have you come here before, when I was here?" Igor asked lecherously.

Erica blankly stared back at him and shook her head "no."

"You are a very beautiful woman. You could be rich."

"Rich?" Erica questioned.

"The girls who work upstairs make much more than the dancers."

"Upstairs?'

"That's where my best girls entertain those special clients," Igor said with a broad smile.

"But I've never . . ." Erica blushed with embarrassment.

"You mean that you have never been with a man before?"

Erica dropped her head and stared at her feet.

"Do not worry my little one. We can take care of that." Igor slid his arm through Erica's arm and patted her hand. He guided her towards the door.

"You will be my best girl."

An excited Igor escorted Erica toward the apartments out back and took her to the unit on the far end of the building. He removed a key from his pocket, unlocked the door, and the two entered the room that reeked of stale perfume and bad incense. A large bed, situated to the far left of the room along the outside wall, took up most of the space. The lighting low and the windows covered with heavy, red curtains marred with greasy stains gave the room an eerie texture. A small dresser with paint peeling off the sides sat in the corner. There were two worn sitting chairs, one near the door with a broken leg and the other in the opposite corner from the dresser. They were the only things in the room that matched. A small sink, mounted on the wall directly across from the front door, had been white at one time, but now colored orange from rust caused by a constantly dripping faucet. To the left of the sink, a small bathroom that contained a toilet and a shower with disgusting, brown mold covering the shower curtain. A two-foot-by-two-foot window above the toilet functioned as the only ventilation. Erica crossed the room and sat in the chair next to the dresser.

"I will be gentle with you. You are very beautiful, and I would not want to ruin you for my best customers. Do as I say and everything will go well for you," he said as he unbuttoned his shirt. "Come on now. Get undressed. I don't have much time. I need to get back to business."

Igor turned his back on Erica and sat on the bed, removing his shoes and socks. Igor twisted his head around and observed her still sitting in the chair.

"Let's go, my little one."

Erica began to fiddle with her bra. Satisfied that she resigned herself to participate, Igor went back to removing his socks. He unbuckled his pants and stood up. By this time, Erica had slipped to the other side of the bed directly behind him. Grasping the piano wire, the ends wrapped around each hand, Erica climbed onto the bed, just as Igor began to unzip his pants, and snapped the wire over his head with her arms crossed at the wrists and yanked it back at the same time she uncrossed her arms, tightening the wire across his throat. Igor's girth knocked Erica off balance when he jerked his body in response to the attack.

The two tumbled backward, hitting the bed stand, sending the lamp crashing to the floor. Igor rolled off the bed and pulled at the wire with his left hand as he dug into his pants pocket with the right hand, retrieving his pistol.

Igor rose to his feet firing wildly around the room. Erica, desperately hanging on to Igor, continued to choke him with the wire.

"This is for my father, Goran Sekulic," Erica grunted through clinched teeth.

Erica tugged harder on the wire, hard enough that it cut into her hand.

Outside, Dimitri walked back to the club when he heard the shots coming from the room at the end of the building. He ran up closer to the apartment door and heard more shots coming from inside.

Igor flailed wildly, then lost consciousness and fell to his knees. Erica tied the wire off by twisting it several times. Outside, Dimitri kicked at the door, trying to break in as Erica twisted the gun out of Igor's hand and fired two shots into the door. The banging stopped.

Erica jumped off the bed and grabbed her shirt from the chair. Three shots were fired into the door lock from the outside. From the corner of the room, Erica fired the final round into the door and ducked into the bathroom, slamming the door behind her. In one deft move, she sprang onto the toilet and out through the window doing a summersault, landing on her feet, and off running.

Dimitri burst through the door and rushed to the bathroom, kicking it open only to find that Erica had escaped. Victor was at the apartment front door as Dimitri came out of the bathroom. He turned to the armed men that were with him.

"Spread out; she can't get very far. I want that new bitch alive."

Erica ducked around into the alley of the warehouse next to the motel structure where she could hear the sounds of Victor shouting instructions to his men. I need to get to a populated street and blend in, she thought to herself.

Erica had to start taking chances. This did not go down as she had planned, and the time to improvise was immediate. She kept close to the warehouse wall, making sure she stayed in the shadows as she cautiously made her way to the main thoroughfare.

The men scattered in all directions. Victor entered the room where his cousin, Igor, lay dead with the bloody wire wrapped tightly around his neck.

"My god, what a mess," Victor said.

"What do you want to do?"

"Get one of the men to stand guard and make sure no one comes into this room. I'll make arrangements to get the body disposed of before the police come down on us."

Dimitri nodded and turned to leave the room.

"Dimitri!" Victor barked. "I want that girl found, do you understand?"

Dimitri turned back to Victor, seeing the anger in his eyes. Deep down inside, he knew that Victor would take great pleasure in torturing Erica before he killed her.

After getting one of the least reliable men in Igor's employ to keep guard on the murder room, Dimitri found Victor at the desk in the little office attached to the storage room in the basement of the club.

"I've got a man at the room, and I've got someone getting us a new door so we can lock the place up before morning."

Victor looked up from the desk. "Good. I've got Igor taken care of. A man owes me. Get out there and find that girl."

Dimitri turned and left the office, closing the door behind him. Victor sat back in the office chair, put his hands behind his head and chuckled as he propped his feet up on the desk.

As Victor saw it, he was now in charge of the whole operation. He looked around the room. His empire now— every filthy piece of it.

———————————————

Using dumpsters and parked vehicles as cover, Erica maneuvered to a street with more traffic than typically found around the club. There were restaurants and bars on both sides of the street with outdoor seating and plenty of patrons. Erica slipped into one of the bars and proceeded directly to the rear exit. The rear door of the bar dumped her into a small, narrow alley that connected to the other establishments along the street. The second building down from the bar was a populated restaurant.

Erica slipped in the rear door and found herself in the restaurant's kitchen. As she moved around the tall, metal racks of canned goods and pots and pans, she saw the doorway that led to the dining room. As she made her way toward it, she suddenly came face to face with a young busboy carrying a tray of clean glasses.

"Can you help me?" Erica asked, looking around confused. "I was looking for the ladies room but—"

"It's the door to the right. People do that all the time. Just go out this door, and it's directly across," the busboy said, pointing.

Erica smiled at the busboy and walked purposefully out of the kitchen. The busboy's eyes followed Erica as she left; admiring Erica's shape as she strutted out still in her skimpy short skirt and tied off blouse she wore on stage, completely forgetting he was on the job.

"Those glasses aren't going to stack themselves." The cook's deep voice cracked like a bullwhip and the boy just about tossed the tray into the air.

The startled boy bolted out of the kitchen, perilously trying to balance the tray in his hands.

Erica made her way into the almost full seating area. At the front of the restaurant, large windows were folded open on this warm night. Erica surveyed the interior.

As Erica turned to her left, she noticed a coat and hat rack next to where she stood. Hanging on the hooks were various clothing items. Erica eyed the length of the rack and stopped on a short, blue, denim jacket hanging from one of the hooks that looked to be just her size. She casually reached out her left arm, behind the clothing hanging there, and felt for the denim jacket. Erica slipped the item off the hook and slid it to her. She draped the jacket over her left arm and then casually walked to the front door of the restaurant. As she reached the front door an older waiter, bald with a bushy, white mustache smiled and bowed to her.

"Was everything to your satisfaction, miss?"

"Quite superb, thank you."

The waiter slipped the denim jacket off her arm and held it out for her to put on. She slipped each arm into it with a smile and muttered, "Thank you."

"Please come again." The waiter bowed, and Erica strolled out of the restaurant and into the street.

Erica walked into a small convenience store half a block down from the restaurant and made a complete tour of the place. Walking between shelves of snacks and canned goods, magazines and newspapers, Erica was careful to take notice if anyone had followed her.

She left the store and observed the people moving about the street. No one seemed to be in a hurry or seemed to be looking for anyone. Erica assumed that Victor's men would be looking for her at cabstands or bus stops. She would have to make the long trek back to the university dorm mostly on foot. Erica wouldn't feel safe waiting at a bus stop until she had put several miles between herself and this part of town. Mixing in with the foot traffic, Erica started toward the dorm.

Dimitri, having left Victor's office, headed straight for the kitchen. He remembered seeing Erica arriving at the club with a backpack always over her shoulder. A quick search of the kitchen paid off, for there in a corner wedged between shelves and the wall a black backpack. With no one in the kitchen, Dimitri took the backpack from its hiding place and quickly darted out into the alley. He slung the backpack over his shoulder, trotted down to the end of the alley, and made a right turn into a large, unpaved area surrounded by a falling-down, rusty, chain-link fence.

In the fenced-in area were several cars of various makes and models. Dimitri walked up next to a faded, light blue BMW, circa 1983. He unlocked the car door with his key, opened it, and tossed the backpack on the passenger's seat. Dimitri slid behind the wheel and started the car.

The car was in gear before he had the door closed, and Dimitri slammed down the accelerator, spinning his tires as he rapidly backed the car out of its parking slot, causing the car to slide around 180 degrees.

Slamming the gearshift into first, he tore out of the fenced-in parking area, cranked a right turn, and came out on the street that paralleled The Nest. Dimitri drove about six blocks before he stopped in front of a warehouse closed for the night. He turned on the dome light and opened Erica's backpack.

Inside the backpack, Dimitri found a lady's compact; lipstick; two bras, one red and one black with frills on them; and matching lacy panties. A pair of black, high-heel, stiletto shoes; a chocolate bar; a pack of gum; a small notebook; a cotton, waist-length jacket; a map of the city; a medium-sized pocket knife, which Dimitri slid into his pants' pocket; and the one item that Dimitri hoped he would find. Dimitri held in his hand, the clue to Erica's destination, a key from the Birkan Dormitory at the University of Istanbul. Dimitri quickly shoved the items back into the backpack and sped away from the curb, pointing his car in the direction of the university.

The ever-vigilant Erica boarded a crowded bus several miles from campus. She squeezed herself in the back amongst several young college students, hoping to blend in. She rode the bus, warily observing everyone entering and exiting before she finally got off four blocks away from the university. Cautious to the end, she made her way toward the campus.

At nearly 11:30 p.m., the streets were void of any pedestrian traffic as a watchful Erica walked along the dark street.

Erica had to be extra careful not to attract attention, but in her short skirt and denim jacket, she stood out like a sore thumb. Erica ducked in an alley between buildings to get off the main thoroughfare.

As she came out on the next street, she stayed in the shadows as much as she could, then darted across the street into the adjacent alley. As Erica crossed the street, the street lamp illuminated her for just a second, but that second just long enough as a light blue BMW drove across the intersection just a block away from Erica.

Erica could see the roof of the dorm as she emerged from the alley when she heard the whine of tires losing their grip with the road as the light blue BMW, headlights off, came roaring toward her. Erica froze for a split second then jumped back into the dark alley. The BMW slid sideways and came to a screeching halt—the nose of the car facing toward the alley Erica had run down. The headlights came on, and stark white light illuminated the alley.

Erica turned back and looked over her shoulder as she ran. The car's engine roared to life, and the tires screamed as the car raced down the alley toward a fleeing Erica. In seconds, the car was no more than fifty feet away from her, as she turned left down another alley.

Locking up all four wheels, the BMW slid past the alley as the car strained to come to a stop. Once stopped, the car roared again and backed up to the alley entrance.

With one swift move, the car spun around to face the alley and immediately raced towards Erica. Erica turned to look over her shoulder, and the bright lights of the car nearly blinded her.

As she sprinted headlong down the alley, the headlights of the car illuminated the path ahead. Erica had turned down a blind alley and was trapped, a dead end. She stopped a few feet in front of a brick wall twelve feet high that blocked her escape, and she had no weapon. Erica only had a second to think as the car closed in on her. She picked up a two-foot piece of wood from the ground and smashed the window on the building to her right. Glass splattered everywhere, but the window still mostly intact. The BMW's tires squealed, came to a stop four feet from Erica. The door swung open, and Dimitri leaped out. In an instant, Erica looked down the barrel of a very large pistol.

5

My name is Adrijana Erica Sekulic

ERICA GLANCED at the broken window. Could she jump through it? It was at least five feet off the ground. Throw the wood at his head and then break for the window, the thought that raced through her mind. She lifted the piece of lumber over her head.

Erica's eyes darted around the alley as she took a deep breath, her muscles tightening.

"If you want to live, get in the car," Dimitri yelled.

Erica hesitated for an instant, ready to throw the wood.

"I can't miss from here," Dimitri cautioned. "Put it down and get in the car. It's your only chance, or I'll just shoot you now. What is it going to be, Angel?"

Erica dropped the piece of wood on the ground. Dimitri motioned to her with his gun to walk toward the car. Erica came even with the car and stood there looking at Dimitri.

"Open the door and slide down as far as you can, so no one will see you."

Erica opened the door and realized her colossal error. Her backpack lay on the passenger seat, unzipped and the contents obviously rifled through. Erica got into the car and reached for the backpack.

"Leave it alone. Just do what I tell you and you won't get hurt," Dimitri barked.

Erica squeezed herself into the seat between the backpack and the door, positioned the seat back as far as it would go, and closed the door.

Dimitri slid into the driver's side, holding his gun on Erica. Without taking his eyes off her, he closed the door, grabbed the backpack and tossed it into the back seat. He put the car in reverse and backed up the alley until he had enough room to turn the car around and drive out of the alley.

"Where are you taking me?"

"Shut up!" Dimitri snapped. I don't want any trouble from you."

Dimitri looked down at Erica hunched in the passenger seat. "Farther."

"What?" Erica asked.

"Get down farther, and sit on your hands. One sudden move and I'll shoot. Don't test me."

Erica slid further down on the seat and put her hands under her butt. Dimitri guided the car swiftly through the dark streets, tossing Erica around in the process. All Erica could think about, her backpack in the seat behind her. If only I could get my hands on it, she thought. The knife in the side pocket—maybe it's still there. Erica looked up at Dimitri as he drove, the automatic on his lap, his finger in the trigger guard. This was not a good situation, but Erica would just have to bide her time and wait for the right moment. Erica tried to clear her mind. For now, she must summon the patience of a saint so she could be ready for the moment of opportunity that would eventually come. Any time, at any second, Erica would need to recognize the opportunity and act decisively. Erica took a deep breath and waited for what seemed an eternity.

The car finally came to a stop. Not a word exchanged for the twenty minutes Dimitri twisted and turned through the streets of the city.

"Stay down until I tell you it's okay," Dimitri demanded as she reached to open the car door.

Dimitri parked in the car lot of a medium-sized apartment building in a respectable neighborhood. He took a long look around the area for any sign that they were followed. Not a person in sight as Dimitri shut the door. Keeping his attention on any movement, he walked around to the passenger side, opened the door, and motioned with his gun for Erica to get out. Erica slid out; Dimitri shoved her towards the apartment building's rear entrance, keeping a safe distance from her to prevent any attack. The two stopped at the apartment's rear entrance.

"Open it."

Erica opened the door and entered with Dimitri close behind. Once inside, Dimitri waved his gun to the stairs.

"Third floor."

Erica and Dimitri climbed the metal stairs. When they reached the landing, Erica opened the door.

"Left, apartment three-sixteen."

The two walked down the dimly lit corridor and came to the corner apartment. On the door in black were the numerals, three-one-six.

"Up against the wall, face first," ordered Dimitri.

He shuffled the keys in his hand and selected one, slipped it in the lock, and turned. Dimitri gave the door a slight push and the door swung wide open. Sticking his hand inside the apartment while keeping his gun trained on Erica, he flicked on the apartment lights.

"Inside."

Erica stepped away from the wall and slowly entered the apartment.

"Stand in the middle of the room with your hands clasped behind your head."

Erica complied. Dimitri stared at her, shaking his head. He ran his right hand through his hair and let out a big sigh. The apartment, small and shared a living and dining room area. A tiny kitchen located in the corner of the apartment, with a small refrigerator and a two-gas-burner stove cramped in the corner. A shelf separating the kitchen from the dining room served as a small bar. The couch sat along the far wall, behind that wall the bedroom and across the hall from the bedroom, a small bathroom.

Dimitri took a few steps across the room to the couch, pulled off two of the seat cushions, and tossed them across the room next to the steam radiator.

Erica watched with darting eyes as Dimitri approached her, the muzzle of his gun constantly facing her. "What are you going to do to me?"

"Shut up. You'll talk when I tell you to talk," Dimitri snapped.

Dimitri grabbed Erica by the wrist forcefully and dragged her to the radiator, throwing her down on the couch cushions. He reached into his back pocket and slid out a pair of handcuffs, slapping one of the cuffs around her wrist that he held and the other to the heavy, steel pipe coming out of the floor attached to the radiator. Dimitri tightened the cuffs and then walked to the kitchen, opened the small refrigerator, and retrieved a plastic bottle of water. Striding back to the apartment door, Dimitri tossed the water bottle at Erica's feet.

"I'll be back later. Don't go anywhere."

"You filthy Turkish bastard," Erica hissed, spitting at Dimitri's feet.

Dimitri stepped out of the apartment and closed the door behind him. Erica heard his key turn in the lock and the sound of his footsteps echoing down the hall until the apartment was silent. Erica pulled on the handcuffs, testing the radiator strength. No possible way she could expect to free herself without a key. Erica relaxed and made herself as comfortable as possible on the couch cushions. Only the sound of the city traffic and the occasional police siren broke the monotony.

The following morning the apartment door slowly opened and Dimitri poked his head in and found Erica asleep on the couch cushions, still cuffed to the radiator.

Dimitri quietly entered and closed the door behind him without making a sound. He tiptoed to the kitchen and as quietly as he could, filled the old-style, percolator coffeepot with water. From a tin can on the counter, Dimitri filled the metal basket with coffee grounds and put the pot on the stove. Finding a pan in the cabinet next to the stove, Dimitri opened the refrigerator and retrieved and small bowl with several eggs in it.

The smell of fresh-brewed coffee permeated the small apartment, the aroma bringing Erica out of a deep sleep. As the fog cleared in her head, she suddenly became aware of her surroundings. The memory of her capture flooded back into her consciousness, causing her to lurch forward, forgetting she had been handcuffed to the radiator. Erica let out a painful groan as she quickly jerked back when the cuffs snapped tight around her wrist. Dimitri came in from the kitchen with two coffee cups in his hands. He set the cups on the dining table just a few feet from Erica and then stepped by her. He stopped in front of an oak-wood cabinet four feet wide, two and a half feet tall, and two feet deep. There were two doors on the front of it with small brass knobs in the center. It rested in the corner of the room.

Dimitri took out a set of keys from his pocket and selected one, fitting the key into the small lock in the right cabinet door. He swung it open, reached in, and retrieved a small, leather wallet from the top shelf.

Closing the cabinet door halfway, Dimitri then stepped back to where Erica lay on the floor. He flipped open the wallet and held it out to Erica. With her free hand, Erica took the wallet from Dimitri. Her eyes immediately widened as the light from the lamp reflected off the polished silver and gold badge housed in the leather, left pocket of the wallet. In the right hand pocket an identification card. In the upper right corner a one-inch square photo of Dimitri looking back at her in a serious pose and to the left of the photo the owner of the card's vital information. 'Name: Dimitri Plavakos. Rank: Detective 3rd Grade. Istanbul Police.' The official seal of the police department superimposed over the inscription.

"You're a cop?" Erica remarked with astonishment.

"Undercover. Your stupidity could cost me eight months of work trying to bust Igor's organization," Dimitri hisses at her. "Just what the hell do you think you were doing?"

Erica shifted her body, trying to make herself more comfortable. Dimitri notices her cut hand.

"You're hurt. I'll get something for your hand." Dimitri went into the bathroom and after a few moments returned with a white box in his hand. He knelt down in front of Erica and removed a bandage and a bottle of antiseptic from the box.

"I'm going to take off the cuffs. Don't try anything."

"We're on the same side . . ." Erica looked at the ID Card. "Dimitri."

"We'll see about that."

Dimitri unlocked the cuff from Erica's wrist. He reached up to the dining table and handed Erica a cup of coffee. As she drank the coffee, Dimitri cleaned and bandaged Erica's cut on her hand. He stood and placed the first-aid box on the table. "Sit. I've made us some breakfast."

Erica rose and took a seat at the head of the small table. Dimitri took a few quick strides to the kitchen, returned a moment later with two plates of eggs, and toasted rye bread. He placed one of the plates in front of Erica, who immediately picked up the fork on the table and dug into the plate of food. Dimitri sat in the chair to Erica's right. He took a long drink of his coffee.

"Why did you kill Igor?"

"You get right to the point, don't you?" Erica retorted between bites.

"I was starting to making progress, and in one dumb move, you may have just ruined everything."

"It doesn't take a genius to figure out Igor was involved in prostitution," Erica snapped.

"Prostitution is just a small part of what he's up to. There's drugs, money laundering, murders, and human trafficking. You knew what you were getting into. You planned to kill him. Why?"

"It's a long story."

"I've got plenty of time," Dimitri said as he took a sip of coffee.

Erica continued to eat her breakfast.

"You have a choice. Tell me why you did this and I may be able to help you. Don't, and I can turn you over to Victor and maybe I get into his good graces by finding you; or I can charge you with the murder. I'll give you a minute to decide."

Erica stared at Dimitri for a moment and then took several more bites of her breakfast. Sitting back in her chair, Erica picked up her cup of coffee and took a drink. She set the cup of coffee back on the table.

"So, what's it going to be?"

"I thought you said I had a whole minute?" Erica quipped sarcastically.

Dimitri slapped his hand hard on the table, causing the coffee to spill over the lip of her cup. Erica flinched.

"Talk to me!" Dimitri yelled intensely.

Erica sat in her chair, motionless.

Dimitri rose from the table and in one swift motion, grasped Erica's right wrist, and slapped on the handcuff, twisting her arm painfully behind her back, causing her to let out a short scream. Quickly, Dimitri grabbed her left wrist with his left hand.

"You're under arrest for the murder of Igor Tepic," he said as he tightened the cuff on her left wrist.

"What are you doing?" Erica demanded.

"I don't need this shit."

Dimitri picked up his cellphone and punched in numbers. "You're under arrest, and I'm calling headquarters to come and pick you up."

"You don't understand. You can't do this," Erica pleaded.

"I just did."

"Please! We're on the same side. I'll tell you what you want to know."

Dimitri stopped dialing and set the phone down on the table.

"I'm listening."

"Can you take these off?"

"The cuffs stay on. Start talking," Dimitri said as he sat in his chair, his eyes locked onto Erica.

"I am the daughter of Colonel Goran Sekulic, the former security chief to the prime minister of Serbia. My name is Adrijana Erica Sekulic."

"Sekulic and his daughter were killed over—"

"My mother was killed, but my father and I left Serbia after he recovered from his injuries. The reports of our deaths were released to the press because my father wanted to protect me from Andrus Skoffski, who wanted us dead."

"What does that have to do with Igor?

"Igor had been my father's personal driver and part of the traitorous plot to assassinate the president and take over the country. Igor is a coward and a genuine piece of shit, and he betrayed my father, which resulted in the death of my mother, so I killed the bastard. Happy?" Erica fired back, her eyes flashing anger. "My mother was innocent, and they killed her, and I vowed to avenge her death."

Dimitri took a sip of his coffee. He looked at her body language to see if she had been making up the story. As a trained police officer, he recognized the truth when he heard it.

"Okay, tell me the whole story. Start from the beginning."

"I've told you enough."

"I can help you. Don't you understand that? I've kept my eye on you since the day you started. I knew you weren't like the other girls. I've been protecting you," said a frustrated Dimitri.

Erica took a deep breath.

"My father became the head of security for the prime minister. He was extremely popular in the government and was high on the list of considered political appointees, but that wasn't my father," Erica said proudly. "He became the most trusted man in Serbia, but also the number-one target of Andrus Skoffski, the secretary to the Serbian minister of defense. My father told me Skoffski hated him and saw my father as a threat."

"Did your father tell you why Skoffski hated him?' Dimitri inquired.

"Skoffski knew my father found out about him. On the day of my tenth birthday, Skoffski tried to assassinate President Milosevic, and my father knew it, but he was betrayed by my father's second in command, Major Mikael Vukuvic, who was Skoffski's spy."

"What happened next?"

"My father told the president of the plot. Skoffski and Vukuvic knew that the coup had been doomed to failure, so they tried to kill my father along with some other officials who got in their way. Igor was in on the plot and set my father up that day. Vukuvic attacked our house with a rocket-propelled grenade. My mother killed and my father never completely recovered from it. He had severe headaches the rest of his life."

Erica sat back in her chair, taking a deep breath. The thoughts of the attack that killed her mother brought up feelings that were still painful.

"My father took me to a small town on the border of Serbia and Romania where we lived for the next eight years. No one knew where we had gone. We just disappeared. My father was always aware that if they could find us, Skoffski and Vukuvic would have us killed as payback for foiling the coup. At twelve, my father started training me to defend myself. I studied martial arts, weapons, from hand guns to assault rifles and even explosives, but I'm best at the crossbow."

"Impressive," Dimitri mused.

"It wasn't just all weapons. My father was a very smart man. He taught me five languages: English, French, Italian, Russian, and Spanish, and I can speak them fluently. He introduced me to fine arts until a few months ago. Skoffski found out where we were living and sent some men to kill us. I escaped, but they killed my father."

"Do you know where Skoffski or Vukuvic are?"

"I don't even know what they look like. I never saw Skoffski, and I can't find any photos of him. I only met Vukuvic once when I was maybe six years old, so I wouldn't be able to recognize him if he came into this room," Erica said flatly.

"How did you find out Igor was in Turkey?" Dimitri asked.

"My father got a tip from a source of his just a few months before they killed him."

"That could be how they found out where you were living. Very interesting story."

"It's all true," she said earnestly.

"I believe you."

"I'm sorry I spoiled your operation."

"Don't be. I can fix that. That's not your problem."

Dimitri rose from the table and unlocked the handcuffs. Erica rubbed her sore wrists.

"I need you to stay here for now. Don't go outside; don't look out of the window, and try not to make a sound while you are here alone. This is where I really live. I have a hotel room on the other side of town I use while I'm working undercover. I'm going back to the club to tell Victor that you were able to get away."

Erica shook her head.

"I will get back here when I can. There's food for you to eat, so you'll be fine for a few days."

Dimitri disappeared into the bedroom. A few seconds later, he returned with a cellphone in his hand and set it on the table. "If anything happens, dial one and I will be called. If I need to talk to you, I will call, and you will see my name appear on the screen. No one knows this number, so I will be the only one calling. I must go now."

Dimitri patted Erica on the hand. "Don't worry, everything will be fine. Just do what I tell you."

Dimitri quickly slipped out of the apartment, locking the door behind him. Erica sat at the table wondering just what her fate had in store for her next.

Erica spent the next day and night locked inside Dimitri's apartment, watching television programs and pacing the living room floor. The following evening Dimitri called the cellphone he left with her to tell her that he would be coming by the apartment around seven.

The thought of seeing Dimitri again after two days of solitude excited her. She eagerly put the small kitchen to good use with enough food in the pantry to make a nice dinner of Serbian baked beans with red cabbage.

When Dimitri opened the door to the apartment, the rich aroma of beans and bacon greeted him. The small dining room table set with plates and silverware, and much to Dimitri's surprise; Erica had found a lone candle he never thought he had in the place.

"Sit. Dinner is ready," a smiling Erica said to Dimitri.

"Smells wonderful. I haven't eaten all day," Dimitri admitted as he locked the door behind him. Dimitri sat down at the table as Erica moved to his side.

"Would you like some wine?"

"Yes, that would be fine."

Erica poured red wine into Dimitri's glass then into her own. Dimitri sat back and sipped his wine, letting the stresses of his undercover work slip away.

Taking Dimitri's plate, Erica deposited a portion of beans and cabbage onto the plate and placed it in front of him. He inhaled the rich aroma, picked up his fork, and scooped up some of the food. He looked up at Erica, who stood there waiting for the verdict.

"Aren't you eating?"

Erica slid her chair up to the table. She looked at Dimitri, as he tasted the warm forkful of beans. He stopped in mid-bite and scowled. Erica nearly panicked.

"It's not good?"

"It's delicious," Dimitri said, laughing.

"You were just joking with me?"

"Just a little. This is very good; you will make some man a wonderful wife."

"I have much to do. I can't think about that, Erica said morosely.

"You can't let this anger and revenge consume you, Erica." Dimitri said sternly, "It will destroy you."

"It will not destroy me. I will not let that happen."

Dimitri knew from her reaction that this is not the time to pursue this line, and he quickly changed the subject.

"I've talked to some people. I've got a safe place you can stay," Dimitri said brightly.

The irritating ring of Dimitri's phone interrupted his conversation. He picked up the phone and looked at the display.

"Yes!" He listened for a moment. "I'll be there in twenty minutes."

Dimitri stuffed the phone in his pocket.

"Victor's discovered you were staying at the university dorm."

Erica stiffened. The moment of normalcy had ended, again. Dimitri got up from the table.

"No! Sit!" Erica demanded. "My father always said, if you don't feed your body, it will fail you. You need your strength. So eat!"

Dimitri looked at her, dumbfounded. Then he let out a small laugh, sat down, and dug into his plate of food.

Erica awoke in Dimitri's bed that morning. She inhaled deeply and noticed that the apartment dark and deathly quiet.

She reluctantly got up and opened the blinds covering the bedroom window. The sun had just come up. It gave the outdoors a golden glow. Erica went to the bathroom and flipped on the light. The light hurt her eyes for a moment, but in a few seconds, her eyes adjusted to the brightness. She turned the shower on, then walked into the kitchen and started a pot of coffee.

When Erica returned, the water had steamed up the bathroom. She slipped into the shower and let the hot water caress her face and cascade down her body.

After a hot shower, Erica made up the bed, had just come out of the bedroom, when she heard the lock of the apartment door click and the door swung open.

Erica stopped for a moment, expecting Dimitri to come through the door, but no one came in. She froze for a moment, terror welling up in her stomach. Then Dimitri staggered into the room clutching his left side, bleeding from a bullet wound.

6

Mother of God! Where'd you learn to do that?

ERICA RUSHED to Dimitri and held him up as she helped him to the couch, kicking the door closed with her foot. Dimitri flopped onto the couch in severe pain.

"My god, Dimitri. What happened?"

"One of Victor's men. My cover's been blown. We need to get you out of here."

"But you're hurt? You need a doctor."

"Not yet. I've got to make sure you're okay first," Dimitri groaned as he dropped his head back on the couch cushion. "There's a first-aid kit under the bathroom sink."

Erica ran to the bathroom and ripped the sink cabinet door open, grabbed the first aid kid, and rushed back to the living room. Dimitri, teeth clenched tightly, endured the pain as best he could. Erica opened the first-aid kit and grabbed the small bottle of alcohol.

"This is going to hurt," she said.

Dimitri nodded his head and braced himself. "Okay, go ahead."

Erica gently lifted Dimitri's bloody shirt up and over the wound until it was completely exposed. She opened the bottle and poured the alcohol into the ugly looking hole in Dimitri's side. Dimitri stiffened against the pain, but didn't cry out. With his shirt up, and leaning to his right, Erica could see that the bullet had gone completely through him with a small entrance wound in the back of his left side. The larger exit wound in front.

"The bullet went clean through," Erica reassured as she doused a sterile bandage with alcohol and cleaned the entrance wound on his back.

Dimitri didn't react as much this time. His body had become numb to the pain.

"I can pack it with gauze, but that's not going to stop the bleeding completely."

Erica spread a generous amount of antibiotic ointment over the wound, then packed it with sterile gauze and taped it secure. She turned Dimitri to his right to get at the wound in his back and repeated the procedure.

"I need to get you to a hospital," Erica said, concerned.

"It'll be alright for a while. You need to get out of here. Grab your backpack. We've got to go now! I'll take you to the place where you can stay."

Erica helped Dimitri down the rear stairs of his apartment building, her backpack slung over her shoulder. When the two reached his car, Dimitri handed Erica his car keys.

"You'll have to drive." Dimitri looked Erica directly in the eyes. "You can drive, can't you?"

"My father taught me to drive when I was fourteen."

Dimitri opened the passenger-side door, cautiously slid his body in, and closed the door as Erica got behind the wheel and started the car.

Erica steered the car through the busy streets of the city until they reached a crowded commercial neighborhood where the block, packed with buyers and sellers, haggled with each other at the top of their lungs, the noise a deafening tumult. They could only inch the car along as the congestion brought traffic nearly to a stop.

"Turn right at the next corner. We need to get around this." Dimitri groaned.

Erica guided the car through the busy streets of the city. Dimitri struggled to stay alert and awake, the pain beginning to take its toll.

Erica continued driving, and for the next ten minutes, the only conversation Dimitri's directions. They pulled up to a stoplight across from the entrance to the D-100 Highway. As they waited for the light to change, a black sedan slammed into the rear end of the car, sending them into the intersection. Several cars crossing the intersection braked and swerved to avoid hitting the little BMW, but a small truck clipped the back bumper, knocking it off, spinning the car around to face the black sedan. Erica locked eyes with the driver of the black sedan; there, staring back at her, Victor.

Erica slammed the car into reverse, pushed the accelerator to the floor. The tires screamed leaving a trail of blue smoke as the car launched itself up the on-ramp backward. Victor slammed his foot down on the accelerator, sending the sedan into the intersection and sideswiping a taxi, in hot pursuit of the BMW, ripping off his side mirror. The car fishtailed as the two vehicles flew up the on-ramp face to face at increasing speeds as they merged onto the highway.

"Holy shit! What are you doing?" Dimitri exclaimed as he pulled out his gun.

"Hang on!" Erica yelled over the whine of the engine.

Like a professional stunt driver, Erica firmly grabbed the emergency brake and pulled hard while simultaneously yanking the steering wheel to the left, causing the car to spin 180 degrees. In one smooth motion, she slipped the gearshift lever into third gear and accelerated immediately, shifting into fourth, and pulling away from Victor's sedan.

"Mother of god, where did you learn to do that?" Dimitri said, terrified and impressed at the same time.

Erica weaved through slower-moving traffic with Victor hot on their tail. Dimitri reached up and started to crank open the sunroof.

"What are you doing?"

"Let him get a little closer."

"Why?" I can outrun him," Erica yelled emphatically.

"Trust me. Let him get closer," Dimitri shouted as he climbed up through the sunroof.

Erica positioned the BMW in front of Victor's sedan and eased off the accelerator.

Victor closed the gap between the two cars. Erica watched in her mirror as the sedan inched closer, the evil sneer on Victor's face sent a chill up her spine.

Dimitri suddenly popped up through the sunroof and emptied his automatic pistol into the windshield of the sedan. The sedan lurched to the left and slammed into the center divider, flipping over several times, bursting into flames. Cars speeding along the highway spun out of control, trying to avoid the careening heap of burning metal. A semi heading in the opposite direction braked abruptly, causing it to jackknife, hitting several cars traveling next to it. The BMW sped away to freedom and left in its wake a mass of twisted wreckage on both sides of the highway. Dimitri slid back into the passenger's seat, exhausted.

"You think you used enough bullets there?"

"I got him, didn't I?" Dimitri groaned, wincing in pain.

Erica glanced in his direction, and her eyes widened as she saw the passenger seat drenched in blood.

The little, banged-up BMW pulled into the parking lot of the closest surgical facility, Cerrahi Hastanesi. Erica jumped out of the car and slung the backpack over her shoulder. Dimitri lay passed out in the passenger seat.

Erica waved for a man dressed in scrubs who stood near the entrance to the hospital smoking a cigarette.

"I need help. This man has been shot," Erica yelled to the man.

He dashed to the front entrance and yelled instructions to the people inside.

A female nurse and a male orderly rushed a wheeled stretcher out of the hospital and followed the man down to the car.

"He's been shot, and bleeding badly. He's a police officer," Erica said, backing away from the car.

The two men raced to the car and carefully lifted Dimitri out of the vehicle and placed him on the stretcher.

"Go! Take him inside. I'll get his belongings," Erica ordered.

Erica watched as the three hospital attendants wheeled the unconscious Dimitri into the hospital. Once they passed through the doors, Erica turned and trotted to the nearby bus stop and boarded a waiting bus.

The rain poured down the night Erica landed at Newark International Airport from London after twenty-two hours of travel. She tried to hail a cab, but in this weather, there wasn't one to be had, so Erica jumped on a shuttle, taking her to one of the downtown hotels.

Alone in her hotel room, Erica took stock of her finances. She had very little money left and one lead: Tommy Lassiter. Erica picked up the hotel phone, held it in her hand for a moment, and then dialed.

7

This job is not for everyone

THE NEXT AFTERNOON, Erica took the bus to Alexandria, Virginia, then a cab at the depot, and went straight to the VCS Corporation, located in a business section of the city; the tan and gray building stood six floors high with their parking lot located in the front. Erica paid the fare and entered the building's main lobby. A tall African American man, mid-thirties, dressed in a very official navy blue uniform, wearing a gold badge over his left shirt pocket, greeted her. He sat behind a semicircular counter with a shiny black, stone-like counter top.

"How can I help you today, miss?" The security guard inquired, his deep, baritone voice echoing through the lobby.

"I'm here to see Mr. Lassiter."

"Sign in, please," the man requested, pointing to a registration book on the counter.

As Erica signed the book, she could see that the security guard had a bank of computer screens all along the length of the counter, each connected to several security cameras around the buildings perimeter. Erica set the pen down after signing and looked up at the guard, who handed her a visitor badge to clip onto her lapel.

"I'll need to look inside that backpack, miss."

Erica handed the backpack to the guard. He took the bag and placed it onto what looked like a copy machine.

He pressed the glowing button on the small control panel, and the machine buzzed for a few seconds. Then a green light lit up on the panel's upper right corner. He took the bag off the scanner and handed it to Erica.

"Sixth floor. Elevator to your right."

Erica thanked the man and marched to the bank of three elevators. She pressed the 'Up' button, and in a few seconds, the elevator doors opened. Erica took the elevator to the sixth floor. She stepped out facing a small lobby area with current magazines fanned out across a coffee table with comfortable-looking couches on either side. Two leather chairs were in the corners of the lobby opposite the couches. Erica approached the girl behind the reception desk protected by a glass enclosure that ran from desktop to ceiling with a small opening in front of her. The area reminded her of a teller station at a bank. To the right of the reception area a single door.

"I have an appointment with Mr. Lassiter."

"Please, have a seat."

Erica took a seat on the couch nearest the door and surveyed the lobby. Artwork decorated the walls and located across from the couch where Erica sat, a coffee station. Coffee sounded good to her, so she got up, made herself a cup, and returned to her place on the couch.

Erica sipped on her drink, appreciating the high quality of the brew; much tastier than the muddy water she had been subjected to for the last forty-eight hours. It must have been ten minutes before the door next to the receptionist opened.

Erica turned to the door and there stood a man about fifty years of age, gray at the temples, just a shade less than six feet tall. He had a muscular in build, but not overly so, for his tailored navy blue suit fit perfectly, void of any bulges. His face square, with a dominant chin, which had a slight cleft at the base. His medium brown eyes were calm but these the eyes of a man who missed nothing. In one brief glance, his eyes took in everything to the smallest detail. So this is Tommy Lassiter. Erica thought to herself. No wonder why my father trusted him, for he has the presence of a man who knew what he was doing and he knew how to do it well. Lassiter made eye contact with the girl behind the glass for an instant and then turned to Erica, a warm smile washed across his face as he stepped toward her, as she rose to her feet.

"Tommy Lassiter." He said as he extended his hand. "Thank you for coming in."

Erica and Tommy shook hands, both recognizing firm confident handshakes.

"Thank you for seeing me, Mr. Lassiter."

"Call me Tommy. Mr. Lassiter makes me feel like I'm an old man," he said smiling. "Let's talk in my office."

Tommy turned toward the door with Erica behind him, and when they were just a couple of feet away, the girl behind the glass pressed a button. The sound of a buzz, followed by a distinct click, and the door swung open into the offices of the VCS Corporation. They walked through the doorway and turned right, down a long hall.

"You can only imagine my shock when I got your call. I thought you and your parents were dead." Tommy said. "You look so much like your mother."

"I guess I do."

"I was friends with your mother before she met your father. She told me about the first time they met."

"Yes. I know the story. My father told her that he would marry her on their first date," Erica replied smiling.

"That was your dad. He knew what he wanted, and he went for it."

Tommy indicated with an open hand for Erica to enter the first office on their right and he followed her in.

"Have a seat," he said, as he closed the door behind them.

"So what can I do for you?"

"I'm searching for the men that were responsible for my parent's deaths. My father trusted you with his life, so I know I can also trust you. Vlado Nikic my father's aid is living somewhere in this country. I'm not sure where Petkovic is. I need your help to find them."

Erica's eyes quickly darted around the office that looked like any other company office with large windows from floor to ceiling along the outer wall that allowed the occupants to look out over a section of the city. As she watched, Tommy took a seat in an oversized desk chair that seemed to surround him when he sat in it. The large rectangular desk in front of him made of rosewood had a high gloss polish. Only a few items occupied the desktop. A gold pen and pencil set, black metal mesh in-out basket with several eight and a half by eleven sheets of paper in it, and a brass clock-barometer combination that rested on the desk, to his left, everything neat and in its place.

"The years that we spent in Romania, my father trained me. He wanted to make sure that I could take care of myself. He always knew that someday Skoffski would show up." Erica recounted as she sat down in the leather armchair on the right side of Tommy's desk.

"I see. I learned a lot from your father myself. He was one of the best." Tommy recalled, gently rocking in his oversized chair. "But I can't in good conscience, even think of helping you at this time. I'd be signing your death warrant." Tommy intoned casually.

Erica's shoulders dropped as she slumped down into her chair.

"It took Dimitri only ten minutes to know where to find you after you killed Igor. You were noticed wandering around town in a very provocative outfit."

"You know about that?" Erica questioned.

"It's my business to know everything. If Dimitri hadn't been a police officer, you'd be at the bottom of Marmara Bay right now. You blew a fifteen-month sting operation and nearly got a very good cop killed in the process. You're just not ready for this kind of work. "

Erica's head drooped as she inhaled and let out a deep sigh. Lassiter leaned back in his chair, brought his hands together, in a steeple position and sat motionless for a brief time before he spoke.

"However, if you come work for me, I can give you the training you will need to get those bastards."

Erica's head shot up, her eyes exploring Tommy's face.

"Let me tell you about VCS. We are a highly specialized Black Ops organization. We charge top dollar because we are that good. When a job is extremely difficult, or an operation would be too harmful to diplomatic relations between countries we are called in. We do have a private security division, mercenaries as you would commonly call it, but my division handles espionage and assassinations." The words rolled off his tongue as if he had said them a million times before. "I can openly tell you about this because if you ever went to the press with this information, there are so many layers to how this operation works, that it would take a team of investigators twenty years to trace anything back to us."

"I understand," Erica replied.

"If you've been keeping up with the news in the last few days, you'd be aware of some of our recent operations."

"You were responsible for the Pakistani Vice President's assassination?"

"Yes." Tommy said. "Afghan Rebels took the blame, so we were able to kill two birds with one stone, so to speak."

For the next ninety minutes, Erica listened intently as Tommy explained, in detail, the training she would need to go through to become a field agent with VCS. When he finished, Tommy sat back in his plush chair for several moments and then leaned forward, looking straight into Erica's eyes.

"This job is not for everyone. From what Dimitri told me about Istanbul, you have the potential for this kind of work," Tommy acknowledged. "You've had a lot of training so far so you'd be ahead of the game. This has to be your decision."

"I want to do it," Erica responded eagerly.

"I just told you that you may be assassinating someone, wouldn't a little time to think about this be in order? I'm going to give you seventy-two hours to decide," Tommy said as he removed a leather document case from the center drawer of his desk.

The case, approximately ten inches wide and fourteen inches long, had a flap that snapped into a buckle to close the case.

"There is a key to a hotel in town. Fifteen hundred dollars in cash and the key to a vehicle that you will find parked next to the main entrance of the building." Tommy referred to the case in his hand.

"There are also several documents in here that I want you to read very carefully. Spend the next few days to do whatever you need to do—clear your head. You have an appointment with me at four p.m., Thursday. You can give me your decision then."

Tommy rose from his chair, walked around, and stood in front of Erica, holding out the leather case to her.

"Think carefully." Erica took the leather case from Tommy and looked at it for a long moment.

"I will," Erica said, as she stood and extended her hand.

The two shook hands.

"If you have any questions, here is my number. Call me anytime, day or night," Tommy placed his card in Erica's hand.

Over the next six months of intense training, seven days a week, in the art of espionage and covert operations, Housed in a small efficiency apartment not far from VCS headquarters, Erica studied her field operation manual every night until she went to bed. Her training covered surveillance techniques, information gathering, encrypting messages, shaking a tail, martial arts, weapons and computer hacking. Erica quickly became proficient in all of these aspects, including disguises. Tommy was emphatic in emphasizing this advantage to her. As a woman, Erica needed to hone that skill, as it would prove valuable in the years ahead. Erica could enter a building from the front door and by the time she reached the rear door she had transformed herself into a different woman— a powerful asset for women in this line of work.

With the training completed, Tommy presented her with a small briefcase that contained her identities: passports, driver's licenses, library cards, everything an undercover operative would need to prove who they were to the authorities. There were six identities alone for U.S. citizens and half a dozen more for the four other countries where she could speak the native language. Erica now readied for her first assignment.

One week later, Erica reported to the VCS conference room on the sixth floor. The rectangular room had a large mahogany table in the center. The center of the table housed the controls to the state-of-the-art electronic equipment located on the far wall, where two large flat screens were mounted.

The wall of the room that served as the enclosure along the hallway had thick glass walls with a glass door that could be electronically locked from the inside. With the flick of a switch, the glass turned opaque to give the occupants of the room privacy. As Erica approached, she could see two people in the room. Tommy Lassiter and another man had taken seats at the table. As Erica entered the room, the two men stood.

"Good morning, Erica. I'd like you to meet Ford Reagan," Tommy indicated the man standing to his right.

Ford Reagan, twenty-six years old, stood six feet tall had short, cropped, dirty-blond hair and piercing, blue eyes. Ford's face had an even proportion and a distinct sense of calmness to it. The kind of face you'd like your doctor to have, assured and capable. Capable was Ford's middle name, and the best VCS could offer. Ruthless and professional, Ford is the guy they call on when the assignment is tough.

"It's a pleasure to meet you," Ford spoke in a quiet voice.

"Nice to meet you," Erica said as they shook hands. Erica sat down in the seat where a black, leather document folder rested on the table.

"If you'll open your folders, I'll start the briefing," Tommy said as he activated the flat screens on the wall. "This is a pretty simple operation, kind of a chance for Erica to get her feet wet."

Ford turned his attention to Erica and gave her a smile. Erica gave a slight smile back, feeling a bit of apprehension while anticipating her first mission.

"We've reason to believe that Al Maashallah, a known terrorist group, is being funded by an unknown organization somewhere in Europe." Tommy pressed a button on the remote control in his hand, and news footage of a car bombing appeared on the screen that credited to the terrorist group. "What we do know is that the money is being funneled through a business run by this man."

Tommy pulled up a photo of a man having dinner at a restaurant.

"This is Sergio Fortuna. He owns an electronics business in Barcelona, Spain. To put it simply, this will be a burglary. We want you two to break into Mr. Fortuna's home, then extract the information on his personal laptop that contain bank accounts and vital information to all of his contacts. To get into his place, you will have to disarm the security system. Feel free to take any valuables; this has to look like a simple burglary."

Tommy turned to Erica.

"You're ready. Everything you need to know is in the file. Good luck! You two leave tomorrow for Spain."

Erica and Ford boarded a flight back to the U.S. from Barcelona just seventy-two hours after they had arrived.

The operation went off without a hitch. Fortuna was conveniently away from his home the night Erica and Ford broke in. Erica hacked into Fortuna's laptop while Ford ransacked the place. She electronically uploaded the information contained in the laptop's memory to a VCS operative, then destroyed the flash-drive she used to copy the information.

The following morning, Ford contacted a fence that he had established a relationship with and sold off Fortuna's valuables, expensive jewelry, a rare coin collection and cash. It all amounted to nearly fifty thousand dollars. Ford anonymously donated the money to a local children's hospital before leaving the country.

Erica and Ford sipped cocktails as the airliner cruised at thirty-five thousand feet above the Atlantic.

"That was rather boring. I thought there would have been more excitement," Erica commented with an air of disappointment.

"That's usually how it goes; just a matter of routine. It's not like the movies, all car chases and close calls."

"I feel guilty about taking the money I'm getting paid," Erica said, turning her attention to the plane window. "I guess I expected a more satisfactory feeling."

Ford pushed his seat back and closed his eyes as he sipped his drink.

Chapter 8

All Kinds of Wrong

ONE WEEK AFTER Ford and Erica returned from Spain, they were preparing for another assignment. A radical survivalist group in Montana was in the market for weapons.

Erica and Ford sat in the conference room, their attention directed toward Tommy.

"We've got a government contract to fill. The ATF has been stretched pretty thin trying to keep up with the rise in domestic terrorists. You two will be going undercover posing as weapons dealers. The plan is to deplete the 'Freedom First' organization's bank account by selling them worthless weapons. They are a small group, and cleaning out their monetary supply will do immeasurable damage to the organization."

Erica and Ford left for Montana three days later and established themselves in a hotel in Great Falls. For two weeks, Ford went around town showing off some weapons that any survivalist would give his right arm to own.

One afternoon Ford and Erica were finally contacted by one of the group members, a young man trying to impress his superiors.

Shortly after three o'clock, Ford and Erica were sitting in their hotel room when a knock came at the door. Ford looked at Erica.

"You think we got one?"

"Only one way to find out," Erica said with a coy smile.

Ford slid off the bed and crossed to the door. He peered through the peephole and saw a younger man nervously twitching outside in the hallway.

"What do you want?" Ford asked through the door.

"Uh, y'all got some toys for sale?" the male voice inquired a little too loud.

Ford opened the door and took a long look at a twenty-two year old, Daryl Dugan. He stood about five foot ten, thin, and wiry—the kind of guy that looked like he only took a bath on Saturdays whether he needed it or not. He had a scruffy beard that only grew in random spots on his face and missing a couple of teeth.

Daryl was not the brightest bulb in the box, but all in all a good ol' boy. Once he heard about the strangers in town selling weapons, he decided to take the bull by the horns and set up a meeting with Ford and Erica.

"You don't strike me as the kind of guy who can afford the kind of toys I'm selling."

"Well, you just can't tell a cover by its book, now can ya?"

"Are you trying to say, you can't judge a book by its cover?" Ford mocked.

Daryl, caught a little off guard at his attempt to sound intelligent, hemmed and hawed for a moment, looking down at the floor.

"You selling guns or not?" Daryl asked emphatically.

Ford grabbed him and pulled him in the room, shutting the door and locking it.

"Why don't you announce it to the whole hotel?" Ford said in a hushed but stern voice.

"Who you kiddin'? The whole town knows y'all are up here selling guns and whatnot."

"Well, I don't need the authorities and every local yokel coming up here. These are premium weapons, and we're not having a yard sale."

"You ain't gotta worry about the sheriff. He's a big believer in the Second Amendment."

"Let's stop talking and get down to business. You got cash, farm boy, or are you just small potatoes?" Erica uttered impatiently.

"My name's Daryl Dugan, and I'm with . . . uh, how do you say, a local militia. I came to set up a deal with my colleagues and y'all," Daryl said with as much confidence as he could muster.

"My name's Nixon, and that's my partner, Betty," Ford motioned toward Erica.

"So when is this meeting?" Erica said doubtfully.

"How's three o'clock tomorrow over at the Lazy Moose Tavern? It's that old, red barn-looking building at the end of Main Street. You can't miss it. Got a real big moose over the front door."

"We'll be there," Ford said as he opened the hotel door, ushering Daryl back out into the hallway.

———————————————

At just a few minutes before three o'clock the following afternoon, Erica and Ford arrived at the tavern and made their way to the bar, taking seats on stools at the far end. Looking around the establishment, they found it sparsely populated. Two older men in coveralls and dirty baseball caps sat at a table drinking beers, discussing the local gossip. A couple of younger patrons shooting pool on the coin-operated table stopped their game when one of them saw Erica enter the bar. Once she took her place at the bar, the young men returned to their game.

At the corner of the bar near the entrance sat an old man in his sixties, talking with the bartender. Further observation revealed the place your typical local dive bar. The building, old and well worn, with sawdust strewn on the well-traveled, wood plank floor smelled of stale beer. The selection of beverages limited to maybe a dozen or so bottles of hard liquor and three brands of draft beer. Ford nodded to the burly bartender, a man in his late forties, bald on the top of his head, with bushy salt-and-pepper hair covering the sides. His classic beer belly fought hard against the light blue, button-down shirt that bulged out at his navel, straining the buttons to their max.

The man took several steps toward Ford and Erica and stationed himself between the two, but focused his attention on Erica, chewing on a gnarled toothpick stuck in the corner of his mouth.

"What can I get ya?" he asked in a raspy, baritone voice, taking the toothpick from his mouth.

"I'll take a whiskey, water back," Ford replied, turning to Erica, who sat at his left.

"Same," Erica said.

A smile appeared at the corner of the bartender's mouth. He turned and walked a few steps toward the center of the bar, sticking the toothpick back into its former resting place. The bartender selected a bottle from the shelf with his right hand and grabbed two shot glasses with his left and plodded back to Ford and Erica. He set a shot glass in front of each of them, then poured the liquor into the glasses until they spilled over, keeping most of his attention on Erica.

"It's my best stuff." The toothpick bounced in his mouth as he spoke.

He bent over, retrieved two eight-ounce glasses from underneath, and placed them firmly on the bar. Keeping his attention on his two new customers, the bartender reached to his right and grasped the beverage gun in its holder.

Placing the gun over the water glasses, the bartender sprayed water into both of the glasses at the same time, unconcerned with the amount of water spilling onto the bar.

"That'll be four bucks."

Ford reached into the left pocket of his jeans and pulled out a wad of cash. He peeled off a five-dollar bill and placed it on the bar. "Keep it."

The bartender took the money off the bar and backed away, taking another long look at Erica. He rang up the purchase and put the bill in the cash register, then tramped to the other end of the bar and returned to his conversation with the old man in the corner.

"That was a bit uncomfortable," Erica said in a barely audible tone.

"Gave me the creeps."

Ford and Erica threw back their drinks and waited. Nearly ten minutes passed, and Erica started to feel like this was just a ruse.

Just when Ford started to wonder why they were just sitting at this bar marking time, a door in the rear of the room opened, and out walked Daryl. He scanned the room then noticed Ford and Erica sat at the near end of the bar from where he stood. Erica sensed a shift in the energy of the room, glanced over her shoulder, and noticed Daryl shuffling towards the two of them.

She nudged Ford with her elbow, and he turned. Daryl stopped at the edge of the bar to Erica's right, placing his elbows on the bar rail.

"Nixon, Betty, how y'all doin'?"

"We're fine. What's the deal?" Erica asked impatiently.

"I got a couple of guys who want to meet you, out back."

"Well let's get this started," Ford said as he slipped off the stool.

"You wait here," Daryl told Erica. "We just want to talk to Nixon."

"Listen plowboy, we're partners."

"It's okay, Betty. I'm just going to listen."

Erica gave Daryl a look that made him take a step backward.

"I'd be careful how you speak to her, Daryl. She could kick your ass from here to Sunday," Ford said with a wink toward Erica.

The two men strode to the rear of the room, Daryl leading, Ford close behind. Daryl opened the door he came out of just a few minutes earlier and held it open for Ford to enter. Ford found himself in a storage room that also served as an office. Behind a battered desk sat a large man with a round, red face and deep-set, brown eyes. He wore a sweat-stained khaki shirt with the two top buttons open, exposing the collar of a dingy, white t-shirt. Over the left pocket hung a gold star with the word 'Sheriff' etched in black. Next to him stood a younger man, slim with thin, brown hair and a pointed chin, who also dressed in a khaki shirt with a star over his left pocket, but his read: 'Deputy.' Leaning against the wall a slender, tall man with greasy, black hair and a long, thin nose, smiling a toothless smile at Ford as he entered the room.

Seeing the badges, Ford abruptly stopped, his eyes darting between the two policemen.

"Daryl, I thought we understood each other . . ."

"Relax, son, and have a seat. We're all friends here," the man wearing the sheriff's badge said.

"What's this all about?" Ford asked.

"I'm Ernie Biggs. This is my Deputy, Elvin Shanks. Back there is E.J., my nephew. I'm the general of this here little organization. So you've got some weapons to sell?"

Ford took a seat in an old, wooden chair in front of the desk.

"I do, but my merchandise doesn't come cheap, and just so we understand each other, it's a package deal—all or nothing."

"Let's not worry about that for now. If you got what I'm looking for, son, I can pay your price. Tell me what you got, and let's talk turkey," Biggs said, flashing a toothy smile.

"Okay, then," Ford relaxed into the chair, "but I'd like to bring my partner in. I don't want to leave her in the dark."

"If it's all the same to you, Nixon—love that name by the way—I rather we leave the business to just us men. This is no place for a woman."

"Especially one that looks like that!" Daryl chimed in.

"Simmer down there now, Daryl," Biggs said, as he took back control of the conversation. "So tell me what's in your inventory."

"I got ten AR-15s, eight AK47s, two fifty-caliber sniper rifles with night scopes, and two M-136 anti-tank guns," Ford said as if reading off a grocery list.

"That's a hell of a haul, son. What's your asking price?"

"Eighty-five grand—and that includes ammo and the truck. In cash on delivery—not a penny less. Non-negotiable."

Biggs took a long pause, staring at Ford. "What say you give us a sample of the goods before I go shelling out that kind of dough."

"Absolutely. I'll have my partner go get something for you to play with." Ford pulled out his cell phone and called Erica. "Betty, honey, would you be so kind to bring in a sample for these gentlemen," Ford said, disconnecting the call.

"She'll be here in a jiffy."

For the next three minutes, the men in the room just stared at each other without uttering a word between them. Suddenly a knock at the storage room door interrupted the silence. Daryl scuffled to the door and opened it slightly to see who had knocked.

"Just let her in, Daryl," Biggs, barked with a hint of exasperation.

Erica walked in holding a long, rectangular, cardboard box. Biggs rose from his position behind the desk. She placed it on the battered desk, pulled a knife from no one knew where, and commenced to open the box, revealing an AR-15 in mint condition. She took the all black weapon out of the box, reached in her back pocket, and pulled out an ammo clip, slamming it into the gun.

"The AR-15 is a lightweight, 5.56 mm, magazine-fed, fully automatic rifle with a rotating-lock bolt, actuated by direct impingement gas operation. It is manufactured with the extensive use of aluminum alloys and synthetic materials. On full auto, this would cut a man in half. Have fun gentlemen," Erica said as she tossed the rifle to Sheriff Biggs.

He took a deep breath, exhaled as he walked around the desk, and stopped, standing above Ford. "Son, if this toy proves worthy, you got yourself a deal," Biggs said as he extended his hand out to Ford.

Ford reached for Biggs' hand as he stood up with a big smile.

"That sure is a lot of money, Ernie," Elvin remarked.

"Elvin, didn't anyone ever teach you to keep your mouth shut when men are doing business?" Biggs said as he shot Elvin a "shut the fuck up" look, then smiled a big, good-ol'-boy smile at Ford.

"Sorry, Sheriff."

"We'll have Daryl holler at ya tomorrow," Biggs stated as he looked at Erica, impressed with her performance.

"Till then, Sheriff," Erica said.

"You can call me Ernie, little lady. I like your style."

Erica and Ford entered their rental car parked outside the Lazy Moose.

"You got all that, right?"

"Loud and clear," Erica responded as she pulled a tiny earpiece out of her right ear. "This has all kinds of wrong written all over it."

"We're going to have to keep on our toes. This is just too easy. They're going to make a play for the guns."

"I'll rig the truck."

"Yeah, that's probably a good idea," Ford said as he started the car. "You wanted excitement . . . Here you go."

Erica laughed a good-natured laugh.

The following evening, Ford received a call from Daryl that the deal is on, and they were to deliver the guns to a farm about thirty miles north of town.

Ford and Erica geared up for the evening's excitement, testing their communication equipment and rechecking their weapons.

"Truck's wired," Erica affirmed in full warrior mode.

"You know they're going to keep us separated again, so stay sharp."

* * * * *

The sun had just set behind the ridge as Ford drove the 1993 GMC box truck up to the gate of a farm. Erica followed close behind in the Ford Taurus rental car. The red glow of the sunset seemed to set the sky on fire, a fire similar to the one burning in the pit of her stomach. A slow, aching burn boded no good will for her and Ford.

"It looks like there are two guards at the entrance." Ford's voice came through Erica's earpiece crisp and clear.

"Are they armed?" Erica responded.

The headlights illuminated one of the guards standing in the center of the dirt road as Ford approached the gate. He waved his hand out in front of him, indicating for the vehicle to stop.

"Both, with assault rifles."

Ford rolled down the driver's side window, and the man who stopped the truck approached. Erica's car pulled in behind Ford, her stomach smoldering with anxiety.

"You Nixon?" the man, fifty plus, pot-bellied with a full beard, peered inside the vehicle.

"I'm Nixon, and that's my partner behind me."

The man, his beard streaked with gray, turned his attention to Erica's car just a few feet off the truck's bumper.

"Drive straight up the path, and you'll see the lights to the house on your left. They're waiting for you up there. The girl stays here."

Erica heard every word in her earpiece as she sat expressionless behind the wheel. The second guard, in his early thirties, muscular with a shaved head, walked to the driver's side of Erica's car. The older guard lumbered to the metal gate baring the entrance to the farm and swung it open, then signaled to Ford to proceed to the farmhouse. Ford put the truck in gear and drove through the gate, following the dirt path, driving past a rusted, once red 1996 Jeep Cherokee.

"I'll give you a head count when I reach the house," Ford's calm voice reported in Erica's ear.

Erica eased the car closer to the gate as the older guard closed it.

"You're to wait here, missy," the man commanded as he walked to the passenger's side of the car.

Erica pushed the power window buttons and lowered both door windows. The older man stuck his head through the passenger-door window.

"What's the deal? Why can't I go up to the house?"

"I'm doin' just what I've been told. You just sit tight until your boyfriend gets back."

"That's my partner, not my boyfriend, buddy!" Erica snapped.

"Whatever. You stay here!"

Erica opened the car door and slid out. She wore a solid red shirt, sleeves rolled up past her elbows and the top three buttons undone.

Even in the diminishing light, the two men could clearly see that she wasn't wearing a bra. The shirt tied off at her waist, displaying a well-defined midriff. Tight-fitting jeans accentuated Erica's shape with black, high-heeled boots completing the ensemble. The two men exchanged lustful looks, and then both returned their attention to Erica, wanton desire in their eyes.

Erica glided to the front of the car and leaned up against the fender, stretching her long, shapely legs, provoking a look between the two gate guards. Removing a pack of cigarettes from the left breast pocket of her shirt, Erica shook the pack a couple of times, bringing several cigarettes out over the lip of the pack. She selected one and placed the filtered end between her lips.

Digging her right hand into her tight jeans, Erica managed to remove a Zippo lighter. She flipped open the cover and ignited the lighter, touching the flame to the end of the cigarette. Erica took a long draw, bringing the cigarette to life then snapped the lighter closed and slid it back into her pocket.

As Ford slowly drove down the path, he glanced in the side mirror and could clearly see the flash of light coming from Erica's Zippo. "I can see the house. It'll just be another minute."

The two guards couldn't take their eyes off Erica as she leaned back on the fender of the car, impassively smoking. Off in the distance they could hear the sound of the truck's motor getting softer as it neared the farmhouse. After a moment, the only sound heard were crickets chirping.

"This is it," Erica heard Ford say in her earpiece.

The front door to the farmhouse opened, and out stepped Biggs, Daryl, E.J., and Elvin. Ford could see three more men inside the house.

"I've got seven," Ford whispered.

Biggs walked briskly to Ford, with Daryl just a step behind him. E.J. and Elvin positioned themselves on the porch of the old farmhouse. The area nearly completely dark with the only light coming from the inside of the house and from a light fixture mounted over the door of the barn about forty yards to the right of the house. Both the house and barn were weatherworn and in need of repair.

"Right on time. Good to see you again, Nixon," Biggs said with a broad smile across his round face as he stepped off the porch that listed to the right.

"I don't believe in wasting time," Ford said as he shook Biggs' hand, noticing the faded white painted house and peeling red window trim.

"The merchandise is in the truck?"

"It's all there, in the back," Ford confirmed as he tossed a thumb over his shoulder. "You got the money?"

"Us country people move a little slower. Don't be in such a hurry all the time," Biggs remarked as he turned, "Take a look inside, Daryl."

Ford tossed Daryl the keys to the truck.

"Come on into the house. We'll have a little drink, and while Daryl is checking the inventory, you can count the money."

"My partner is waiting at the gate."

"The boys will keep her company. It'll be no more than ten minutes."

The first stair plank missing as Ford stepped over it and up onto the porch. He noticed Elvin and E.J. smiling at him as if he was the guest of honor at a barbecue where he would serve as the main course.

Biggs opened the door to the house and motioned him in with Elvin and E.J. on his heels.

"Damn, Sheriff! Is this a family reunion?" Ford exclaimed as he indicated the other men in the house. "Are there anymore I should know about?"

"Nope, this here's all there is. That's Bud, Bobby, and his little brother, Jed."

Ford looked around the room. He noticed Jed, a scrawny little guy about five-five with long, black hair and beady, green eyes, sitting in the corner sweating bullets.

Bobby, a bit larger build than Jed, had the same black hair but cut shorter. He looked like he got the lion's share of looks and brains growing up in the family, which wasn't saying much. He stood next to Jed, nervously twitching like he had to go to the bathroom. Then there was Bud. At six-three, he looked like a linebacker—gruff, a full red beard, and resembled the Brawny Towel man. He eyed Ford as he would a rare steak ready for carving.

"Well, I see all your cousins, but no money. If I were a betting man, I'd swear I just walked into a trap."

Everyone laughed heartily.

"Relax, Nixon. You're amongst friends."

Erica, hearing the laughter, realized she had to move and move now. As she drew another hit off her cigarette, she looked at the two watching her.

"I'm sorry. Would either of you care for a smoke?"

"I'd take one," said the guard with the shaved-head as he stepped up to Erica.

Erica took the pack from her pocket, shook up a single cigarette, and offered it to "baldy."

He leaned his rifle up against the rental car, took the cigarette, and put it in his mouth. Erica pulled the Zippo out of her pocket and in one move flipped it open and lit it, then held the flame to the end of the cigarette. He took a long puff, blew out the smoke, and smiled a rotten-toothed smile.

"You're kind of cute. How about a kiss, sugar?"

He laughed an embarrassed goofy laugh. "Sure," he drawled.

Erica reached up and placed both hands on his cheeks, and as the young guard closed his eyes with anticipation, Erica slid her right hand under his chin and her left hand on the back of his head, and in one blinding move snapped his neck.

Before the older guard realized what happened, Erica spun around and with a powerful roundhouse kick, slammed her boot into his throat, crushing his windpipe.

Erica quickly opened the back door of the Taurus and retrieved a 9mm pistol and small Uzi, both equipped with silencers, and a pair of night-vision goggles.

She flung open the gate, strapped the Uzi over her shoulder and sprinted across the open field toward the farmhouse.

As she neared the house, she ducked behind a tree where she saw Daryl exit the truck and walk to the black barn door that hung slightly off its hinges.

It took a profound amount of struggle as Daryl forced the creaking and scraping door to open wide enough to get the box truck through. Erica bolted toward the farmhouse as Daryl got back into the truck. She stalked towards the front porch of the house and stopped just a few yards from the window when she heard Biggs in her earpiece.

"Elvin, show 'em the money. It would be rude not to show you the cash even though we have no intention of letting you leave with it."

Erica heard laughter again in her ear.

"E.J., signal the boys to take care of that little bitch down at the gate."

E.J. went out onto the front porch with a flashlight and began to signal in the direction of the gate. Erica took aim and squeezed off a single round, hitting E.J. in the middle of the forehead. E.J. dropped the flashlight and fell down the wooden steps, causing them to shatter.

"What the hell?" said Biggs. "Bobby, look and see if twinkle toes hasn't fallen off the porch."

Erica saw Bobby move to the window, and as he peered out, she popped one round in his forehead just above the bridge of his nose, making a perfect hole in the glass. Bobby stiffened.

"Well? Is he okay?" Erica heard Biggs say.

Bobby rocked and slowly fell backward, away from the window, crashing to the floor. Jed screamed like a girl and rushed to his brother's side.

Erica then heard a scuffle, in the next instance a bright flash of light, and a shot rang out. Erica burst in the room. The first thing to catch her eye was Elvin sitting up against the wall, facing her with a large hole in his chest. Gasping for breath on his knees Sherriff Biggs, his hands clutched his throat.

In the center of the room, Jed hovered over his dead brother in hysterics. Erica saw Bud wrestling Ford, trying to get control of the gun in Ford's hand. They were bouncing all around the room, crashing into everything in their path. Unable to get a clear shot, Erica turned her attention to Jed, as he fumbled in the dim light to get his rifle aimed at the struggling pair. Erica pumped two quick shots into Jed's chest, dropping him to the floor with a resounding thud.

Bud wrestled Ford to the floor and had him pinned, but Ford managed to kick up his leg and knock Bud off him, rolled over to get up when Biggs leaped onto his back and knocked the gun out of his hand. Biggs picked up the gun at the same time Erica got a clear shot at Bud. Erica fired once; then one more quick shot followed, but Bud continued to stagger to his feet. Two more quick shots popped, and Bud collapsed to the floor.

"Put the gun down!" Biggs voice rang out. Erica turned to the sound and froze, her 9mm held in both hands in the firing position. Biggs had his revolver held just an inch from Ford's temple.

9

The warmth of another

ERICA HELD her ground, her gun trained on Biggs as her chest heaved, taking in volumes of air.

"Take the shot, Erica."

Erica inhaled a deep breath and held it.

"Don't be stupid, girly. Put it down! Now!"

"Take it!" Ford shouted.

Erica exhaled her breath, rigidly holding out her arm directly at Biggs head. Her stiff body relaxed for an instant as she dropped her shoulders and slowly lowered her arm.

"Smart move, missy. Now gently set the gun on the floor," Biggs sneered.

It would have taken an atomic clock, separating time into thousandths of a second, to accurately calculate the sequence of events that followed. Biggs blinked his eyes once and opened his mouth to put forth his next demand, and in that microsecond, Erica raised her arm and fired a shot that hit Biggs directly between his eyes. For an instant Biggs just stood there motionless, his eyes wide open, dead on his feet. Ford, confused for a moment, had not realized Erica's shot had hit its mark, and turned just as Biggs hit the floor.

"Grab the money, and let's get the fuck out of here,' Erica barked, her adrenaline pumping, heart pounding.

Ford grabbed the suitcase of money, and the two headed out of the house, stepping over bodies as they went.

Jogging down the dirt path toward the gate, Erica abruptly stopped.

"Daryl is still in the barn. What should we do?"

"Blow it. This whole thing has turned into one big clusterfuck?" a weary Ford said.

Erica dug into her back pocket and slid out her cellphone, then punched two numbers. A moment later, in the distance the ring of a cellphone cut through the night followed by a massive explosion.

"Damn girl! Use enough C-4 there?"

"Wasn't me. What the hell were they keeping in that barn?" Erica said as she looked back at the giant fireball in the sky.

Ford and Erica raced to the entrance of the farm. The gate remained wide open, the way she left it when she sprinted to the house. The two guards lay motionless where Erica left them, dead.

"What are we going to do about them?" Erica questioned Ford, concerned.

"Load them into the Jeep."

They stuffed the bodies of the two guards into the Jeep Cherokee along with the suitcase of money.

"Give me your gun. Get into the car, and follow me," Ford ordered as he jumped behind the wheel of the vehicle.

Ford sped down the interstate with Erica following in the Taurus.

"Here's the deal," Erica heard Ford's voice say in her earpiece. "We're going to stage an accident. These two bozos tried to make off with the money after the gun deal went bad. They killed the sheriff and the deputy, but unfortunately, they were killed in a car accident. I'll get this info to Tommy so he can give the ATF a heads up."

After staging the accident with the bodies of the older bearded gate guard and the young rotten-toothed guy, Erica drove south on the interstate while Ford nursed his pounding head in the passenger seat.

"You saved my life back there. When this whole thing went to shit, you came through like the cavalry." Ford moaned.

"I was on edge the whole time."

"You kept your cool; that's what's important. You didn't panic." Ford took a long look at Erica. "Thanks. I couldn't have a better partner."

Ford's compliment pleased Erica. They were on the same level—partners, comrades, a team; something that Erica never had before. She felt she had always been on her own, but now she had someone . . . someone who respected her.

They drove for an hour and a half until they reached Helena. Erica found the best hotel in town and booked two adjoining rooms. Still pumped up on adrenalin, Erica dragged Ford into the hotel bar for a drink. They ordered cocktails and found a booth in the back corner to give themselves some privacy.

"Are we good with Tommy?"

"I told him we walked into a trap, but we were ready," Ford said as he took a drink of his scotch. "The authorities will get a tip where they can find the Jeep tomorrow."

Ford placed his glass on the table then looked Erica in the eyes.

"I let him know that if it wasn't for you, I'd be long dead by now."

"Thanks for that. Coming from you, it means a lot to me," Erica said uncomfortably.

Maybe it had been the excitement of the mission. Or the near disaster that they had somehow survived. Or maybe just that Erica and Ford were together, and this togetherness made Erica feel a bit apprehensive. When you're responsible for someone staying alive, your connection with them automatically becomes stronger.

Erica looked at Ford, really for the first time. She noticed things she had never noticed before. He had a small scar on his forehead just above his left eye. For some reason, it just seemed to appear as the two sat in that booth, enjoying their drinks. The uneasy feeling come from the fact that she wanted to be close to Ford, wanted to feel him close to her. It was disconcerting to her, but she hoped to extend the evening. Ford however suggested they get some rest.

At the doors of their adjoining rooms, they bid each other a good night sleep and vowed to meet for breakfast the next morning.

In her room, Erica dressed in just a camisole and panties. She could hear Ford moving around next door. Something inside Erica made her knock on the adjoining door. She didn't know why or what she would say when Ford answered the door, but she knocked anyway.

Opening the door in bare feet, dressed in blue jeans and a white t-shirt, Ford eyed Erica up and down.

"Hey."

"I was really scared tonight."

"Being scared is natural." Ford reassured her.

"I didn't think I could get to you in time." Erica admitted still suffering from the ordeal.

The two comrades stood in the frame of the door for what seemed an eternity before Erica spoke.

"I don't want to be alone."

Ford stepped back as he opened the door wider and Erica entered. He took her into his arms and gently kissed her. She kissed him long and hard, feeling his strong arms wrap around her with a squeeze that made her feel safe and electrified. In Ford's arms she felt something she had never felt before, the warmth of another human being caressing her in a romantic way.

There was no mistake; Ford had become aroused. These feelings were all very new for her, but they made her feel alive. Her skin tingled all over her body, and she felt excitement and power like never before.

He picked her up and carried her to the bed. He laid her down gently and turned off the lamp on the bed stand. The light coming from Erica's room gave Ford's room a soft, warm, golden glow. Ford crawled on top of her, kissing her more passionately as his hand caressed her pert breast.

Erica moaned with pleasure, looked up at Ford as he pulled his t-shirt over his head, exposing his muscular pectorals. She ran her fingers through his lush chest hair, then took her fingernails, and pulled them down hard toward his pants.

"Oh my god!" Ford groaned. She unbuckled his belt and unzipped his trousers. Ford couldn't believe what was happening to him.

"I want to remember you, always," Erica said with a warm smile. Erica ran her hand down the front of his pants. "Did you bring your gun to bed?"

Erica struggled to pull his pants down. Ford took her hands in his and bent over to kiss her fingers. He slid off the bed, slipped off his jeans, and revealed his tight gray briefs. The bulge under those briefs enormous, stretching the fabric to its limits.

"Maybe you should think about buying larger underwear. Isn't that uncomfortable?"

"They were fine up until about ten minutes ago."

Erica took hold of the elastic band in his underwear, and it started to tear as she stretched it over his throbbing tool. Ford lay down beside Erica in bed; their eyes locked. Erica sat up and crossed her arms, grabbed the bottom of her camisole and pulled it off over her head and revealed her perfect breasts. Ford reached for her, but Erica slapped his hand away.

"Wait," she said with a disciplinary tone. "All in good time."

"Those are perfect," Ford declared as Erica straddled him on the bed.

Erica took his hands and slid them up her body. She sat on his bulging package, grinding away as Ford caressed her ample breasts. Ford had enough and sat up, wrapped his arms around Erica's body. He flipped her over onto her back—the soft thick pillows enfolded her head. Slowly and gently, Ford slid Erica's delicate panties down her thighs, over her knees, and inched them down to her ankles. Taking her left foot into his hand, he slipped her panties off her foot. Kissing her instep, his lips gently caressed her toes. Ford then reached for the right foot, slid the panties off, and gently kissed that instep.

Ford slid his hands up her legs, caressing, just barely touching her soft, smooth skin that stirred a desire Erica never experienced before.

Ford's fingers explored her, arousing Erica's passion to the breaking point. Finding her G-Spot, a moan echoed within the room. It took a moment for Erica to recognize the voice; it was her own.

"Oh yes! I want you now!" Erica whispered.

Ford hovered, gazed into her eyes. He lowered himself to her and kissed her as she wrapped her legs around him. He penetrated her slowly and gently. Erica's entire body released all of the trials and tribulations of the last eight years in one orgasmic wave of ecstasy.

Erica woke first the following morning, still in Ford's strong arms, arms that cradled her as a soft, feather-down comforter cradles a newborn. Erica felt reborn, a new person, a new woman; the world different today because she was different.

Careful not to wake Ford, she eased out of bed and tiptoed to the bathroom—turned on the light and stood in front of a full-length mirror that covered a section of the wall opposite the door. Her naked body appeared more mature to her this morning. She no longer saw Erica, the virgin girl in the mirror; she saw Erica, the woman. She opened the shower door just an arm's length to her left and turned on the water. She waited no more than two minutes before she tested the water with her hand and found it warm and inviting.

She left the water running, went back into the room, and stood for several moments, watching Ford sleep. Quietly, she crawled under the sheets and pressed the length of her body against his. Nudged close to his ear, Erica gently blew air up and down his neck. The rush of warm air caused Ford to stir a bit.

She did it again, a little bit more forceful this time, and Ford opened a tired eye. He turned his head to Erica, and she kissed him softly on the lips. Ford smiled and wrapped his arms around her.

"I have the shower going and ready," Erica whispered.

"You waited for me?"

Erica nodded and kissed Ford on his cheek.

"Come on. Let's get up."

Erica rolled out of the bed and bounced into the bathroom.

Ford propped himself up on his elbow and watched Erica move across the room until she disappeared into the bathroom. Smiling to himself, Ford threw the covers off, trotted into the bathroom, and found Erica already in the shower.

Over breakfast, the two spoke little, wondered what each other thought about the previous night. Erica, not wanting to bring up any expectations for what may transpire in the future, having no experience in the ways of romance, could not put a coherent sentence together.

"Mmmm, good coffee," Erica said as she sipped from her cup.

"Yeah, I think its French Roast."

"I love French Roast."

Ford smiled at her then took a sip from his cup.

"I love French Roast?" Erica mumbled to herself. "That was stupid."

"I'm sorry, did you say something?"

"No, just good coffee." Erica smiled an awkward smile.

That's the best you could come up with? I love French Roast? Erica thought to herself. He thinks I'm an idiot. Now, he's never going to want to have sex with me again.

"Good bacon, too," Ford said as he stuffed his face.

"I love bacon," Erica uttered without thinking.

Oh, my god! Did I just say that out loud? Look at him. He's just wolfing down those eggs like I'm not even here. That plate means more to him than me. He hates me, Erica thought. I am an idiot, and he knows I'm an idiot. What's going on with me? What are these feelings? I can't control myself, or my mouth. Is this going to happen every time I have sex? I don't think I like this. I mean, I liked it, but I don't like this. Oh, for Christ's sake, shut the fuck up. Did I just tell myself to shut up? Stop!

"You okay?" Ford asked, noticing something strange about Erica's demeanor.

"Fine. Yeah. Peachy."

Peachy? Did I just say peachy? I've never said peachy in my entire life. But today I decide that I am just peachy! God help me. I'm losing my mind, thought Erica. I had sex, and now I'm losing my mind over a man . . . a very attractive man. I mean, when he took his shirt off . . . Oh my God, who are you talking to? Shut up! Just shut up! Shut the fuck up!

"Are you sure you're all right? You've got a weird look on your face."

Shit, he can hear me, Erica thought.

"No, I'm fine. I always look like this after sex . . . after I've had sex. I mean, after . . . Oh, yes, more coffee please," Erica said to the waitress, who suddenly appeared at the table with a coffee pot in her hand.

On their way to the airport, the radio reported the incident on the farm outside of Great Falls with no report on the missing Jeep Cherokee.

The events of the last twenty-four hours took its toll on Erica. Fatigue quickly set in, and only thirty minutes into the flight, Erica fell asleep. Ford lifted the chair arm so he could hold her in his arms as she slept, dreaming pleasant dreams—dreams that took her back to the happy days of her childhood: her mother, her father, school parties, and play dates with her friends. She dreamed of Ford: the warmth of his eyes, the strength of his being. When she awoke, she was disappointed to discover that the blissful experience, that seemed to make time standstill, had been just a dream. Her compensation—she awoke in Ford's secure arms.

The next two months consisted of additional training, candlelight dinners at Ford and Erica's respective apartments, cocktails and dancing on Friday nights, site-seeing on Saturdays and Sundays. For the first time in her life, Erica was in a relationship. The first time that she could remember, she hadn't obsessed about the death of her parents or about the revenge she had been seeking for the last two years. Her mind now bathed in thoughts of breathtaking sunsets, the sound the crickets made as they chirped on a warm evening, and the vibrant colors of fall as the trees turned.

During these days of Erica's discovery about herself, she and Ford worked together on two assignments. First, another "without a hitch" intelligence-gathering operation in Iran that gave Erica an appreciation for Ford and his ability to take things as they came without complaint. The second did not go as well; unexpected circumstances caused the situation to become serious. Erica's next assignment to head up surveillance and monitor the video and audio feed as Ford infiltrated the Chinese Embassy in Montreal, Canada and plant a listening device. The objective—to gain evidence of the Chinese Government's intentions in a business deal with Canada that could possibly jeopardize U.S. military secrets. To insulate itself from anything that could go wrong, the CIA hired VCS to take on this mission.

Ford entered the embassy through a service entrance left unlocked by a custodial worker VCS had put on their payroll months earlier. Everything went as planned when things started to go wrong. All missions are susceptible to happenstance. Ford had been inside a good ten minutes when a drunk driver lost control of his car and smashed into the gate of the embassy, starting a fire that set off the embassy's security system.

The embassy immediately put all staff on full alert. Officials as well as security officers began to scurry around the embassy. Ford found himself trapped inside with the Montreal Fire Department and Police Department just minutes away from the location.

Erica contacted Ford on the communicator, warning him of the situation. Ford decided to finish the job and not extricate himself from the embassy. Erica panicked. She bolted out of the surveillance van and raced to the service entrance unnoticed. She entered the embassy and quickly maneuvered through the building to Ford's location. She didn't get very far before she met Ford approaching her in a hall. Ford grabbed Erica's arm and dragged her back to the service entrance, noticeably upset. They hit the door just before the entire embassy shut down. Ford and Erica lost themselves in the crowd that gathered to gawk at the accident.

Ford and Erica returned to Virginia twelve hours later, arrived at VCS early that morning, and were told to meet Tommy in the conference room. When Erica and Ford approached, they could see Tommy Lassiter as he paced the conference Room. Ford opened the door for Erica, she stepped in with Ford just a step behind her. Tommy paced, took no notice of them.

Ford and Erica exchanged looks then cautiously sat down in the two chairs closest to them. Tommy continued to pace. Erica and Ford continued to watch. It would have been fair for someone observing from the outside to conclude that the two were watching a tennis match, each of their heads moving from left to right in a rhythmic fashion.

Tommy abruptly stopped his pacing. He stared out of the window for several moments before he spoke.

"I'm going to have to make a change," Tommy said, facing the window. "I'm not happy about it, but it's something I have to do."

Tommy turned, faced the young pair, leaned over and put both hands on the polished, mahogany table, never taking his eyes off his employees. Some time passed without Tommy saying a word.

"What kind of change?" Ford asked, unable to stand the silence any longer.

"You two are my best operatives. You know that. You also think you're so cleaver, you think you can get away with things without me finding out about it."

Ford and Erica exchanged looks, concern on their faces.

"It strikes me as ill-advised to try and put one over on the person who probably knows more about you than you know about yourself."

"I don't understand," Erica said.

"You two are a couple; that's a fact. You can try to deny it, but what's true is true," Tommy stated, then turned his attention to Erica.

"You left your post when things got tight at the embassy. That's rule number one. You should have never left your post, period."

Erica looked down at her hands.

"And you." Tommy said, his searing gaze on Ford. "You had an obligation to do what?"

Tommy's gaze felt like the sun at high noon on the Sahara Desert. Ford swallowed hard, took a deep breath, and then blew it out. "Report any breach of protocol."

"So you do know the procedure. You were senior on this operation, and I had to get a debrief from a communications tech." Tommy raised himself and paced the floor again.

"Both of you are now emotionally compromised. I can't send you out as partners again, for the company's sake and for yours. You can no longer make detached decisions that are required in the business we do because you're attached!"

Tommy stopped in front of Erica and Ford.

"You will both be assigned new partners," Tommy said.

"You don't have to do that, Tommy," Ford urged, as his eyes met Erica's. "We can work this out."

"No. I don't think so. It's not that you two are an item; it's just that you kept it a secret. I can't trust you two to make the right decisions because of your newfound relationship."

Tommy took a seat at the head of the conference table.

"You can still see each other, get married. I don't care. Do what makes you happy. It's just that you can't work as a team any longer. That's my decision, you're both on probation," Tommy continued, taking a deep breath. "I'm sorry. That's just the way it has to be. Now, get back to work. I want a full report from both of you on the embassy mission by the end of the day. Omit nothing. Understand?" Tommy demanded pointing his finger at the both of them.

Ford and Erica nodded, rose from the table, and exited the room without a word.

For the next few weeks, Erica and Ford were forced to work a desk, researching, calculating coordinates, and other menial jobs for other agents' assignments, which proved very boring for the both of them.

The only good thing out of this punishment was that the two got to spend more and more time alone together in the evenings to explore their relationship and each other. They went shopping, spent evenings out in restaurants and clubs, went dancing, ice skating, and best of all, Ford took Erica to her first circus. They were like two teenagers with a free pass to see the world, and they crammed it all in as fast as they could.

One night Ford, assigned to the decoding room coding a pile of messages, slaved away, but no matter how fast he worked, the pile never seemed to get any smaller. Buried in this mundane task, Ford had enough of his punishment, so he stormed up to Tommy's office.

Erica had been busy in the kitchen making a special dinner for Ford that evening, when he appeared in the doorway with a huge smile on his face, a bottle of wine, and flowers in his hand.

"You brought flowers?" a surprised Erica said.

"And your favorite wine."

"Well, you're late. So pop that baby open and sit because dinner has been ready for a while," Erica playfully scolded as she kissed Ford.

"I've got news," Ford said, beaming.

"News? Good news or bad news?"

"Of course it's good news. Who'd bring wine and flowers for bad news?" Ford joked as he popped the cork on the wine.

"Okay, so tell!"

"We're off probation! I have an assignment next week."

"I thought we had two more weeks?"

"That's why I'm late. I got so fed up decoding code like a first-year drone that I stormed up to Tommy's office. I said, 'Listen, we've had about all of this punishment we're going to take. We need to be back in the field, or we're done!' Tommy looked at me—you know the way he does when he's got something on his mind he wants to say but he never says it, right?" Ford imitated the look.

"That's the one." Erica laughed.

"Then after a moment he quietly said, 'okay.'"

They hugged and kissed several times.

"I'm hungry." Ford said with a twinkle in his eye.

"Let's eat," Erica said as she kissed Ford again.

They talked and laughed through dinner, Ford imitated Tommy's look several more times, and Erica made poor attempts at Tommy's look. They kissed, drank, and were the epitome of two lovebirds on a prom date.

"Tommy brought something up a few weeks ago that's been on my mind."

Ford gently brushed Erica's hair out of her face.

"What did he say?" Erica asked, curiously playful.

"He said he didn't care that we were a couple. And it made me think that maybe we should take this relationship to the next level."

"What does that mean?"

"Well, Tommy didn't care if we got married," Ford said sheepishly.

"What?"

"Maybe we should think about getting married."

"Maybe? Maybe we should think about getting married?"

"No."

"What? Now you don't want to marry me?"

"No, that didn't come out right. I love you, Erica." Ford dropped to one knee.

"Will you make me the happiest man on earth and be my wife?" Ford asked as he pulled a small, black box out of his pocket.

Erica began to hyperventilate. This was the farthest thing from anything she had ever dreamed of, let alone ever imagined. Someone said he "loved her." She hadn't heard those words since she was a child. Erica struggled to hold herself together, but the emotions came up like a volcano about to erupt. Ford opened the box and revealed an extravagant but modest two-carat, Marquis-cut diamond ring. Erica had never seen anything as beautiful in her life and gushed with a torrent of joy and giddiness, speechless.

Ford slid the ring on her trembling finger. By now the tears of happiness streamed down Erica's face and she threw her arms around Ford.

"Yes, yes, yes, I'll marry you!" she blubbered through sobs of joy, and smothered him with kisses.

10

A Shroud of Dread

THE NEXT SEVERAL months were filled with new discoveries for Erica. The entire universe changed; flowers smelled sweeter, the sun brighter, and life's road now paved with happiness as far as the eye could see. Ford and Erica both got along well with their new partners. Ford worked again with the man who trained him five years ago, and Erica quickly realized that Ewan Steward would be a man whom she could learn volumes. Ewan had been an operative with MI-5 and his insight regarding world events differed from most of the other operatives at VCS. Erica attributed that to Ewan's European background.

Erica and Ford's assignments were routine in nature, mostly intelligence gathering for clients, having to do with weapons trafficking to terrorists groups. Ford made two quick trips during those months to Algeria and Turkey. Erica hadn't thought about Turkey, or Dimitri, for a long time, but knowing Ford's destination brought back those memories. They seemed so long ago now, so far away. Erica's passionate desire for revenge replaced with a passionate desire to experience life and all that life had to offer.

It had been years since Erica stopped to listen to the squeals of little children as they played in the park, but in today's world Erica stopped to indulge herself in that exquisite pleasure every chance she got.

Children. Kids. Having a kid? Raising a child? There a thought that wasn't possible six short months ago. The thought just ambled into her mind just as easily as one would stroll into a cafe or market. A baby. She and Ford could have a baby? Let's get the wedding over with first, thought Erica as she laughed to herself. We have a ways to go before kids enter the picture. This was indeed a new experience, thinking about her future. What that future had in store for her, she didn't know. Erica had so much to tell, but who was there tell it to—no one.

* * * * *

VCS acquired a contract to promote a regime change in Ecuador. Ford, heading up the operation left for Quito. The opposition party, Los Lobos needed sophisticated surveillance and a person to handle it and VCS the obvious choice. This mission was highly clandestine; Ford and his three-man team, to put it simply, were to initiate a coup and overthrow the current ruling party. It would be a long six weeks for Ford and even longer for Erica since the two hadn't really been apart since Montana.

Four weeks crawled by with only limited contact between Erica and Ford; all contact only during what could be called, "working hours". The two never had a chance to speak privately during that time.

Erica decided to take some time off and took a leisurely trip through the Blue Ridge Mountains. The time spent in the outdoors gave Erica energy, and she was able to cope with her separation from Ford much easier.

She took photos and picked up souvenirs of her sojourn to share with Ford when he returned from his mission. Erica walked about two feet off the ground, and nothing could cast a pall over her joy. She decided to sit in a park and enjoy the last of the sunlight. It was early fall, and the sun low on the horizon. Forty minutes passed quickly, and clouds began to roll in from the north, that brought a damp chill into the air. Erica pulled the collar of her jacket tight around her neck as she briskly walked across the thick grass on her way to her vehicle. There wasn't a noticeable gust of wind or a rumble of thunder off in the distance that stopped Erica in mid-stride; something much more subtle halted her advance. The sky, the odor of the damp grass, the chill in the air suddenly reminded her of that day she returned from the village, that day the men came to her father's house, that day they murdered her father. A shroud of dread engulfed her.

Fear suddenly pierced her heart. Instantly she was there again, feeling those feelings, but these feelings were immediate, fresh, like they were happening now. Erica dashed to her car and drove all night, straight through to Virginia, with a sense of trepidation that sat in the pit of her stomach like a chunk of rough granite.

At four-thirty in the morning, Erica arrived in Alexandria. It was still deathly dark and quiet. A random vehicle passed along the street from time to time. She turned into the parking lot of her apartment complex when her cellphone chirped.

She received a text message from VCS. There had been an emergency, and she needed to report to the facility immediately. Erica turned her car around, and six minutes later, she parked in front of the VCS building.

The building was a madhouse of activity, with everyone on high alert and security extremely tight. Erica rushed into the building and legged it to the control room. Several technicians were there, all with worried looks on their faces. Tommy stood by a computer screen in a rigid pose, left arm across his mid-section, his right hand on his chin. Only his eyes moved when Erica entered the room. She took a half dozen steps to Tommy and stopped when he turned to her.

"What is it?" an apprehensive Erica asked.

"Come with me," Tommy said sternly as he turned and walked to the door.

Erica had some difficulty just keeping up with him, as his strides were long and quick.

"Has something gone wrong?" she said urgently.

Tommy opened the door to a small office and walked in, Erica on his heels.

"Tell me what's going on, Tommy."

He turned to face Erica, set himself and took a deep breath.

"There is just no good way to say this, so I'll just say it."

"Tommy! What the hell . . .?"

"Ford's dead."

"What? You lost contact? The communication is dead? What are you saying?" Erica asked perplexed.

"Ford's dead. There was an agent for the president in with Los Lobos. Ford suspected something like that, but they got to him before he could smoke them out."

"Maybe he's just hurt." She said as her arms flailed in the air.

She looked around the room for something to make sense of this horrible news.

"No Erica. He's dead. It's been confirmed."

"Then we need to get down there," she slammed her fist on the desk.

"We're not going anywhere. We've been compromised. The mission is over. The whole team is dead. There's nothing we can do. We go down there now, we start a war."

"If you kept us together, this wouldn't have happened," Erica hissed, pointing an accusatory finger at Tommy's face.

"You can't say that, Erica. There was no way you could have done anything. You'd be dead too," Tommy pleaded.

"I should have been there," Erica proclaimed as she opened the office door. "I'd rather be dead than live without him."

Tommy stood for a moment as he heard Erica's footsteps echo down the hall. Tommy sat down in the desk chair, placed his elbows on the desk and held his head in his hands.

Erica, visibly upset, stalked silently through the dozens of desks in the operations bullpen to her station, threw her purse underneath her desk, dropped into her chair, and began furiously typing on her keyboard.

Ewan sat at his desk just across from Erica. He was thirty-five years old, but looked younger. He stood five foot ten, built on a narrow frame with black, short-cropped hair and a tightly trimmed 'soul patch' under his lower lip. Ewan had light brown eyes that when he smiled revealed thin crease lines at the edges that made him look as though he squinted from the brightness of the sun.

"I'm sorry, about Ford," Ewan consoled. "You shouldn't be working."

"I'm fine," Erica mumbled.

Ewan rose and stepped around his desk and sat himself on the corner of Erica's desk.

"You're not fine. This has been a terrible shock. I can't even begin to imagine how you feel. You should go home. There's nothing here you can do."

"Go home to what? He's not there. He's not going to be there," a weary Erica said as she continued to search her computer for information. "Tommy has locked me out of all the intelligence info having to do with Ford's operation. He thinks I'm going to go down there and take care of those bastards."

"Will you? . . . Go after them, I mean?"

"Yes, but that's not the point."

"You should get some rest and calm down. Go home, and we can talk about this tomorrow. You're just all in right now and can't think straight."

"I know, you're right," Erica agreed.

Ewan gave Erica a warm, knowing smile and a supportive shoulder squeeze, then got up off the corner of the desk and returned to his station. Erica took her purse and withdrew from the bullpen without another word.

When Erica got back to the apartment, she frantically paced up and down every room. She poured herself several glasses of scotch, but could not shake the feelings that bounced around in her head. Those thoughts of the future with Ford, marriage and babies were gone. A home, a new life, gone.

After several hours, completely exhausted, Erica slept on the couch and awoke shortly before 1:00 p.m., hungry and needing a stiff drink. She selected a frozen pasta alfredo dinner from the freezer, popped it in the microwave, then poured herself a double-scotch over ice. She slammed down the first drink and started on her second double when the microwave announced her dinner ready for consumption.

Erica was hungry, but she only poked at her dinner, nothing appealed to her; even the third scotch held no satisfaction in its amber liquid. Halfway through the pasta and on her forth scotch, Erica startled by the irritating sound of the apartment door buzzer, looked at her watch-only one-forty-five. The last thing she needed right now, a visitor at the door. The buzzer buzzed again, this time more insistent than the last.

Erica took another drink from her glass, hoping the person on the other side of the door would just go away. The buzzer sounded again; followed by the ring of her cellphone that alerted her she had just received a message. Erica picked up her phone, and on the screen, she read: 'I'm ringing your door. I know you're home. Ewan.'

Erica rose from the table and shuffled to the door. She swung it open, and there stood Ewan with those smiling eyes, leaning against the door jam. Erica ushered him in and immediately made him a drink.

"So what do I owe this pleasure?" Erica asked as she poured a double-bourbon.

"Just wanted to talk to you. Could I have water on the side please?" said Ewan as he sat down on the couch.

Erica handed Ewan his drinks and stood in front of him.

"So talk. Tommy wants you to make sure I'm okay?"

"No one knows I've come to see you," Ewan said as he looked at both of his hands, each with a glass in it.

Unable to find a drink coaster on the coffee table, Ewan placed the water glass on top of a magazine then took a drink of his bourbon. Erica still hovered over him.

"You're making me nervous. Why don't you sit down?"

Erica took a few steps back and dropped into an overstuffed easy chair diagonally across from the couch. "So what is it you want to talk about?"

"I can help you get the info you want."

Erica sat up, suddenly interested in what Ewan had to say.

"I can keep one of the techs busy while you download what you need."

"Why are you doing this?"

"We're partners, and partners are supposed to help each other," Ewan said.

An almost imperceptible smile appeared at the corner of Erica's mouth.

"Tommy's got to look out for the interests of VCS. As much as he would like to, he can't get involved. You know you'll need to resign."

"Yes, I know." Erica replied.

"I can give you the name of a mate of mine. He works freelance and can get you assignments, that is, if you want to."

"Thanks. I really appreciate this, but won't this get you into trouble?"

"Not if I can help it," Ewan quipped as he rose from the couch.

Erica got up from her place. The two faced each other and touched their glasses together in a toast of comradeship, then simultaneously drained their glasses.

The following morning, Erica sat at her desk when Ewan signaled he would make his move. Ewan went to one of the techs and told him he had an issue with his computer. Ewan had run a program just a few minutes earlier that he was sure would cause his station to lock up then placed a keystroke copier under his keyboard.

When the tech checked out Ewan's computer, he needed to login with his password to unlock it and then bring it back on line.

Once the computer got back up and running, Ewan convinced the tech to grab a cup of coffee with him, before he returned to his station. In the few minutes that Ewan and the tech were in the lounge, chatting and fixing coffee, Erica sat at Ewan's computer. She pulled up the keystrokes the tech used and gained access to the files she needed. She downloaded the files and returned to her desk just as the tech and Ewan returned. Erica gave a wink that indicated she had what she needed.

"You know, I'm not feeling well. I'm going home," she muttered to Ewan with a knowing glance.

Ewan nodded and gave her a smile as Erica grabbed her bag with a determination to seek vengeance on those responsible.

* * * * *

On the next morning, the door to Tommy's office burst open, and Erica blew in like a hurricane off the cost of North Carolina.

"Did you give up knocking?" Tommy said, not looking up.

"I don't have time for bullshit etiquette," she quipped.

Erica reached into her jacket pocket and pulled out a business-size white envelope. She took a step forward and placed the envelope on Tommy's desk.

"It's my resignation. I kind of envisioned throwing it at you, but . . ."

"I think you're making a big mistake. I'm not speaking as your boss right now, I speaking to you as a friend and colleague. Don't do this," Tommy pleaded. "You're asking for more trouble than you can handle. And if you go down there, you'll be all alone on this one. We can't help you."

"I won't be able to rest until this is over. As long as Ford's killers are alive, I wouldn't be a good agent anyway."

Tommy slid open the middle drawer to his desk and produced an envelope of his own. He held it out to Erica across his desk.

"There's a check in there for all you've done. The only other thing I can say is . . . be careful."

Erica took the envelope from Tommy and nodded. She turned and stepped to the door.

"Erica . . .," Tommy implored, as he searched for something he didn't know how to say.

Erica gave a half smile and disappeared into the hall.

11

Settling The Score

ERICA FLEW to Panama then used one of her fake passports to book passage to Ecuador. She established herself as an Ecuadorian citizen, employed as an archeologist for the María Augusta Urrutia Museum in Quito.

She arrived in the port city of San Lorenzo, bought a ticket on the Buscar, a rough ride, and packed with tourist. Due to Erica's ability to speak the language, she blended in and arrived in Quito virtually unnoticed.

Once in the city, she booked a room at the Hostal Casapaxi. The room so small you had to walk out in the hallway to change your mind. The bed small, but surprisingly comfortable, with a nightstand and small chair as the only furniture in the room and small rectangular cut in the wall that served as a closet to store your bags.

A very loud, multi-colored curtain, indigenous to the local area, covered the opening. In the corner of the room, a little sink barely big enough to wash your hands. The shower and toilet facility a common area down the hall shared by the four rooms located on the floor.

Erica locked the door behind her after she entered the room. She went to the window and opened it, the cool mountain air rushed in, much nicer than the hot, steamy air of San Lorenzo. She slipped her laptop from her travel bag and fired it up, then activated her mini-satellite transmitter. It took only thirty seconds for her laptop to come online, spurring Erica to start feverishly punching at the keyboard. If luck was with her, and the stars were aligned, Domingo Solis would still be in the city.

Erica poured over the intelligence material with a fine-toothed comb; the smallest detail not overlooked. The leaders of Los Lobos were killed, captured, or scattered to the winds. All Erica had to go on, a photograph and her satellite tracker. She decided to take some chances and narrow her search. Erica gleaned from the intelligence that Domingo liked to party and frequented the nightspots around the city.

La Bunga, Arribar, Cubano, and Sapphire, according to Ford's reports, were the clubs where Domingo met Ford and his team over the weeks that they were in the country. Erica would start tonight with a steak-out of the first club on her list, La Bunga.

La Bunga wasn't busy that night; the crowd inside sparse. The establishment modest and friendly, had a large bar resting in the center of the space, in the shape of a rectangular box where the bartenders would work from the inside. The wooden rack hung over the center of the bar, held a variety of beverage glasses. Below the bar and on top of the refrigerators, liquor bottles lived on shelves. Erica took a stool at the bar and ordered a drink. The bartender, Paulo, young, tan, was always smiling. Erica made small talk for a while before she broached the subject of Domingo Solis.

"Solis been in today," Erica said in fluent Spanish.

"Haven't seen him in a few weeks. He must be busy."

"Busy," Erica said as she took a drink from her glass.

"Why do you want to waste your time on him? He'll just run around on you. You should think about someone like me," Paulo replied, smiling.

Erica began to assemble a better picture of Solis. He betrayed his women as well as he betrayed his compatriots.

"I need to deal with Domingo first."

"If I see him, who should I say was looking for him?" Paulo inquired as he put his elbows on the bar, leaning forward, to get closer to Erica.

"I'd appreciate it if you didn't say anything," Erica replied.

"I get that a lot," Paulo laughed.

The fact that Erica, a new girl in town didn't go unnoticed. She received a great deal of attention from the men in the club, none of which were able to give her any information on the whereabouts of Domingo. He lived somewhere in the hills, but no one wanted to volunteer any more information than that. Before she knew it, Paulo announced, "Last call," so Erica called it a night and planned the resumption of her search the next evening.

Around town the next day, Erica learned that not many of the residents of Quito knew of the coup plot against the president. As far as the city was concerned, it was business as usual. The city teemed with tourists, and Erica decided to blend in with the crowd, visiting some of the attractions the city had to offer.

She spent several relaxing hours at a museum of Pre-Columbian Art. In the evening, she had dinner at a local restaurant then made her way to Arribar.

Arribar a much different establishment than La Bunga; all loud music and jammed with tourists. Arribar must have been in all the guidebooks. It attracted just about everyone who visited the city: Germans, French, Americans, and Asians. Erica had a cocktail and pressed the bar staff for information. An older waitress told her that Domingo hadn't been in lately because so many tourists were in the city.

He liked to hang out at Sapphire these days, the waitress told her, because of the girls and the private rooms available in the club. She guessed that he would be there at least twice a week but maybe more if Domingo had not left town.

Erica took a cab across town to the Sapphire Club to find the place jammed with people. The club larger than most; two bars, and plenty of strategically placed TV screens programed to present various sports events, from soccer, to bull fights, to baseball. Erica roamed the club, scanned every male face, as males dominated the clientele. Erica spotted a waitress as she entered the ladies room, followed her in to get a closer look at her uniform. The wait staff at Sapphire wore an outfit, designed to imitate a maid's garb. All black, a short skirt, with a white laced apron in front.

Each of the waitresses wore a bright colored, pink, orange, or yellow straight-cut wig on her head, and their facial makeup reminded one of an ancient Egyptian princess. Dark eyeliner accented the eyes and brought the outline of the eye to a point on either side of the head. Lashes were long and dark, creating a very exotic effect to the face. Erica struck up a conversation with several of the women, and she discovered that Solis frequented the club on a regular basis, but his usual appearance would be on Friday nights, so they expected him to be in the club the following evening. Erica had the information she needed. Tomorrow she would plan her attack.

The next day Erica shopped. She purchased a black maid's uniform identical to the costume worn by the wait staff at the Sapphire Club and had no problem procuring a pink wig. Erica did however need to take scissors to it to make it resemble the wigs worn by the staff. Back at her hotel room, Erica prepped herself for the evening. She laid out a sexy, tight, silver dress, black shoes, and a sterling silver chain necklace. Before she left for South America, Erica had the jewelry specially designed for her purposes, particularly a silver chain, with a thin steel wire woven through it, capable of suspending more than two-hundred pounds. This would be Erica's weapon of choice for tonight.

Erica arrived at the Sapphire just after dark with a medium-sized, black bag slung over her shoulder. She wandered through the club. Solis had not arrived as yet, so Erica settled down with a cocktail at the bar. It didn't take long before the young guns started to hit on her. Firm and relatively polite, Erica fended off their advances. Two drinks and forty-five minutes later, her prey sauntered into the establishment.

Domingo Solis stood five foot nine, carrying two hundred and twenty flabby pounds on his corpulent body. His round face sported a patchy black beard, and slicked-back black hair made him looked unkempt. When he smiled wide, he revealed his two gold front teeth, and Erica knew she had her target. According to Domingo's profile, he was the type of man that never saw a peso he didn't like.

Domingo could be bought, and bought cheaply and when they discovered that Domingo supplied guns to Los Lobos, the Ecuadorean Government put him on their payroll. All he had to do was let General Infante's staff know what Los Lobos' plans were. When Ford and his team showed up, like a good little rat, Domingo immediately informed Infante that American mercenaries were allied with Los Lobos. Domingo led Ford and the team into a trap set by Infante.

Erica held her ground at the bar for a good twenty minutes, just biding her time, observing Domingo throwing his weight around along with copious amounts of the blood money he earned. Erica's patience paid off. Domingo noticed her and approached her at the bar.

"Hola, señorita!" Solis said, his gold teeth flashed.

"Are you just going to stand there smiling all night or are you going to buy me a drink?" Erica remarked in Spanish with a flawless Columbian accent.

"Carlos, another round for the lady!" Solis laughed. "I've never seen you in here before. What's your name?"

"Marisol," Erica offered up playfully. "What's yours?"

"I am Domingo! Your prince charming." He laughed again with the confidence of a Matador.

The two of them made small talk for a while, and with every drink Domingo's confidence grew and his hands roamed freely, groping Erica at every opportunity.

"You are the most beautiful girl I've ever seen, and I've seen beautiful girls before, but you truly are the most beautiful one ever!"

"Domingo?" a female voice shrilled from behind him.

Domingo turned and discovered a very attractive young Ecuadorian woman standing behind him. About twenty-five with long, curly black hair and deep, brown eyes, with lips were as red as roses, and her cheekbones were very distinguished. She wore too much makeup and smelled as if she put the entire contents of the bottle of perfume on moments ago.

"Teresa! What are you doing here? Didn't you get my message? You're supposed to meet me at Cubano at ten o'clock." Domingo turned to Erica and winked. "I'm just having a drink with my cousin, Marisol."

"I don't think this is your cousin!" Teresa snipped, pissed off. "I think this is another one of your putas!"

"Hey, that's no way to talk about Marisol. Tell her. Tell her you're my cousin," Domingo said, as he signaled Marisol with his eyes to play along.

"I am his cousin, on his mother's side. Just in town until tomorrow," Erica smiled.

"I don't believe either of you. I'll be at Cubano when you want to apologize to me for being a shit," Teresa pronounced as she stormed off.

"Who was that? Your wife?"

"Ah, no. She's just a girl I know. Not like you though. You have class and sophistication. You are something special."

"Ha, I bet you say that to all your girls."

"We should go someplace else, and I'll show you that you are special," Domingo said with a suggestive golden smile.

"Honey, you've been kind of entertaining, but I come at a high price. I don't think you've got what it takes . . . moneywise."

"Oh, so that's how it is? I've got plenty of dinero." He dug into his pocket and extracted a wad of cash that could choke el toro. He starts to peel off large bills and pile them on the bar next to Erica's glass.

One by one, he piled on the bills as Erica watched, unfazed by the cash. As the pile grew higher, Domingo started to get nervous, when it didn't impress Erica in the least. Finally, Erica scooped up the money and stuffed it in her bag.

"Okay, big boy, let's go. My place or yours?"

"No, there are rooms in the back. We can do it right here," Domingo said, grabbing Erica's hand as he lead her off. The two swam through the sea of people, as they danced to the pounding music, until they reached the back of the club where the private rooms were located.

A guard stood at a velvet rope that closed off the secured area. A six-foot-seven, very dark man known only as Hector gave Domingo the universal guy's head nod of approval as he opened the rope and gave Erica a lustful up and down glance.

Domingo entered the first room that had an open door, and a second later, a gorgeous waitress wearing a pink wig appeared with a tray of liquor selections, setting the tray on a low, black table. She turned to leave as Domingo slipped her some cash and a big smile. The room eight feet wide and ten feet deep, and covered in crushed red velvet. The walls, the chair, and the couch were red velvet. The far wall in the room was all mirrors, the side wall, a built-in coatrack. Domingo stepped to the door and slid the heavy bolt-lock closed. He turned back to Erica, who at this time had unclasped the silver necklace from around her neck. Domingo approached her lecherously and put his hand on her hips. Erica smiled.

"This is for Ford," Erica purred.

He leaned in to kiss her then stopped, puzzled.

"Ford?"

In a microsecond, the silver necklace tightened around Domingo's neck, crushing his throat. He struggled, but it proved futile. In moments, Erica ended his worthless life. Erica pushed him into the coatrack, unwrapped the silver chain from around his now bloody neck, and dropped it on the floor. Taking a lamp from the table, she ripped the cord from it and wrapped it around his neck. She strung Domingo up on a hook like a slab of beef. Without a moment's hesitation, she stripped off her dress then removed the pink wig and maid costume from her shoulder bag. She put the outfit on and stretched the wig on her head, shoving her own hair underneath it. It took no time for Erica to complete the make-up portion of her disguise. She picked up the silver chain, shoved it in her bag along with her dress and slung it over her shoulder. She grabbed the serving tray from the table, and exited the private room. Erica closed the door behind her then took a magnet from her purse. Holding the magnet on the outside of the door, opposite the bolt lock, Erica slowly moved the magnet across the door. On the inside of the room, the bolt slid into the locked position. Erica tried the door — it was locked.

She turned and strutted out of the private-room area and walked by Hector, who only saw a pink wig and maid's costume and took no notice of the girl who wore it. Moving through the crowded club, Erica headed straight for the kitchen, where she set the tray on a counter and glided out the back door. Once outside, Erica ditched the wig in a trashcan, dug into her bag, and retrieved a sweater. Slipping the sweater over the uniform, Erica emerged into the street and mixed in with the evening revelers as they crawled from club to club. Erica made it back to her hotel room in twenty minutes, her bags packed in minutes. Just fifteen minutes later, she boarded the Buscar to San Lorenzo, where she spent a long restless night.

Before Erica boarded a plane to Venezuela the next morning, she checked news of Quito on her laptop. The story of Domingo's murder appeared in the Ecuador Reporter. According to the publication, a prostitute at the Sapphire Cub for non-payment of services murdered Domingo Solis. His body discovered in a party room. The body wasn't discovered until a female acquaintance of

Solis' went to the club to look for him. The security staff at the club had to break down the door, as it had been locked from the inside. The police were on the lookout for a tall Columbian woman for questioning, after interviewing the bartender who served the woman drinks and remembered she spoke with a Columbian accent.

Erica closed her laptop when she heard the announcement for her flight to board, an empty feeling in her heart. She had avenged Ford's death, but it did little to cure the ache in her heart. On the plane Erica tried to sleep, but her mind kept replaying the loving moments she and Ford spent together as a couple. She looked down at her left hand time and time again over the duration of the long flight. Her third finger naked and seemed alien to her. Procedure called for operatives to leave their personal belongings behind before they left on a mission, but Erica wished she had broken that rule. She wished she had the ring with her now, to comfort her, to bring Ford closer to her, to make her feel less alone.

Erica returned home late in the afternoon, exhausted from her journey. She entered her empty and quiet apartment that now seemed foreign to her. All the contents belonged to her, but at the same time they seemed strange. Those were her chairs, her couch, her bed, her clothes, but they were barely recognizable. It felt like she had never really lived there before; she didn't belong. Erica collapsed onto the couch and just sat there for more than an hour. Since the day Tommy told her Ford had been killed, Erica had been functioning on adrenalin and sheer will. She had nothing left. She couldn't muster the energy to walk to the bedroom, let alone plan what she would do with the rest of her life. Erica was dead inside, a virtual zombie.

She knew she should cry—cry for her loss, cry for Ford, cry for her parents, but Erica was dry. She couldn't cry. The world had taken too much from her; she had nothing left to give. Erica would move about the world now: eat, drink, sleep, interact with others, but only on a surface level. Deep down inside she had become a machine—a cold, emotionally detached machine.

Erica wasn't the type of person to put a gun in her own mouth and pull the trigger. She would live out the rest of her days empty and alone. She would try to correct the wrongs in the world with the slight chance it would give her some kind of closure, a release from the pain she carried with her every day. As Erica sat staring blankly at the far wall, something caught her attention. Her personal cellphone flashed on the living-room table. Erica suddenly became aware that she plodded toward the phone. When she reached the table, she looked down at it, not knowing what to do. She stared at the device for several minutes before she saw her hand reach down and pick it up. Erica had no control over her body; it operated without brain commands. With the phone in her hand, Erica focused on the display screen. It indicated that it had received a message recently. Erica entered in her code, and the message appeared. 'Ewan suggested we should talk. Call me. Seth Fogarty.' Erica watched as her fingers dialed Fogarty's number.

12

Assassin For Hire

THERE WERE SEVERAL rings on the other end of the line before Erica heard a deep, raspy voice—the kind that years of cigarettes and whiskey honed.

"Fogarty," the voice said.

"Hello? This is Erica Drago, Ewan's friend."

"Miss Drago, I'm glad you called. Ewan speaks very highly of you."

"What can I do for you?" She asked.

"Actually, it's what I can do for you. Nice work, by the way, down in Ecuador. I like your style. I could use someone with your talent. Whadya say?"

"You get right to the point, Mr. Fogarty."

"Call me Seth, please. You want to hear more?"

"Sure. Why not," Erica replied bluntly.

"I get calls all the time from people—very important people who have problems and need those problems dealt with. You follow?"

"I'm listening."

"That's where you come in." Fogarty said, "I'm basically a head hunter. I put people together. There's plenty of business to go around. Once I put you in contact with a client, the specifics—fee, timeframe are on you. You handle your end any way you see fit."

"So, I'm completely in charge?"

"It's like a dating service. You don't like the date, pass, I'll get you another one. There are issues being taken care of daily," Fogarty stated with a slight laugh. "So, can I count you in?"

"I'm in."

"I'll be in touch," Fogarty said and hung up.

Erica heard the phone beep and read: 'Call ended.' She stared at it even after it went to sleep, not quite able to ascertain what just happened.

Erica took some clothes, her toiletries, and packed them in one bag, everything else in her apartment left behind. She told the apartment manager that she could have whatever she left behind. Sell them and give the money to charity, or offer the place as a furnished apartment; it didn't matter to Erica. She would never come back. She got into her car and drove west. Erica would disappear—disappear from a world where people fell in love, married, and lived a life of mortgages and PTA meetings. A world she could never experience. A world that now could only be possible in her imagination.

With those thoughts pushed deep into the recesses of her brain, Erica dialed her cellphone.

"It's Ewan."

"I spoke with Fogarty. Thanks for the introduction."

"If you need anything, just let me know." Ewan replied.

"There is something you can do for me."

"Name it."

"Dig around when you can. I want to find Vlado Nikic and Milan Petkovic. It's time they pay for what they did to my family." Erica declared with such venom that it sent and icy chill down Ewan's back.

Erica exited a do-it-yourself carwash in Los Angeles after the long cross-country trek with that one bag in the backseat of her rental car. No trash, no fingerprints; nothing in the car could be traced back to her. The car would be dropped off spotless, as Erica started a new life, if you could call it a life, from scratch. Not a thing from her past came with her, not even her diamond engagement ring.

Los Angeles, California, the perfect place for Erica to disappear into with 468 square miles and over twelve million people in the surrounding metro area to get lost. Plenty of room and plenty of people and a place where a million others come to leave their past behind and start fresh. In Los Angeles, you could reinvent yourself on a daily basis, all you needed to do, print up a new business card.

Five weeks had passed without word from Fogarty or Ewan, when Erica received a call from her former colleague.

"Hey, it's Ewan, have to make this quick. I have good news and bad news on Petkovic."

"Tell me." Erica demanded.

"The good news is he's dead. Died in a car crash."

"What's the bad news?"

"He was killed instantly. Didn't suffer," Ewan joked. "But this will make it better. I have a location for you on Vlado. He's living under the name of Nick Lekas, in Syracuse, New York. He owns a pizza shop a few blocks from the university. Besides spinning pizza dough, he runs a gambling operation in the back room."

Within forty-eight hours of the call, Erica boarded the mid-night flight east.

* * * * *

Erica arrived late in the morning at the Syracuse airport. She rented a car and headed toward the college campus that a short drive from the airport. She parked on the street a few doors down from Nick's Pizza and pulled out her smartphone—retrieved a picture Ewan had sent her of Vlado as he appears today as 'Nick'. She waited.

Hours went by—the sun had set and finally the neon light that read; Nick's went out. Erica got out of the car and made her way to the alley behind the restaurant. She saw a pot-bellied man in an apron and white shirt dump a trashcan into a large dumpster, then went back inside — the screen door slammed behind him.

Erica eased up to the door and slipped in, mindful to keep the screen door from slamming shut with the heel of her shoe. As she made her way through the kitchen, she noticed a large carving knife resting on the stainless steel table. She picked it up and moved toward the doorway that led to the dining room. Just then, Vlado appeared in the doorway and froze when he saw Erica.

"Who the fuck are you?"

Without hesitation, Erica drove the knife into his chest, "This is for my father, Goran Sekulic."

Vlado's eyes locked on Erica's and in pain grabbed for her, "I was only following orders."

He grunted — fell to the floor and a long slow last breath left his body.

The next morning, the Syracuse Journal reported of the tragic death of a beloved pizzeria owner killed in an apparent robbery gone wrong.

Weeks bled into months and months bled into years as Erica took on assignments from various sources, including several from foreign governments. She exposed politician's scandals with compromising photos that caused several prominent government officials to tender their resignations.

To take out a terrorist cell leader, in the market for radioactive material to produce a dirty bomb, Erica posed as a government employee who could get him into a secure nuclear facility in Miami. She continued to hone her skills as an undercover operative and became one of the most sought after freelancers in the business.

The time passed for Erica like a glacier moving across the poles, imperceptible. She had nothing in her life to mark the time: no birthdays to celebrate, no anniversaries to remember; she just existed.

She had money in her bank account—actually, several bank accounts in several different names, but money nonetheless to go places and see things. But Erica had no place she wanted to go and nothing she wanted to see. One afternoon, she received a phone call from Ewan.

"How you doing, kid?" Ewan's cheerful voice hummed in Erica's ear.

"One day at a time, my friend."

"I've got a job for you. This has to be kept on the down low. Are you aware of Congressmen Bennett's situation?"

"His intern disappeared . . . a couple of years ago?" Erica remarked.

"Right. Well she didn't disappear. She was removed, so to speak. This comes from high up, I mean really high up. They want him eliminated, neat, clean, no sign of foul play. Right up your alley."

"Get me the details, and I'll do it."

Erica packed a bag for D.C. when her phone rang.

"Hey, I'm sending you some details about a new job." Forgarty said.

"Well, it will have to wait. I'm headed east on another matter."

"How long will you be away?"

"At least a couple of weeks."

"Well, they really want you, and your special skills."

"Then they're just going to have to wait." Erica scoffed.

"Okay. Tell you what, I'll still send the information, set up a contact, and you take it from there," Fogarty said.

"You going to do the phone under the park bench again?" Erica said wryly.

"Why not. If it ain't broke, don't fix it.' Fogarty laughed. "This guys a real scumbag; planted a bomb and killed twelve oilrig workers off the coast of California just to get a story to bring down the company. They need it to look like an accident."

"Okay. Just send it. I gotta go."

All packed, Erica headed to the airport bound for Washington D.C. to exact justice on one, Congressman Wilton Bennett.

13

Jason Comes Up Empty

JASON GOT INTO his Prius and left the hotel with a purpose. The flow of information from inside Global Energies had dried up. The only thing he had obtained from Jennifer was that Peter had been on vacation and unable to be contacted. Jason punched in the address for Peter Walker's residence and made his way to the San Fernando Valley.

The ten-minute drive took thirty minutes because traffic in Los Angeles is as unpredictable as the stock market on a Friday afternoon. The time in traffic hadn't given Jason any ideas of what he thought he would find once he got to Peter's home. Jason exited the freeway and pointed his car in the direction of the Encino hills. The streets as usual, congested with vehicles of every shape and size, but as Jason continued up into the residential hills, the roads emptied and he entered a quiet, tree-lined street. The neighborhood of high-end homes, the smallest probably selling for over a million dollars, were obscured by large, older trees and high walls for privacy. As he directed his auto higher into the hills, the homes got larger and more expensive. You could recognize the homes with pools from the small pickup trucks parked and loaded with pool supplies in front of them throughout the neighborhood.

Jason turned his vehicle down a cul-de-sac and stopped in front of the first house to the right of the circle. Jason's eye immediately caught sight of a pink tricycle on the lawn of a modest older house that belonged to Peter Walker. The house a tan stucco design with a two-car garage and the second story located above the garage. The cement driveway stained with oil pools indicated that two cars had parked side by side. By the looks of the condition of the property, the house must be over twenty years old.

Jason got out of the car and looked back down the street. The entire San Fernando Valley displayed itself before him as he took in the view. A slight breeze rustled the leaves of the trees along the street, but that wasn't the only sound Jason picked up. He also heard the sound of a little girl giggling. As Jason stepped closer to the front door of the Walker house, the sound of the little girl's voice became louder. Jason strolled up to the door and pressed the doorbell. He heard the chimes announce his presence to the occupants. Only a few seconds passed when Jason heard the sound of a sliding door on the other side of the house open and slam shut. The rapid footfalls of a child running toward the front door followed. The latch clicked back, and the large door slowly opened. A little, brown-haired girl about six years old peeked around it.

"Hello," the girl chirped.

"Well, hello to you. How are you today?" Jason asked, smiling.

"Fine."

Jason heard the sound of heavy footsteps as they approached the door.

"Who is it, honey?" came a female voice from inside the house.

"A nice man," the little girl said, turning toward the voice.

A heavyset Hispanic woman, about fifty years of age wearing a simple floral dress with an apron tied around her waist, came to the door and stood next to the little girl. "Can I help you?" she asked, putting her arm on the little girl's shoulder.

"My name is Jason Brent. I'm a reporter," Jason said while he held out a business card to the woman. "I'm looking for Peter Walker."

"He's not here. I'm the housekeeper. Would you like to leave a message?"

"Peter was helping us with a story, and I was just trying to follow up with him on a matter."

"Mr. Walker is on a business trip and can't be contacted, but if you'd like to come back or call this evening, Mrs. Walker could probably give you more information."

"Mrs. Walker will be home when?" Jason inquired.

"She's at work and I don't expect her until late."

"I see.

"She will be working tomorrow until six."

"I'll come back tomorrow around six. I'm sorry; I didn't ask your name."

"Margarita."

"Thank you, Margarita." Jason bent over to come eye to eye with the little girl. "And thank you."

"Lena."

"Thank you, Lena." Jason reached and shook her hand. Jason went back to his car and picked up his cellphone. He dialed a number and waited for the call to go through.

"Jen! Just stopped by the Walker's house. The housekeeper told me that Peter is on a business trip, and his wife is here. I'm coming back to talk to the wife tomorrow when she gets home from work. This is weird. Hope your meeting is going well. Talk to you later."

Jason disconnected the call and pondered the situation for a moment. What kind of business trip could he be on that he can't be contacted, Jason thought to himself. Jason started his car and headed home, baffled.

14

Her Next Target

ERICA WALKED briskly into the baggage-claim area of LAX after she landed from her Washington D.C. flight. A middle-aged man, medium build, dressed in a black suit with a white shirt and black tie stood by the baggage carousel, a white card with the name 'SPENCER' on it held under his chin. Erica, in a professional manner, approached the man.

"I'm Miss Spencer."

"Very good, miss. Do you have bags?" he asked as he tried to get a good look at her under her big, floppy hat.

"Just this."

The man took Erica's bag and indicated for her to follow him. They walked out of the baggage-claim area and into a waiting black Lincoln Town Car. He opened the rear door, and Erica got in, the chauffeur closed the door behind her. As the car moved out into the airport terminal traffic, Erica laid her head back on the seat and closed her eyes.

The Lincoln rolled down the 405 freeway into West Los Angeles the day sunny with a cool breeze wafting off the ocean. Erica realized her cellphone had been off since she boarded the plane, so she reached into her purse and turned it on. It buzzed right away with an incoming message that read: 'Ad placed in Westside Daily. Fogarty.'

"Driver, can you find a newsstand, please?"

"Sure. There's one up here on Santa Monica."

The car exited the freeway and turned left, moved west on Santa Monica Boulevard, then came to a stop at an outdoor newsstand.

Erica got out of the car and surveyed the plethora of magazines and newspapers. She selected the Westside Daily. The front page led with the story of the untimely death of Congressman Bennett, which brought a slight smile to Erica's lips. She handed the clerk two dollars, and returned to the car.

"Driver, can you just give me a minute?"

"I'm yours all day, ma'am," responded the driver.

She quickly thumbed through the pages until she came upon the Lost and Found section. Halfway down the page, she stopped on an ad that read: 'Found: Heart-shaped pendant with gold chain. Inscription inside. To claim, call LA Library.'

"Driver, take me to the downtown, Los Angeles library."

"Yes, ma'am."

The car made a U-turn away from the curb and headed east down Santa Monica Boulevard towards downtown. Erica reached into the car's minibar and poured herself a drink, then sat back for the time-consuming drive to downtown.

The town car stopped at the curb in front of the main branch of the Public Library on Fifth Street. "Drive around the block. I'll only be a few minutes and should be out by the time you come back around," Erica told the driver as she exited the car.

Erica took the elevator to the basement of the library and purposefully strolled through the aisles of shelves filled with books, knowing exactly where she needed to go.

She glided to the reference section that appeared as if no one had been there in years. She looked around to make sure no one watched her. She then reached for a large book titled Western Times and Water Wars: State, Culture, and Rebellion in California.

Erica opened the volume to the back where a pouch, that contained several maps, was located. Among the maps, a six-by-eight inch manila envelope. Erica retrieved the envelope and slipped it in her purse. She placed the book back on the shelf and casually walked to the elevator. As the elevator doors opened, an attractive man stepped out.

He took notice of Erica as she stepped into the elevator, turned to her, "Excuse me, can you tell me where . . .?"

Erica, kept her head down, pressed the 'Lobby' button before the man could finish his sentence. As the elevator started up, she could clearly hear the man say, "What a bitch!" Erica smiled.

She strolled to the curb outside the library and arrived just as her car pulled up. Before the driver could get out, Erica had already jumped in the back seat.

"Take me to the Standard."

"Yes, ma'am."

The driver merged the car into traffic and headed to the Standard Hotel, only about six blocks away. He maneuvered through traffic, dodged slower cars and pedestrians like a New York cabbie.

The town car rolled up to the main entrance of the Standard and stopped. The driver jumped out, opened Erica's door, and then stepped to the rear of the vehicle and retrieved her bag from the trunk. Erica, two crisp one-hundred-dollar bills in her hand took her bag from the chauffer.

She held the bills out. "Thank you! You were a real doll. I'm sorry; I didn't get your name?"

"John," he said as he took the money.

"Well, John, I'll make sure to ask for you next time."

"Thank you very much. Please, take my card."

He gave a slight bow, got into the car, and swung away from the hotel entrance as Erica entered the lobby. The valets were very busy tending to new arrivals and departing guests. She walked into the lobby and as she passed, a trashcan threw the business card John gave her in and then promptly walked back out of the hotel and up to the first cab, she saw. The driver puffing on a cigarette as he leaned against the cab read a newspaper with the headline: 'Congressman Bennett's Death Kills Energy Bill.'

"Can you take me to the Ritz Carlton?" She said, as she slid into the back of the cab.

"Absolutely," he said in a very thick Persian accent, then tossed his cigarette on the ground and stepped on it.

The cabbie wasted no time in shuffling into traffic as he whipped around cars and trucks as if they were not even there. The Ritz was only about ten blocks away, and he got there in less than four minutes.

The cab stopped in front of the hotel. Erica, with her bag in one hand, slipped the cabbie a twenty-dollar bill.

"Keep the change," she said, as she exited the cab.

As Erica walked to the lobby doors, a bellhop approached her to take her bag. Erica waved him off and entered the hotel, heading straight to the elevators. She pushed the 'Down' button and waited. Just then, an attractive man pushed the 'Up' button. Tall, blond, and fit—the kind of person that figured women who saw him thought he was fifty shades of, "I want some of that." His cockiness oozed out of him like a bad odor.

"So, you in town for business or pleasure?"

The word pleasure had such a degree of creepiness that it sounded as if your alcoholic, pedophilic uncle had asked if he could smell your panties.

Erica stepped into the elevator and pushed 'P3.' "Fuck off," she said with disdain; all the while, her head kept down, the brim of her hat used to hide her face.

As the elevator started down, Erica could distinctly hear the man say, "What a bitch!" She laughed a small laugh.

The elevator doors opened to a dark parking level. The lighting scarce, and the parking level only half-full. Erica quickly stepped to a late model, light blue Chevy with white interior parked in a corner space. The car so inconspicuous that a typical owner would walk past it several times before realizing this is their car.

Erica got in and tossed the hat in the back seat, started the engine, and then removed the blonde wig she had been wearing. She plucked out the pins that held her hair up and shook her head out, ran fingers through her hair to comb out her silky, black locks. She flipped down the sun visor and found a pack of American Spirits cigarettes and a gold plated nametag. She pinned the tag on her left breast pocket, then lit up a cigarette and backed away from her parking space after completing the total transformation. To anyone that would see her, they would assume just one of the hotel staff on their way home after a long shift. As she exited the structure, she turned toward the 110-freeway on-ramp. She tuned in the radio, and Mahler's Fifth symphony in C Major filled the car. She took a long drag on the cigarette and then tossed it out of the window. She leaned back in the seat as she exhaled the smoke, taking in the music. She drove for several miles, then when the car passed under a freeway sign that read: 'Mt. Washington', Erica steered the car off the freeway onto the Mt. Washington exit. She continued away from the freeway and into the residential neighborhood, taking a road that wound its way up into the hills.

She turned onto a narrow, quaint street with very small houses. The yards of these houses were filled with more trees than most Los Angeles neighborhoods and lent the area a rural quality, a quiet community where the residents mostly kept to themselves.

The houses were close but were isolated enough that the residents had plenty of privacy. This, the kind of neighborhood Erica liked, a comfortable and tranquil place where she could mentally escape.

Erica turned her car into the driveway of a small, beige house with dark brown trim and an attached garage. She brought the car to a stop and hit the remote garage door opener and carefully drove her Chevy inside the garage and closed the door behind her. Erica grabbed her bag and purse as she got out of the car, entered the house, dropped her bag by the kitchen door and trudged directly to the kitchen where she deposited her purse on the table. She wearily walked down the hall and entered the bathroom. She reached into the tub and turned on the water, adjusted the faucet to the proper temperature.

In the vanity under the bathroom sink, she pushed cleaning items aside and reached into the deepest part of the cabinet to extract a jar of bath salts.

She uncorked the large, round stopper off the top of the jar and dumped a good portion of the contents into the tub, then picked up a box of matches that rested on the tank of the toilet. Erica lit several candles stationed around the compact but ergonomic bathroom.

Erica checked the tub water and, satisfied with the temperature, exited the bathroom, leaving the water running and candles lit.

She trundled into a small, sparsely decorated bedroom. The room neat, clean, and everything in its place that made you think you'd walked into a convent.

There wasn't a thing in the house that gave any clue as to the type of person who lived there—no photos or personal items except for a five-by-seven photo of a family that came with the frame. Erica had made absolutely sure that if she had to leave in a moment's notice, nothing left behind would be useful in an effort to discover her true identity.

She kicked off her shoes and took off her dress, tossed it on the bed; panty hose and undergarments quickly followed. Sliding open the closet door just across from the bed, Erica reached in, yanked a cotton robe off its hook, and slipped it around her, the sash secured around her waist. Her closet also a representation of her lifestyle with all her clothes neatly hung.

None of the clothing items stood out in any way, and upon further inspection you would discover labels of all her garments had been meticulously eradicated.

Barefoot, Erica plodded to the kitchen, opened a cabinet and took out a wine glass. Grabbed a bottle of red wine off the wine rack on the counter and headed back to the bathroom, on the way removed the envelope from her purse and slipped it under her arm.

Once in the bathroom, she shut off the water and turned on her iPod that rested in a Bose speaker caddy on the vanity. The bathroom filled with the strains of Mozart as she opened a vanity drawer where she kept a corkscrew for this type of situation. Erica deftly opened the wine bottle like a sommelier at a fine restaurant and poured herself a glass. She let her robe drop to the floor glanced at the reflection of her amazingly fit body in the mirror, then slid into the warm tub.

Erica quaffed a measure of wine and swirled it around her mouth, slowly letting it slide down her throat. After a few minutes of sheer bliss, Erica reached for the envelope and looked at it. Then she slipped her finger under the flap and opened it. She pulled out a photo and there, staring back at her, Jason Brent, her next target for assassination.

Erica would eventually read the file on Jason Brent like a suitor on a dot-com dating service with every detail, gone over and processed to the nth degree. Jason Brent an investigative reporter with connections to major news outlets that included Reuters and UPI. He had written several high-profile articles for The New Yorker, Newsweek, and Time Magazine. Jason's primary subjects were companies that had abused the environment and focused on bringing them to justice any way he could. When corporations saw him coming, they shut their doors.

Erica tossed the envelope across the floor and slid deeper into the hot tub. Thoughts continued to swirl around in her head. Her past had been brought to the forefront of her mind, and she couldn't get her brain to stop reliving it. Where and when Jason Brent would meet his demise would have to wait again until later—much later. For now, Erica needed to shove these painful thoughts back into the secure box from where they had escaped.

Erica blew out the last candle and wrapped her robe tightly around her. She slipped on her fluffy slippers, shuffled into the kitchen and swung open the refrigerator door and peered into it. Most of the shelves were void of food except several stalks of wilted celery, some wrinkled carrots, and a small head of lettuce that had started to go brown. Nothing in the box looked very appealing. Erica tried the freezer next. More choices, but she needed something that could be prepared quickly. Erica shifted the freezer items around and settled on a frozen stir-fry meal. She removed a meal from the freezer and tore open the package, dumped the contents in a bowl, and set it in the microwave oven. She set the timer and padded into the living room, exhausted. She flopped down on the couch and picked up a remote control that rested on the arm of the couch. She pressed a button on the wand, and Samuel Barber filled the room with the somber "Adagio for Strings." Erica laid her head on the back of the couch and closed her eyes.

15

Pieces To The Puzzle

JASON ARRIVED early the next day to his Santa Monica office just off Broadway on Lincoln. He parked his car in the small adjacent parking lot and walked the short distance to the rear entrance of the white-stoned, three-story office building. The old building had undergone many facelifts over the years and now stood as a clean, modernized commercial property. He took the stairs up to the second floor, his footsteps echoed down the tile-floored corridor. Jason stopped in front of door, number 209 and slipped his key into the lock. He swung open the door, and his nostrils reacted to that distinctive musty odor created when a room shut tight for days.

Jason crossed the small office, pulled open the curtains, and opened all the windows fully. Fresh, cool, ocean air filled the office. Jason leaned a bit out of the window and inhaled the salty air. He contemplated taking some time to enjoy a few moments of the beautiful day in Southern California, but there was work to do. Jason planted himself at his desk and fired up his laptop. It only took a minute before he had the computer up and running, and Jason accessed archival files on Global Energies. He decided to start back at the beginning and try to make sense of the information that he had so far.

Global Energies emerged on the business scene just ten years ago. The company had garnished a significant amount of oil leases in Eastern Europe. They were cash rich and were able to make deal offers that other companies could not compete with because they lacked the liquid assets. Jason's research had not been able to determine where Global got their money. The man behind the success of the organization was one Zubin Ratko, the man who pulled the strings of the president of the company, Henry Laski. Laski only represented the face of the company, the figurehead. Zubin called all the shots. No one knew much about Zubin. From the beginning, he had kept himself in the shadows. Trying to get a photo of Zubin proved to be next to impossible, as he never presented himself in public. His right-hand man, and second in command David Edison was as reclusive as Zubin.

As far as Jason had gleaned from his research, Zubin and Edison came from Eastern Europe, but any information that went farther back than ten years proved vague at best. Global opened their first office in Dubai and quickly expanded within a year with an office in London. They had a laundry list of holding companies in its organization that made it very difficult to track any of their subsidiaries back to Global. Jason got an idea. A colleague of his currently located in Dubai could be an asset.

"I'll give him a call and see if he can help out," He said to himself.

Jason grabbed his cell and looked up Greg Baker in the contact file.

"Let's see, it's noon here, so it'll be eleven o'clock in Dubai. He's probably out clubbing."

He found the number and hit 'Dial.' The phone rang several times.

Then, abruptly, a very loud voice yelled into the other end, "Hello!"

The instant the loud music blared through the other end, Jason jolted, held the phone farther from his ear. He strained to hear the voice on the other end through the multitude of sounds. "Greg! It's Jason."

"Mason?" Greg asked.

"No. Jason! Go outside so you can hear!"

"Hang on, I'm gonna go outside so I can hear!"

A long pause followed as the music increased before it decreased, and then the sound of traffic echoed in the background.

"Hey, Mason, how are you?"

"No man. It's Jason Brent, dumbass!' Jason retorted condescendingly.

"Oh, hey man. What's going on?"

"I need some help with a story."

"Well, you came to the right place, brother! You know me. I'm the go-to guy!" Greg said, still yelling.

"Well, I need you to go to the offices of Global Energies and find out everything you can about these guys, and stop yelling."

"You got it, Jason! I still owe you for that time in Mexico City," Greg said in a slightly softer tone.

"I told you never to mention Mexico City to me, ever!"

"Oh, yeah, I forgot. Listen, don't worry, man. I got this covered. Call you back when I got something for you."

"Thanks." Jason disconnected the call. "I forgot how much I really hate that guy."

Jason pored over files and documents that he and the Reuters research staff had accumulated. He followed what seemed like a hot trail that only led him to another dead end. Every trail went cold the whole picture looked like a jigsaw puzzle with half the pieces missing. Nothing he could find substantiated any kind of criminal activity.

Jason, as stuck as he could be and at the end of his rope, could only hope that something could be uncovered, and soon, or this story would be filed away. Once again, his quest for that illusive Pulitzer would elude his grasp.

Jason sat back in his chair right hand stroked his chin, as he tried to think of an angle. Something was missing in this story, and it had to be the key to the whole puzzle. Deep in his bones, he knew that Global had secret illegal drilling operations. They used dangerous and potentially devastating methods of energy extraction that could cause an explosion similar to the one off the California coast or worse, a catastrophic disaster that would kill everyone who worked near the project, as well as permanently destroying the surrounding environment.

They got away with it because Global had successfully insulated itself from the drilling companies in charge of the day-to-day operations. Then funneled contracts with legitimate drilling companies through so many dummy corporations that the sheer magnitude would take a team of accountants thirty years to unravel its complexity and connect it back to Global. Determined to expose them and not to let this story get shelved, Jason had to find something—something that would take this investigation to the next level. Jason pondered as he glanced at the wall clock across from his desk already three o'clock. "Christ, I haven't eaten a thing since breakfast," he said to himself. Jason closed his laptop and slid it into its case

He got up from the desk and slung the strap of the case over his shoulder. Just time enough to get a bite and drive up to the Walker house by six. Jason thought to himself as his stomach registered its complaint loud and clear, reminding him that newsmen as well as armies travel on their stomachs.

Jason finished his late lunch and made a few phone calls before he headed back into the valley to visit with Mrs. Walker. At about six o'clock Jason pulled up in front of the Walker home. He got out of his car just as a late-model, red SUV turned into the Walker driveway. Just a few houses away, a dark, late-model Toyota sedan pulled over to the curb and stopped. Jason approached the SUV as a woman in her thirties got out of the vehicle, looking harried. As Jason got closer, he could see that this woman had lacked sleep for several days.

"Excuse me, Mrs. Walker?"

Unaware that anyone had approach, the sound of Jason's voice startled her.

"Oh my god!" she blurted as she jumped back two feet.

"I'm sorry; I didn't mean to startle you."

"I didn't hear you walking up," Mrs. Walker said, looking up at Jason.

Mrs. Walker looked a lot older than she should, Jason thought. She looked at him through bloodshot eyes—eyes that had more turmoil and stress behind them than anyone could calculate.

"I'm Jason Brent, reporter."

Mrs. Walker gave Jason a slight nod to his statement.

"I wanted to talk to you about your husband."

"You've talked to Peter?" she exclaimed, nearly dropping her purse.

"Well actually, I was hoping you had some information about Peter's business trip."

"I don't know a thing, and I'm worried. Can we talk inside?"

The two proceeded to the front door. Mrs. Walker unlocked the door and entered the foyer with Jason right behind her. Hearing the front door open, Lena came running from the kitchen directly to her mother.

"Hello, baby," Mrs. Walker said as she scooped her daughter into her arms and held her tight. "Were you a good girl today?"

"Yes, Mommy."

Mrs. Walker set Lena down. "You go back into the kitchen and finish your dinner. I need to talk to this man for a little bit."

Lena smiled and waved to Jason and then quickly turned and ran back into the kitchen.

"We can talk in the den."

Mrs. Walker crossed the large living room and entered the den situated on the opposite side of the room's far wall.

"Can I get you something to drink? Coffee?" she asked.

"No thank you. I'm fine. It's Amy, right? May I call you Amy?"

"Yes, please," She said as she took a seat in the leather armchair in the corner of the room, Jason the loveseat along the near wall.

"Peter was helping us with a story, and I had some questions, but we haven't been able to get in contact with him. According to Global, he went on vacation."

"Vacation?" Amy scoffed. "He went on a business trip to South America. He told me that it was some sort of secret. Couldn't let the word get out to competitors as to what he was working on there. He told me it was worth millions of dollars. I don't understand why they would have told you he's on vacation."

"When did you speak with him last?"

"Last week. On his way to the airport. His flight had been delayed. He told me he'd call when he got in if it wasn't too late. He didn't call that night, but I wasn't worried because I thought I'd hear from him the next morning."

"Did he call?"

"No! I tried to call him, but his cellphone just goes to voice mail." Amy became more agitated as the conversation continued. "I called his office, and they told me that they could get a message to him. I waited and never got a call, or a text, not even an e-mail."

"How do you explain it?" Jason asked.

"I can't. This is not like Peter. He talks to his Lena every night before she goes to bed." Her voice cracked. "He's done that since she was born. He's never missed a night until this week. It's been six days now."

Jason too became worried. All at once, this had a sinister feel. He had gotten enough information and reluctant to speculate in front of Amy, he produced a business card from his pocket and held it out to her.

"Here's my number. If you hear from Peter, have him call me, or if you think of anything else you think I should know, call me. I'm going to do some investigating on my own."

Jason rose and offered his hand to Amy. She stood and shook Jason's hand.

"I'd appreciate anything you can do, Mr. Brent," Amy implored as she looked down at his card. "I'm just so worried."

As soon as I find out something, you'll be the first to know." Jason turned and started to leave the room. "I'll see myself out."

As soon as Jason got in his car, he called Jennifer.

"Jason. I got your message. Did you see Peter's wife?" an anxious Jennifer said, answering on the first ring.

"Just pulled away from the house. Mrs. Walker last spoke to Peter about a week ago. He was leaving for South America on business that was hush-hush. The last time they talked, on the way to meet his flight. He never called, e-mailed, or sent a text since. Something is very wrong here."

"You need anything from me?"

"No, I'm good. I'm going to contact that Paulina girl. I've got feelers out, waiting for info to come back. Call you when I've got something."

"Be careful, Jason." Jennifer's voice reflected unmistakable concern.

"I will. Talk to you soon."

Jason disconnected the call. This was not like Jennifer at all. In fact, this could be the first time he genuinely felt that she was indeed scared. Jason felt scared too—scared to think about what might have happened to Peter Walker for helping him get the goods on Global Energies. How many skeletons does Global have in their closets that they would take such risks? Jason had the feeling that illegal drilling might just be the tip of the iceberg, and if he kept peeling the onion, what would he find. Jason's gut told him that he was onto something big, really big. He just might get his illusive Pulitzer.

As Jason drove back to his office in Santa Monica, the dark Toyota sedan mirrored Jason's every move as it followed from a safe distance.

Erica, in the dark rental Toyota, concluded that Jason was driving back to his office by the route he took out of the San Fernando Valley. She hung back, kept to Jason's blind spot so as to not arouse his suspicion. Forty-five minutes later, he swung into his office parking lot. Erica stopped just beyond the corner of the office location and watched Jason, through her driver's side mirror, as he entered the building by the rear door that opened onto the parking lot. Erica waited several minutes before she got out of her car and meandered to the entrance of the building that housed Jason's office. Checking the black, glass-encased tenants' board in the lobby, Erica found the name J. Brent that corresponded to an office space on the second floor. Erica made a quick check of the interior layout of the building and then left by the rear entrance, made her way across the lot and down the street to her parked car. Erica took one last look at the building before she got into her car and headed home to plan her next move.

Inside his office, Jason sat at his desk, banged away on his laptop, finishing an article that would be put out on the wire in the morning. Jason assembled his case against Global, and he upped the ante with the latest installment in the Global story. Jason's next article would cover the mysterious reassignment of Peter Walker. Why did the company send Walker away if they didn't have anything to hide? Jason promised his readers that he would continue digging until they answered some questions or Walker contacted him. As the night wore on, Jason pounded away, strung the limited amount of facts he had together to form a compelling story. Sometime after midnight Jason filed his story and went home to bed. His next move would be to meet with Paulina Gregory and get some answers to his questions.

16

It's Post Time

DAVID EDISON bounded out of the elevator on the executive floor and briskly made his way down the hall, through the executive suite living room, and into Ratko's massive office. Upon entering the office, an angry Ratko greeted Edison. Ratko looked the worse for wear, dressed in a silk bathrobe, his face unshaven.

"About time you got here," Ratko bellowed.

"I rushed over as soon as you called me," Edison replied as he walked to the front of Ratko's desk.

"Have you seen this morning's paper?" Ratko barked as he waved a newspaper in front of Edison's face.

"I came directly here after you called."

"Brent wrote another article. He quoted Walker."

"Walker's been taken care of," Edison responded.

"Well, Brent visited his wife, and he wants Walker to call him. This is getting out of hand, and Brent needs to be stopped."

"That has been put into motion. I have confirmation."

"I'm counting on you cleaning this up," Ratko snapped as he gave Edison a wave of the hand that signaled the conversation terminated.

Edison turned on his heel and marched out of the office without another word.

Erica spent her day poring over Jason's past articles, to get a feel for Jason's writing style, getting a sense of his personality. Wow. This guy's really good, she thought to herself. The more she knew about Jason, the more she developed a cover story that would spark his interest in her—a commonality he would share with her that would draw him in and induce him to want to develop a relationship with her.

By the time she finished her research darkness had fallen, and Erica hungry, threw on some clothes and headed out to a local restaurant, the thought of cooking was not an option at this hour. She had Jason Brent's file tucked under her arm.

* * * * *

That evening, Jason sat at the Oak Room Grill's bar in the Financial District on Hope Street, the hang out for Global Corporate Officers, where Paulina Gregory regularly frequented. She stopped in the tavern most evenings after work to relax instead of fighting the rush-hour traffic driving to her Pasadena condominium. Jason drained his drink and gave a nod to the bartender.

A tall, thin bartender in his fifties moved quickly to Jason, a gin and tonic already in his hand.

"That's what I call service," Jason said, accepting the drink.

"I figured you were good for a second. For first timers, the second one's on me."

"You know most of your customers?"

"The regulars? Absolutely," he said with certainty.

A group of five men entered the bar, gave a wave to the bartender, and then took seats at a free table in the center of the room. A waitress greeted them, as she placed cocktail napkins on the table.

"A lot of the Global people come here?" Jason casually questioned.

"A bunch of the suits, yeah."

"Do you know a Paulina Gregory?"

"P? Sure do. She comes in for a bit almost every night. Stingers on Fridays."

"Excuse me?"

"She only drinks stingers on Friday nights. During the week, she usually has just one mojito. You know her?"

"Actually, no."

Another group of people entered, comprised of three men and three women.

The bartender looked to the group entering.

"What are you, a cop? What do you want with her?"

"It's not like that. I'm a reporter and just want to interview her for an article and thought it'd be easier away from the office. You know, catch her in a comfortable environment," Jason flashed a disarming smile.

"Oh, that's cool! Who do you write for?"

"Freelance," Jason replied. "When Ms. Gregory comes in, maybe you could point her out to me."

"Oh, you'll recognize her. Believe me." The bartender smiled wryly, nodding his head toward the entrance of the establishment.

Jason twisted his body in the direction of the door. Three people entered the bar, two females and a male. The man in his forties had a distinct receding hairline, and dressed in a dark blue suit, white shirt, and red tie.

One of the women looked to be in her late thirties, short blonde hair, wearing wire-framed glasses. The other woman could only have been Paulina Gregory. Tall, with shoulder-length, dark brown hair, she appeared to be in her late twenties. As she spoke to her co-worker, her expressive face made her dark eyes light up when she smiled. She dressed in a black pleated skirt with a white blouse and a red jacket. Paulina is the kind of woman that would catch the eye of any man, even if she dressed in a mechanic's dirty overalls, stunning to say the least. Looks were everything to her: impeccable makeup, perfectly tailored clothes, every hair in its place, and it was no mistake that she walked like a runway model. She sold sex and any man within a ten-mile radius a potential customer.

Jason took another slug of his gin and tonic. This is going to be a little harder than I thought, Jason thought to himself. This woman has it all, and she knows it.

The trio found a bistro table in the corner of the bar, and the two women took seats. The man spoke with the women for a moment and then left for the bar as the establishment began to fill with customers. Jason slid off the stool and walked to Paulina Gregory's table, summoning up every ounce of charm he could muster. Paulina saw Jason approach and surreptitiously eyed Jason up and down. Her female companion, surprised to find Jason at her elbow when he introduced himself, unaware of Paulina's artful perusal.

"Ladies," Jason said as he positioned himself at the table between the two women.

"Oh!" the older woman with Paulina said, as she turned to see Jason standing there. "I thought you were Aaron with our drinks."

"I'm sorry to disappoint. I'm Jason Brent." Jason offered his hand to the older woman first.

She shook his hand, and then Jason offered his hand to Paulina.

She took his hand into hers and gave it a firm squeeze, then straightened up as she took her hand back, gave a smile that told Jason she liked what she saw.

"I understand that you work for Global?"

"That's correct. My name is Gregory, and this is Kathy Lewis," Paulina said before her companion could answer.

"I'm a reporter with Reuters. I had been talking with one of your colleagues about a story idea, and I wondered if you ladies would be available for an interview?"

"You really need to contact our PR Department," Kathy said flatly.

"I can give you a name and number," Paulina volunteered as she fingered a business card from a gold card case in her purse. Paulina wrote a name on the back of the card and then offered it to Jason.

Jason took the card and looked at it. "Thank you very much."

"If you need any assistance, you can always give me a buzz," Paulina insisted, with a smile that said, "Call me."

"Thanks again," Jason said as the man with the trio approached the table. "I see your drinks are here. Have a nice evening." Jason nodded and strode back to the bar and slid back onto his bar stool. The bartender appeared in an instant.

"Hot or what?"

"Hot alright. You'd better hit me again. I need to cool down," Jason said with a wink and a smile.

Jason stopped at a coffee house just a few miles from the bar. With a coffee at his side, he sat at a table in the corner of the shop checking messages on his computer and following up on leads. Jason took Paulina's business card from his pocket and set it on the keyboard of his computer. He read the card carefully: 'Paulina Gregory, VP of Business Relations.' office phone numbers, cellphone number, e-mail address all there on the card. Jason picked up his cellphone and punched in her cell number. Jason typed out a text. 'Nice meeting you tonight. Are you available for a chat?'

Jason only had to wait two minutes before he received a text back. 'Didn't think I'd hear from you so soon. I've just arrived home. Call me.'

Jason dialed Paulina's number. She answered on the second ring.

"It's Paulina."

"Hey Paulina. It's Jason Brent."

"What can I do for you, Jason?"

"You hungry?"

"Yes, why?"

"Have dinner with me. We can talk a little," Jason said seductively.

"I know a nice little cafe in Old Town Pasadena."

"Perfect." Jason replied, "Text me the address, and I'll see you within the hour."

———————————————

Jason sat at the bar in a trendy Pasadena restaurant when Paulina walked in dressed in tight-fitting denim jeans with a cream-colored blouse tucked in at the waist. The top three buttons were undone down the front that drew everyone's attention to the natural jiggle motion created by her womanly strut. Around her waist, a black leather belt decorated with silver studs and a silver buckle. High-heeled, leather-strapped sandals completed the ensemble. She knew she attracted attention, and that's just how she liked it.

Paulina couldn't have been more than three feet inside the establishment when she spotted Jason at the bar. A slight smile crossed her lips. His classic bone structure reminded her of an NFL athlete, the kind of man she liked, the kind of man who looked like he had stamina and she the kind of woman capable of testing that stamina.

Before she took another step toward the bar, she had made up her mind that she would indeed test it, and test it soon. Paulina sauntered up to Jason and planted herself on the stool next to him.

"How many are you ahead of me?"

Jason turned to the sound of her voice.

"Paulina! Just one. What can I get you?" Jason replied as the bartender approached.

"Gin and tonic, with a twist."

Jason nodded to the bartender. "I'm glad you could meet me. I got us a table."

"It was either dinner with you or a date with my microwave. You're much nicer to look at," Paulina said, smiling.

"Thanks, I think."

"So what did you want to see me about?"

"I'm working on a piece about the rise of Global in the energy industry."

"That information is all in our PR Package," Paulina said, sipping her cocktail.

"PR Packages are all the same. I'm looking for some real insight. Do you think you could help me, Paulina?"

"Call me 'P.' All my friends do."

Jason flashed his disarming smile. "Let's have some dinner 'P.'"

After Erica finished her meal, she headed back home and contemplated her next move. She knew where Jason worked, and she knew where he lived. The first problem she would need to solve would be the meeting. How would she meet Jason that would not make him suspicious, not make him leery of her intent? Erica went to her closet in the bedroom, opened the wall safe, and extracted a leather briefcase from it. She sifted through the ID information the case contained. Erica would become Mary Jo Sommerson, non-profit grant writer. Now just how would Mary Jo happen to bump into Jason? Erica had an idea.

Jason and Paulina had a table in the back that allowed for conversation at a relatively normal tone in the crowded and noisy restaurant. Paulina saddled up next to Jason, very close, as if she'd known him her whole life. On the menu, small talk at the start of the meal, and it would be difficult to pinpoint the exact time Jason started probing into the affairs of Global, as he had an impeccable ability to set people at ease. Paulina also had an agenda, and her agenda, Jason Brent. She, the kind of woman who usually got what she wanted, and she wanted him.

"Peter Walker had been a great deal of help, but he went on some kind of trip, and I haven't been able to contact him."

"That's odd."

"That he took a trip?" Jason asked.

"No, that you would be talking to someone from the engineering department. You weren't dealing with anyone in PR?"

"I needed some technical data so . . ."

"That's not a problem. I can get you a name. Peter's no longer with us," Paulina remarked flatly.

"I didn't know. Did he get fired?"

"Oh no, nothing like that. He took another job, in Saudi Arabia, or South America. I don't remember which, but he left a couple of weeks ago."

"If you could do me a big favor," Jason said earnestly.

"If I can, sure."

"Can you find out what company Peter got a job with? I would be indebted to you."

"I think I can do that," Paulina said with a slight smile, "but what are you going to do for me?"

A puzzled look came over Jason's ruggedly handsome face that caused a U-shaped crease to appear at the top of his nose. "Well, what can I do for you?"

Pauline reached under the table and caressed Jason's crotch. Jason flinched a bit with a startled look on his face.

"Will there be anything else, sir?" the waiter asked, appearing out of nowhere.

"No thank you. We have everything in hand," Paulina responded seductively.

The waiter picked up the empty plates and walked away from the table. "My place is five minutes from here. You ride with me. I don't want to let you out of my sight."

Paulina kissed Jason passionately, getting a rise out of him.

"Oh, that's much better," Paulina said with a sinister grin.

"Why don't you get the car and I'll pay the bill. I'm gonna need a second before I can get up," an embarrassed Jason muttered.

A short while later, Jason walked out of the restaurant to see Paulina waiting out front in a white Mercedes convertible, top down and motor running, and so was the car. He slid into the passenger's side, and before he could close the door, Paulina peeled away from the curb, left a long patch of rubber on the asphalt as the car sped away.

Paulina had to have been lying when she said she lived just five minutes away, because it only took two and half minutes before she pulled into her parking garage, or she blew through every stop light on the way. Jason had a difficult time telling since he feared for his life at every intersection. He wasn't sure if this was her idea of foreplay, or just the typical L.A. driver.

Paulina shoved Jason out of the car and practically dragged him to the elevator, pawing him at every chance. Once the doors closed, Paulina pinned Jason against the wall and kissed him hungrily while she pushed the button for the fifth floor.

The elevator doors opened directly across from Paulina's apartment door. Still locked in a lip lock, the two staggered across the hallway as Paulina fumbled for the door key, trying several times to get it into the hole.

"I hope you don't have this much trouble," encouraged Paulina.

"Well, maybe if I'd bought the doorknob a couple of drinks first, it'd be a little more willing," Jason quipped.

Paulina laughed, then finally the door opened and the two entered into her spacious apartment that had a spectacular view of the city.

"Wow, that's a great view."

"Yeah, I know. Terrific," Paulina said, dragging Jason to the bedroom.

Paulina shoved Jason down on her bed and crawled on top of him as she took both his hands and placed them above his head. Before Jason knew it, she had him handcuffed to the brass headboard.

"Jesus Christ! What are you doing?" an apprehensive Jason barked.

"Relax, sweetie. I'm going to ride you like a thoroughbred in the Kentucky Derby."

In the next moment, Paulina grabbed the bottom of his shirt and in one savage motion, ripped it open. Buttons flew everywhere.

"Holy crap, 'P'!"

Paulina then unbuckled his belt and unfastened his pants while she slid them down to his feet. She quickly slipped off his loafers and ferociously pulled his pants and boxers down to his ankles. Now lying completely naked and vulnerable, Jason's appendage stood at full attention.

"Now, don't you go anywhere," Paulina instructed as she walked away.

"P? What exactly is going on here?" Jason asked with a trace of fear in his voice.

"I'll be right back."

Paulina disappeared into the walk-in closet. Gone for no more than five minutes, she returned in full Jockey Silks. Jason's eyes popped out of his head as Paulina slowly danced her way over to the bed dressed in black, patent leather riding boots. As she stepped up onto the bed he noticed the white, rider's pants were crotch-less. Her white-sleeved, baby blue, polka dot jersey stopped right above her areolas, exposing her very plump breasts. Jason didn't know if he looked at the most ridiculous outfit ever, or he was in the presence of the hottest jockey on the planet.

"Why the number eight?" a befuddled Jason queried, nodding to the number on the jersey.

"That's how many races there are tonight," Paulina said as she slipped the riding crop out of her left boot.

"Oh fuck."

"What's happened here?" Paulina inquired as she took the riding crop and fondled his 'love package.'

Her touch started to arouse Jason again.

"It's post time!" Paulina announced as she mounted her steed.

As the night went on, Paulina rode Jason like Paul Revere on that fateful night in 1776.

After she finished the third race, and Jason spent, Paulina dismounted him, kissed him on the forehead as if he were an actual horse; left him handcuffed to the bed and disappeared into the bathroom. He immediately fell asleep, exhausted.

Jason relived his encounter with Paulina in his active dreams through the long night. Her words repeated in his brain as he slept: "We're in the back stretch now," "Coming around turn two," "Making the turn for home. It's going to be close. It's neck and neck." It was ecstasy and agony even in his dream.

Jason woke up released from his handcuffs, and apparently, toweled off in his sleep and tucked in with Paulina nowhere to be found. A note left by the bed. "Thanks for the ride! You're a real winner."

Definitely one for the books Jason thought.

Sore and moving slowly, grabbed his clothes and dressed as quickly as possible. Unable to button his shirt, he just tucked it in as best he could. He thought to himself that Santa Anita would never be the same.

As he left, Jason looked at Paulina's apartment, noting that her living space reflected her lifestyle. Provocative, sexually oriented artwork hung on the walls, from photographic works to oil paintings. Neat and clean with everything in its place, her apartment projected a warm and inviting feel and showed that Paulina liked the finer things in life and would spend top dollar to get them.

* * * * *

Erica awoke early the next morning with an aggressive "To Do" list in her hand that would challenge the most capable of humans. She needed to find an apartment, get it furnished and decorated, have business cards printed, and a new wardrobe purchased.

It would be a hectic day, but it needed to be done before she would be able to set up "the meet." The faster Erica could get this done, the quicker she could take the next critical step in the completion her contract.

Erica found herself a spacious one-bedroom apartment on Idaho Avenue in West Los Angeles, bordering Santa Monica, less than a mile from Jason's office and about four miles from his home in the Hollywood hills on Electra Drive. Erica paid the first years rent in advance. She next went to a furniture rental business she knew and picked out all her furniture and accessories, including artwork and knickknacks.

Within the next forty-eight hours, Erica moved in as Mary Jo Sommerson, and the next phase of her plan would begin.

Back in his office after his night with Paulina, Jason composed an e-mail on his progress with Global to

Jennifer, when his office cellphone announced an incoming call. Jason quickly glanced at the screen and saw Paulina's number.

"Hey, Paulina," said Jason as he answered the call.

"Hi there, sugar," Paulina replied cheerfully.

"What's up?"

"I was hoping you were," Paulina said wryly.

Jason rolled his eyes. "Well, you know, working . . ." Jason was about to say 'hard,' but thought better of it. "Lots to do, busy day."

"Too bad. Anyway, I did some snooping for you. I thought Walker took another job, like I said, but then someone else told me that his wife called the office several times trying to get a hold of him. This person told me that he told his wife that he went on some kind of trip to South America."

"So he is still with the company?"

"That's the weird part. He's not on the payroll anymore. He's basically disappeared."

"Really," an inquisitive Jason replied.

"I talked to my girl in human resources, and she said they were told to take him off payroll until further notice. Some kind of sabbatical, but I've never heard of anyone at this company taking a sabbatical. What's really strange is they boxed up his personal stuff and put them in the company storage room."

"I'd like to take a look at his stuff? Do you think you can get me in?"

"I don't see why not. Something's funny here, and I'd like to find out myself, and it will give us a chance to play detective. Let's have dinner, and I'll get you in after the offices close."

"Let's do it." Jason cringed as the words left his mouth.

"Perfect. Then we can check out the storage room," Paulina giggled.

Erica shopped for her wardrobe. Only a few items were new; the rest of her closet filled with clothes purchased from several secondhand stores. Erica, meticulous in every detail to make her environment look lived in, left nothing to chance. Erica brought her purchases to her new apartment and began laying them out. The following afternoon the furniture would arrive, and the apartment would be complete.

Erica filled the kitchen with pots, pans, china, glasses and silverware, a coffee maker and dishtowels, all purchased from secondhand stores.

After stuffing her new closet with her clothes, Erica got on her computer and created photographs of herself and her faux friends.

Then Erica cruised over to Jason Brent's office to get a feel for the location. She parked down the block in a position that gave her a clear view of the building and the parking lot. Erica focused her high-resolution camera with telephoto lens on the building housing Jason Brent's office, his Prius, parked in the lot on the side of the building. She snapped off twenty shots that covered the area, the buildings, and the alleys so she would have a working knowledge of all escape routes in case anything went awry. Satisfied with her photo coverage, Erica headed home for the day to study her cover story.

Jason left his Santa Monica office around six o'clock in the evening and drove the surface streets across town to meet Paulina at a local bistro at seven. Accounting for the Los Angeles rush-hour traffic, the drive took nearly fifty minutes. By the time Jason parked, he arrived at the restaurant just a few minutes past seven. Paulina sat at the bar sipping a glass of wine when Jason entered.

"Hey, baby," Paulina said as she slid off her bar stool.

"Paulina."

Paulina wrapped her arms around Jason's neck and planted a deep kiss square on his lips.

Jason's arms went around her waist for a moment, then gently squeezed her left butt cheek, and then pushed her back when he felt that the kiss had lasted long enough. "Save some of that for the home stretch."

"It will be about five more minutes before we get a table," Paulina said as the two stood nose to nose at the bar.

"I could use a drink." Jason took a seat next to Paulina and motioned the bartender to him. "Scotch, please."

Paulina rubbed Jason's thigh from crotch to knee as he scanned the little restaurant. The bar had only two other patrons who sat drinking cocktails. A man in his sixties dressed in a blue business suit and a woman in a blouse and slacks.

"You look a bit off today, honey."

"I'm just a little stiff." Jason replied.

"Well, we do have about five minutes," Paulina said with a devilish grin.

"No, stiff as in sore. You rode the hell out of me last night."

"Well, darling, then we need to get you back out on the track and work out that stiffness."

"I'll be fine," Jason replied with a short laugh and a charming smile.

The bar could only hold maybe five people at a time with the restaurant taking up the remaining space in the establishment. Small tables filled the room, all dressed in starched white linen with a candle in the center. Soft, soothing, classical music played over the sound system as the patrons dined on French cuisine.

"I had to leave early the other morning; had a meeting."

"No problem. I took a cab back to the restaurant," Jason said.

"I thought you might have been upset with me."

"Not at all. We're good."

The waiter, dressed in a black suit, starched white shirt, and black bowtie, interrupted the conversation.

"I have your table, miss."

Jason took Paulina's arm, and the two followed the waiter to their table.

Some ninety minutes later Paulina and Jason finished their meal and had an after-dinner drink before they left the restaurant around eight thirty in the evening. By nine o'clock, they arrived at the Global building. Paulina parked on the first level of the parking structure, and the two walked to the far corner of the garage and exited the door that led to the loading dock.

Jason suddenly stopped abruptly when he saw the security camera mounted above the doors to the service elevator.

"Don't worry. That camera is out. Hasn't been fixed yet. That's the only reason I can get you in," Paulina said as she used her magnetic key card to enter the service elevator.

They took the elevator to the basement of the building. The basement, deadly quiet; their footsteps echoed off the concrete floor as they walked to the locked storage room.

Paulina opened the storage-room gate, and the two entered a large area filled with office supplies on metal shelves. One section of the room, enclosed in a wire cage, had an electronic door lock at the entrance. Paulina punched four numbers into the keypad, and the cage door unlocked. Jason followed Paulina into the caged area, and moved to a shelf at the rear of the cage. The metal rack stood eight feet tall and ran along the entire length of the caged area. Cardboard boxes were labeled on the ends with names. Paulina scanned the boxes and found the box with 'Walker' written on it in black marker. Paulina pulled the box off the shelf.

"Here it is."

Jason took the box from her and set it down on the floor, lifted the cover off, and peered inside. The condition of the items indicated that the box had been packed in deliberate haste. The items piled on top of each other, in random fashion.

The first item that caught Jason's eye, a framed photograph of Walker with his wife and daughter that he removed from the box then looked up at Paulina.

"Why would the company hold onto this stuff? Why not send it to his wife, to his house?" Jason asked.

"It doesn't make sense. If he quit working here, they would let him box the stuff himself and escort him out of the building. If he's on an assignment, his stuff should be at his desk. It's not like we need the office space."

Jason continued to dig through the items in the box; an assortment of note pads, pens, post-it notes, a couple of pieces of mail, paperclips, all the things one would expect in an office desk.

Jason thumbed through Peter Walker's spiral-bound appointment calendar, finding little except for one entry made nearly three weeks back where he scribbled the word 'Argentina.' Jason closed the calendar. Frustrated by the lack of information he'd garnered, he threw it back into the box. The force of the calendar as it hit the side of the box dislodged something from the spiral wire that held the pages together. Jason picked up the book again, and hanging on the edge of the wire, a flash drive. Jason looked up at Paulina; her attention focused on the supply-cage door. Jason palmed the flash drive and put the cover back on the box.

"Well not much help here. We better get out before we get caught."

Jason picked up the box and deposited it where Paulina had found it.

"Not so fast there, mister," Paulina demanded as she cuffed one of Jason's wrists to the storage rack.

"What are you doing?" Jason said, surprised.

"You're under arrest for stealing my heart," Paulina declared as she unzipped his pants.

"Are you fucking nuts? Someone could catch us."

"Then you better confess everything, and fast!" Paulina said as she slipped off her skirt and revealed she hadn't worn panties.

Jason got aroused immediately, and Paulina giggled with great delight, crawled up on him and mounted him.

"I'm gonna have to add a charge of concealing a loaded gun." Paulina moaned as she placed Jason's love weapon inside her.

The two went at it like a couple of bobcats in heat, groaning and grinding each other. As the two reached the height of ecstasy, Jason grabbed the shelf rack for better balance and inadvertently pulled the entire shelf down; boxes fell to the floor with a loud crash.

They laughed and panicked at the same time. Paulina reached down to put her skirt back on, and Jason tried to free himself from the cuffs.

"You gotta get this thing off of me."

Paulina dug into her purse to retrieve the key, laughing at Jason's predicament.

She pulled out the key and unlocked Jason's wrist. Paulina darted to the door as Jason pulled his pants up and struggled to get out the gate, not amused by the turn of events.

"Holy crap! The elevator is coming!" Paulina said in hushed tones.

Paulina and Jason, in a frantic dash, ran back the way they came in just before the elevator doors opened.

Paulina laughed all the way to her car, jumped in, and started the motor. "Quick! Get in!"

Jason jumped into the passenger seat, and before he could close the door, Paulina slammed the accelerator to the floor, spinning the tires. The car lurched and just about tossed Jason out.

17

It's Just A Scratch

THEY RODE in silence except for a few bursts of giggles from Paulina from time to time until they reached the restaurant where Jason had left his car.

"How's Friday?" Paulina asked as if nothing had happened.

"Friday sounds good. I'll call you," Jason said as he opened the car door.

"Don't forget to take your vitamins. I need you to keep up your strength. There'll be races that night!"

Jason smiled and closed the car door. Paulina gave Jason a wink and a smile and pulled away. He stood for a moment, shook his head. What the fuck? Jason thought to himself as he watched Paulina's tail lights fade into the darkness. Keep my strength up? Jason rolled his eyes and rubbed his wrist. 'You're not dull, Paulina. I'll give you that."

Jason raced home eager to open the flash drive he had taken from Peter Walker's personal effects. Once in his apartment, Jason fired up his laptop and plugged in the flash drive. Much to his consternation, the drive had a password. The contents of the drive would have to wait until tomorrow. Jason would have to seek help from a computer programmer friend who could open the drive for him.

Jason grabbed a beer from the fridge and sat in his favorite chair. He immediately passed out from exhaustion before he even opened it.

* * * * *

Erica arose early in the morning, went straight to her apartment in Santa Monica, and spent the entire day putting in the final additions that would make the space looked lived in. Every detail meticulously attended to, from a leftover dinner to an open bottle of white wine in the refrigerator. Soiled laundry had a home in the bathroom hamper; a half bottle of aspirin in the medicine cabinet along with a used toothpaste tube, dental floss, and a nearly empty bottle of mouthwash. Nothing left to chance that could give Erica's cover story away. Bills, magazines, and junk mail staged to look as though Mary Jo had occupied the apartment for months. Erica gave it one last inspection to make sure everything was in its place. With all in order, she prepared to execute phase two.

Jason awoke at nine and made a phone call to his computer genius friend, Franklin Eide. Franklin, the epitome of computer geekiness, right down to the pasty skin color and matted-down, greasy hair, but a genius none-the-less.

"Franklin, I've got a job for you," Jason said cheerfully. "Are you busy? I need this ASAP."

"Sure thing. What is it?"

"I've got a flash drive I need you to open."

"If you want to drop it off, I can override the password and download the data, then e-mail it to you," Franklin said.

"Perfect. I'll get it to you later this morning. Talk to you then," Jason responded, disconnecting the call.

Global Security Captain Wes Palmer, African American, fifty-five years of age that showed every year in his ruggedly lined face. He surveyed the mess left in the supply room cage along with Harold Calvin, the forty-year-old building maintenance man, an unassuming, hardworking man, who took pride in his work shook with rage at the condition of the supply room.

"I noticed the supply room door open, and I looked in, but it was dark. When I turned on the light, I saw this mess." Harold hissed.

Palmer hitched up his starched, creased uniform pants as he nodded his agreement to Harold.

"I told the building manager there should be a camera in this room," Palmer said.

Stepping over strewn office supplies, Palmer looked around the room for some clue as to the perpetrator of this crime.

"Nothing is missing?" Palmer asked as he turned to Harold.

"Not that I can tell," Harold said, shrugging.

Palmer retrieved his cellphone from his front pants' pocket and dialed a number.

"It's Palmer, sir. Nothing is missing, but we did find something interesting. I'll bring it to your office."

Palmer punched a button on his cellphone and slid it back into his pocket.

"If you find anything is missing, call me." Palmer requested as he stepped out of the security cage.

———————————

Jason had to run some errands and left his house, stopped to drop off the flash drive at Franklin's, and by the time he reached his office, had already received an e-mail from Franklin with an attached file that he'd retrieved from the drive. Jason opened it and started to review the information contained therein. Jason took special interest in several dates Walker had recorded in his electronic notes.

Walker had sent a memo to Ratko worried about what dangerous procedures Global used in fracking operations. Walker concluded that the procedures had dangerous implications, and were illegal. He assumed that the field managers were operating outside company guidelines. He also provided Ratko with some evidence that a Global team, through gross negligence, caused the California oilrig explosion that killed a dozen workers. Walker finished his memo with a suggestion to bring in legal counsel before these violations were presented to the authorities.

Jason found another interesting entry that dated back three weeks that stated Mr. Ratko wanted Walker to leave for Argentina on the fifteenth to investigate if similar illegal practices took place at their South American facility. Mr. Ratko informed him that he had a ticket for a seven thirty flight to Buenos Aires, from LAX. Walker would be leaving that evening.

Jason went immediately to work and in twenty minutes compiled a list of airlines with flights that departed for Argentina from LAX. The next step, to find which carriers departed after seven o'clock on the fifteenth. With the list narrowed down, Jason began to call the airlines, checked them off his list one by one, as he went. No one had Peter Walker as a passenger on the fifteenth, nor had Global Industries purchased any tickets.

Jason picked up his cellphone, opened the directory, and called Amy Walker at work. Amy confirmed that Peter did leave on the fifteenth and taken to the airport in a limousine. Jason, back to the grunt work now, with a list of limo companies, calling each one to find out who may have taken Peter Walker to LAX.

Several hours had gone by when Jason trotted out of his office building and down the street to the corner coffee shop. Another beautiful sunny Southern California day a breeze drifted in off the ocean. The air fresh and clean, the sky clear, and Jason needed caffeine, and he needed it now. Jason turned into Beano's Coffee and Cakes.

Across the street, parked in a rented Prius, Erica sat and watched her target. She snapped off a series of high-resolution digital photos. Erica documented every move of her prey in its natural habitat as she compiled a profile of every tendency, to the smallest detail, from the number of sugars to the type of cream he puts in his coffee—even the number of times he stirred before he licked off the stick and tossed it in the trash.

Jason looked a bit more awake after a few sips of coffee. He waved to the young pretty girl behind the counter and headed back down the street to his office. Erica continued to snap away at his every step.

"You're cute, Jason Brent, but you don't know what's about to hit you."

The hours dragged by as Erica kept watch on Jason's office with her high-powered binoculars. The digital clock on the dashboard of the rental Prius glowed 6:52 p.m. when Erica saw the light in Jason's office window go out.

Erica started her car and quickly swung into the small parking area next to the office building, guided her machine close to Jason's vehicle and just grazed the rear bumper as her car passed by his. She quickly exited the car and trotted up to Jason's vehicle with a small pad and pen in her hand. Erica scribbled on the pad as Jason walked around the side of the building toward his car.

As he approached the driver's side, he saw Erica writing on the pad, as she stood next to the front left fender.

"Can I help you?" Jason asked.

Erica feigned surprise as she jumped at the sound of Jason's voice.

"Oh my god, you startled me," Erica said with a slight Texas twang.

"I'm sorry. I didn't mean to scare you," Jason said disarmingly.

Dressed in a navy blue business suit with a starched, white blouse accented with a red and white striped scarf tied around her neck, Erica couldn't have looked sexier. A matching, navy blue, pleated skirt completed her ensemble. Her dark hair pulled back, to show off her silky complexion. Light blush and sparse eye makeup accentuated Erica's natural beauty.

Jason's hair on the back of his neck stood up, and his pulse quickened. It may have been the last bit of sunlight that reflected off the white building wall, for indeed, a glow that surrounded this beautiful woman. Jason wasn't about to let this chance meeting go by the boards without making an approach. Jason wanted to know this woman.

Erica locked onto Jason's eyes, and a twinge of excitement surged through her body.

"I, ah . . . kind of bumped into your car. I think I put a scratch in your . . . ah . . . rear . . . car . . . I mean, bumper," Erica said, fumbling for words, taken aback, as she saw Jason up close for the first time.

Photographs and viewing from a distance didn't do him justice. Jason Brent had an unprecedented charismatic presence.

Jason stepped around to the back of his car and bent down to take a close look at the rear bumper. Erica followed close behind him. Her heart pumped harder. Her breathing became shallow. She took deep breaths to try to regain her composure.

"I just couldn't hit someone who drives an eco-friendly car like myself and not leave a note," she said, in her phony Southern charm.

Jason stood up and turned to Erica.

"You just take it to any body shop you like, and I'll pay for it. I'd rather leave out insurance if you don't mind," Erica pleaded.

"It's just a scratch. I wouldn't worry about it," Jason said with a smile.

"No. I insist," Erica said, looking directly at Jason again with the same electric excitement. "I want to fix your car."

"I couldn't let you do that," Jason insisted, extending his hand. "My name is Jason—Jason Brent."

Erica took Jason's hand into hers, and immediately her knees became weak as she felt the warmth of Jason's hand. The lines that appeared at the corners of his eyes when he smiled reminded her of Ford. Jason's eyes smiled at her just a microsecond before his mouth did.

Her heart beat faster. A chill ran up and down her spine; she connected with Jason as soon as their hands touched. Erica tried to shake off the feeling, but she couldn't. She had felt this with Ford and this feeling disrupted her rehearsed story. Erica forgot the alias she used; she just stared at Jason as they held each other's hands. Name. Tell him your name, Erica's brain screamed at her. What's my name? Mary! It's Mary!

"It's Mary," Erica heard herself say. "Mary Jo Sommerson."

Erica quickly regained her composure and smiled warmly back in character.

"It's nice to meet you. I know I frightened you. Please forgive me," Jason pleaded.

"That's okay. No worries."

Erica suddenly realized she still held onto Jason's hand and sheepishly slid it from his.

"If you won't let me fix your car, let me take you to lunch or something." Erica begged.

"Lunch would be fantastic."

"Good, that's good."

Jason reached into his jacket pocket and produced a business card. "Just call me with a time and place."

Jason smiled, and the jolt of electricity hit Erica again. She stood there for a moment and just watched as Jason reached toward her and took her right hand in his left and placed his business card in her palm.

"Yes. I'll call you," Erica said apprehensively, frantically fumbling in her purse as she searched for her business cards. "I've got a business card in here somewhere."

"Don't worry about it; I'll wait for your call."

Erica slid her purse up on her arm and gave Jason an awkward smile, turned and walked back to her car. Jason watched her walk away, marveled at her shapely, toned legs and the way she floated across the parking lot in her black leather, high-heeled shoes. Jason took a deep breath, wished he had a few more minutes to chat with this gorgeous creature. Erica reached her car, then turned back toward Jason and gave him a little wave of the hand just before she entered her vehicle. Jason stood by his car as Erica attempted to turn her car around without hitting anything unintentionally. She backed the car up a few feet, then inched it forward a few feet, turned to her right and then reversed her direction again. To anyone watching, Erica looked like a high school student taking a Driver's Education Class. Finally, her car, completely turned around, pulled out of the parking lot, giving Jason another wave as she turned onto the street.

Erica hadn't driven more than a block before she let out a primeval scream.

"How could you be so stupid? What is wrong with you?" "Christ, it's like you never talked to an attractive man before. You nearly blew it," Erica yelled as she slammed her fist against the steering wheel. "Couldn't even remember my cover name. Pathetic!"

18

I'm gonna have to kill that bitch!

PAULINA HAD CHANGED into sweat pants and a t-shirt, poured herself a glass of wine, and just put a frozen dinner in the microwave when the doorbell buzzed. She shuffled to the front door wondering, "who the hell this could be" and opened it. David Edison stood in front of her

"David. What a surprise. What do I owe the pleasure? Thought you lost my address?" said Paulina sarcastically.

"What? An old friend can't drop by to say hello?" David uttered as he walked past Paulina, letting himself in. "You alone?"

"Yes. Not that it's any of your business. Do you want something?"

"I just thought we'd catch up," David said as he surveyed the room.

"Catch up? You said we were done. What is there to 'catch up' on?"

"You seeing anybody these days?"

"What do you care?" Paulina snapped back.

"Just making conversation. Oh, here's a bit of news. We had an incident last night at the building. Someone broke into the supply cage."

"You drove all the way up here to tell me that? Still haven't figured out how to send an e-mail."

"Always charming 'P.' Anyway, I planned to put something in the lost and found, but decided it might be incriminating," David said as he pulled the handcuffs out of his jacket pocket and dangled them in front of her face.

Paulina eyed him with a 'go fuck yourself' look as she took the cuffs out of his hand and dropped them on the couch. "Why do you have to be so fucking melodramatic?"

"Why did you have to bring someone into our building just to have sex with him?"

"Because it was fun and exciting! What? Did you forget about all the times we fucked in the conference room? Then sat there during a meeting as Zubin put his Danish right on the table where we had been the night before. You thought that hilarious!"

"Yeah, it was. Just thinking about it is making me hot right now."

"Is that what this is about? You're jealous?"

"Maybe."

"Oh, David, you miss 'P' don't you?" Paulina teased in her little girl voice as she sidled up next to him.

David grabbed her, pulled her in, and kissed her hard.

"Oh my! You got yourself all worked up because you knew I was doing someone else. Poor little David."

"You're a real bitch, Paulina," David snarled as he flipped her around, bent her over the couch, and pulled down her sweatpants in once swift move.

He gave her a little spank on her tush as he unbuckled his pants and let them drop to his ankles.

"You've been a naughty little bitch, and now you're going to be punished," David growled as he aggressively penetrated her.

"Oh, god! That's right, Daddy. Punish me!"

David took his open hand and smacked Paulina on her ass.

"Yes! Paulina has been naughty. I'm sorry, Daddy!"

David slammed into her harder and caused the couch to slide out of position. "You better be sorry! Now tell me who you were with!"

"Just some guy, Daddy. He's no one," Paulina pleaded, taking on the little girl role convincingly.

"Not good enough," David protested as he spanked her harder. "Who is it?"

"He's just some guy I met at the bar," Paulina said, enjoying the game.

"I want a name, you little bitch! Give me a name!" David barked, hitting her even harder.

Paulina really got into the moment, role-playing along with every smack.

"Who is it?"

"Just some reporter."

"A reporter?" David hit Paulina hard. "Are you fucking crazy?"

He hit her again.

"Ow! David, that's too hard."

"Tell me his name!" David shouted as he thrust harder. "Tell me!"

"Jason! His name is Jason."

David stopped thrusting; a shocked look came over his face.

"Jason who?"

"Jason Brent. What the fuck is the big deal? Do you know him?"

David pulled his pants up and buckled his belt as Paulina turned around.

"Why did you stop? That was great!" Paulina said, confused.

"You fucking, stupid whore!" David screamed at her as he hauled off and slapped her across the face.

"Jesus Christ, David! What the fuck?"

"That guy is poison to us! I can't believe you brought a reporter into our building. That guy has been trying to pin something on us for a year! You fucking idiot!"

"How was I supposed to know?"

David hauled off and slapped her across the face again.

"You stop seeing him right now! I mean it, Paulina. End it, or I'll fucking kill you! Do you understand?"

David raised his hand to hit her again.

"I understand! Jesus, David!" Paulina said as she put up her arm to block the blow.

David stormed out of the apartment and slammed the door behind him.

"Fuck you, David Edison," Paulina said as she rubbed her cheek. "You fucked with the wrong girl."

* * * * *

Late morning, and Jason, unshaven and unkempt, had worked two days straight, seated at his desk in his office, on his laptop, tracking down limo companies. He had been trying to find a record of Peter Walker as a passenger on the fifteenth, but his search came up empty. Frustrated, he picked up his cellphone and dialed.

"Hey 'P', its Jason."

"Just the man I wanted to talk too. We're still on for tonight, right?" Paulina said, eager to see him.

"Of course. Pick you up at seven."

* * * * *

The sun setting and the sky full of pink and lavender wisps of clouds gave the air a melancholy feel as Jason pulled up to Paulina's building. He stepped into the elevator and rode it up to the fifth floor. Ringing the buzzer, Jason waited patiently while Paulina took her time answering. Finally, Paulina opened the door wearing a stunning little, black dress as she fixed her earring, her makeup expertly covering the bruise she had on her right cheek.

"Come in, honey," Paulina said, hurrying back into the bedroom, her dress unzipped in the back. "I just need another minute."

"You look amazing in that dress."

"Thank you. You're sweet. My day's been shit! I'm starving, and I need a drink. Zip me," Paulina asked, as she strutted out of the bedroom, up to Jason and turned her back to him.

Jason zipped up her dress, turned her around, and kissed her.

"What do you feel like? Italian? Mexican?"

"How about a nice portion of Jason!" Paulina said with a big smile.

"That's for dessert, darlin'," replied Jason as he kissed her again.

"My, you're awful frisky tonight," Paulina said happily. "I missed you."

"It's only been three days."

"I know," Paulina winked.

David Edison sat in a lounge bar with two beautiful young women on each side of him, a redhead and a brunette of European descent, who could easily be models or mail-order brides. As the two women pawed all over him, his cellphone rang.

"Hold on, girls. But remember where we left off," David quipped, full of himself. "Fred, what do you got?"

David listened intently to the caller.

"I want you to stay on them until she's alone. Got it?" David ordered as he hung up.

"Now, girls, where were we?"

Jason and Paulina sat at a table across from each other as the busy restaurant buzzed, with muffled conversations. Dishes clanged, all around the establishment Italian music played softly overhead.

"Sometimes the people I work for can be real assholes."

"Has this anything to do with the supply cage or the bruise?"

Paulina touched the bruise lightly aware that Jason could see it.

"Yes and no, but I'll tell you; there is something fishy going on at that company."

"More than you know."

"What do you mean?" Paulina said with trepidation.

"Peter Walker gathered some evidence for me on illegal fracking, undocumented drilling, and the truth behind the oil rig explosion off the coast."

"But they know how that happened. We were cleared."

"No, 'P,' it was a big cover-up and Peter had the names of everyone who got paid off, and now he's disappeared.'

"But he may still be on that trip."

"Then why did they clean out his office? Why hasn't his wife heard from him in weeks? He was supposed to have left for Argentina on the fifteenth, but I can't find an airline he flew on. His wife said he got picked up by a limo, and there are no records of any company picking him up; way to suspicious if you ask me."

"Maybe the company limo took him."

"Wait. You guys have your own limo?" Jason questioned, leaning into Paulina.

"Yeah, a couple of them," replied Paulina, a bit frightened by the implication.

"I need you to do something for me, 'P,' but you gotta promise me you'll be careful," Jason said sincerely.

"Okay, but you have to answer a question for me first."

"Sure, anything."

"Are you seeing me just to get information for your story, or is there something else here?" Paulina asked flatly.

"Honestly, 'P,' in the beginning I was just going to ply you with drinks and pump you for information. But then you took me to the races and showed me more fun than I've had in years. I really like you, and that's why I'm asking you to be careful. What I'm going to ask you to do could get you into a lot of trouble."

"I appreciate the honesty. This was a no strings deal from the get go. I just didn't want to be used. What do you want me to do?"

"I need you to find out if Peter Walker got picked up by one of Global's limos and who the driver was so I can talk to him."

"That should be easy. We keep a log."

"Thank you, 'P.'"

"You're cute when you're all concerned," Paulina said as she squeezed Jason's hand.

After dinner, Jason parked his car outside Paulina's building, and the two walked close to each other as another car pulled up and parked across the street.

Jason and Paulina walked through the lobby doors as the gentleman in the parked car snapped photos of them.

A few moments passed when a light came on in a fifth floor window. Several minutes later, the light went out.

* * * * *

"This is so cool. It's really big," the redhead from the bar remarked.

"It's not that big," the brunette said, disappointed.

"I was talking about the T.V."

David Edison lay in his bed with the two girls from the bar. They were drinking champagne as they watched a pornographic movie on a huge flat screen television. Edison's cellphone vibrated on the nightstand.

"Mute that! I have to take this," David snapped. "What is it, Fred? David listened for a moment. "So, he's spending the night? Okay, go home."

David stared straight ahead as he squeezed the cellphone in his hand.

"Get out! Both of you!" David bellowed.

"What's going on?" the redheaded woman asked.

"Get out, now!"

The two girls collected their clothes and left dejected.

"I'm gonna have to kill that bitch," David grunted, and threw his phone across the room in a blinding rage.

19

MARY JO MAKES A DATE

JASON AROSE before Paulina the following morning and made himself at home in her well-stocked kitchen. The aroma of fresh-brewed coffee and frying bacon welcomed Paulina as she entered the kitchen.

"Pour yourself a cup of coffee. I made it strong," Jason said, smiling.

"Smells wonderful. You can come over and cook any time you want. I'll set the table."

After his breakfast with Paulina, Jason went back to his office to go over all the information that he had put together on the disappearance of Peter Walker. Armed with this information, Jason scheduled a lunch with Jennifer at a downtown restaurant. When Jason arrived, he found Jennifer seated at a table.

"Thanks for seeing me on short notice, Jen," Jason said as he slid the chair out from the table.

"You said it's important, but why couldn't you tell me over the phone?"

"Because if I'm wrong, it would make us look bad — maybe blow everything I've been working on for the last year."

"I've never seen you like this," Jennifer said, concerned.

"Peter got onto something big. I hope I'm wrong, but I think someone at Global found out about it, and they took care of him."

"What do you mean by 'took care of him?"

"My gut tells me that they had him killed?"

"What?" Jennifer blurted loud enough that patrons at nearby tables took notice of her.

"Yeah. Whatever he found, it was devastating enough to make someone at Global want Peter out of the picture permanently.

"Jesus, Jason. We're talking murder."

"That's why I have to make sure. Paulina agreed to help me. She's checking the logs to see if Peter used a Global limo to go to the airport on the fifteenth of last month."

"We need to go to the authorities," Jennifer insisted.

"It's all conjecture right now, Jen. I need to get more evidence."

Worried, Jennifer rocked back in her chair, knowing that Jason hit it on the head. Without solid information, no way the authorities would listen to them.

After his lunch with Jennifer, Jason went back to his office and checked his messages. Jason felt an icy stab in his heart when he saw an e-mail from Amy Walker.

Almost afraid to open the file, Jason hesitated, but knew that he had to, and reluctantly clicked on the message. As Jason read, he couldn't believe his eyes.

Amy, relieved to have received an e-mail from Peter forwarded it immediately. To summarize, Peter had apologized for not having contacted her sooner, but his cellphone stopped working, and the area so remote he could not get access to any outside communication until now. Jason immediately called Amy at work.

"Amy, its Jason Brent. I got your e-mail," Jason said pleasantly.

"Did you get a message from him?" an excited Amy asked.

"No, I didn't."

"I wrote him back and told him you had come to see me and you needed to talk to him."

"I see," Jason said, trying to hide his concern. "But I'm sure he'd want to get back to you first. I'm a low priority."

"You should be hearing from him soon."

"I'm sure I will. You take care of yourself. Bye."

Jason hung up the phone, leaned back in his office chair, and rubbed his chin with his hand. "They're covering their tracks, dammit!" Jason said.

Jason picked up his phone and dialed Paulina.

"This is Paulina."

"'P,' it's Jason. Listen, I just wanted you to know that someone at Global is onto me. Be careful."

"Yes," Paulina said in a way that indicated she could not speak freely. "I can have that for you soon."

"Okay," Jason responded, understanding the situation. "Call me when you can talk."

"That would be fine," Paulina said. "Thank you for calling."

Jason became more determined than ever to get to the bottom of the Global conspiracy. Peter Walker, about to go to the authorities and divulge the information he had collected on the oilrig explosion, had been stopped before he could, by someone directly connected with Global. Someone had Peter Walker eliminated. According to his computer notes, he sent Zubin Ratko a memo with his suspicions. Ratko knew everything and likely the one responsible for Walker's disappearance. Jason felt a tingling sensation down his spine, the feeling that signaled he's on the right track, and this story, once uncovered, would be huge. Getting closer by the minute, and on the scent like a bloodhound, Jason covered the office walls with the evidence he collected. Photos were on every wall and strings tying one piece of evidence to another like a jigsaw puzzle half solved. The pieces were right in front of him, but he just hadn't quite put everything in its place, or could there still that one elusive piece missing? Jason racked his brain, as he assembled the pieces the best he could when his office phone rang.

"Jason Brent."

"Mr. Brent, its Mary Jo Sommerson. I wanted to know if you were free for lunch tomorrow."

When Jason walked by the hostess station at the trendy restaurant toward Erica's table, a broad smile washed across his face as they made eye contact. Her heart did several flips inside her chest, causing her to hesitate for a moment before she stood for fear that her knees would buckle and she'd make a complete fool of herself. Christ almighty! Calm down, will you? The voice inside Erica's head warned. You need to keep your wits about you before this all goes to hell.

"It's so nice to see you again, Mary," Jason said as he reached the table and extended his hand.

Erica rose from her chair and reached over the table to take Jason's hand. No knee buckle, no fainting spell—all going well, so far. Jason took Erica's hand in his and gently squeezed it for a moment—it sent a chill up Erica's arm, through her shoulders, down her back, past her hips, and stopping at her knees. Her left knee tingled for an instant.

"Nice to see you, too, Mr. Brent. Sit please," Erica said as they let go of each other's hand.

Sit please, before I fall over this table. Dammit. What is going on with me? that voice chastised again in her brain.

"Jason. Everybody calls me Jason," he said, still smiling. "Do your friends call you Mary, or Mary Jo?"

"Mary's fine," Erica replied, conscious of her accent as she situated herself in her seat. "I want to thank you for being so kind regarding our little accident."

"Not at all. Nothing... really. A little rubbing compound, and it took the scratch right out. I could rub yours too." Jason felt a flush of heat in his cheeks. Rub yours? She's going to call the cops any second now, Jason thought to himself.

"My?" Erica asked, puzzled.

"Bumper. Rub the scratch out of your bumper."

"Oh! No. That's not necessary. The car is fine." Erica smiled. Bumpers . . . We're talking about bumpers. Come on, Erica. Get your head in the game, Erica thought as the waiter approached the table.

The two ordered cocktails and a lunch entre. Jason, for the first time in his life, found himself at a loss for words. He just didn't feel like himself with this woman and couldn't get into a conversational flow. His typical 'impress them topics' had deserted him.

As he fumbled to form a coherent sentence, Erica saw her opportunity to take the lead. "Your card tells me you're a journalist. Are you with one of the local papers?" Erica asked, nearly choking on a forkful of salad when she noticed again how Jason's eyes smiled just a half second before his mouth registered the emotion.

"No. I work for the wire services," Jason said.

For an instant, Erica felt as though she sat across from Ford, at one of those many meals they shared when they were courting. Like Ford, Jason Brent had a quiet, almost shy confidence about him.

She surmised, Jason the kind of person who stayed in the background, not wanting to be the center of attention, taking compliments with a large dose of humility. This totally contradicted the information she had received from her employers who wanted him dead.

Erica already knew this man, knew how to handle him, how to make him feel comfortable with her. All Erica would need to do was project Ford Reagan onto Jason Brent, and her task would be easy, as easy as falling . . . falling in love.

"After college I got an opportunity to get on with UPI as a runner. I learned a lot. What kind of work are you in?" Erica heard Jason say as she brought herself back into the present moment.

"I work in the nonprofit sector," Erica said, focusing her eyes directly at Jason, looking for any kind of reaction from him. "I help write grants, get the organizations to file the proper paperwork, that kind of thing. Primarily, I help in the funding of orphaned children foundations."

"Sounds like fascinating work."

"It's very rewarding. I was orphaned myself, and I know how it feels to be on your own without parents at a young age."

"I know what you're talking about. I lost my parents when in high school, but I was lucky. My aunt and uncle took me in," Jason said, his mind raced back to that day he despondently went to live with his godparents. "You didn't have any family to take you in?"

"No. I was placed in the system, that didn't work very well; bounced around from foster home to foster home. Some of the foster parents I lived with were just taking on kids for the money. A horrible situation, but eventually I got old enough to be out on my own."

"You are doing a great service for the children and the community. You should be proud."

Erica gave Jason an embarrassed smile and looked down at her plate of food. The embarrassment indeed genuine, for the entire story a total lie, as Erica never spent a day in foster care. She never wrote a government grant. Everything that came out of her mouth a lie and by the look on Jason's face, she knew he bought it, and it made her feel guilty.

As the meal progressed, Erica learned more about Jason and his past, and the reason for his desire to become an investigative reporter—his focus on environmental issues. In Jason's his second year of high school, he discovered that both his parents were suffering from cancer caused by the toxins they were exposed to by their employer. Taggert Chemicals operated the plant where they worked with no regard for the safety of the employees.

The equipment they worked with old and worn, could not operate safely. Dangerous toxins were released into the air, and anyone working with this worn-out equipment became exposed to lethal doses of chemical toxins. Once the company made tests and discovered the problem, there were layoffs of most workers directly connected with the faulty equipment. When these workers later contracted serious diseases, the company claimed no responsibility.

Lawsuits followed, but none of the sick ever received a penny of compensation. Jason vowed after the last lawsuit had been dismissed that his purpose in life would be to expose any company's unsafe working conditions and shut them down so others would not suffer the same fate as his parents. Jason's work naturally progressed to company's whose business operations also threatened the environment.

"You're doing good work, Jason." Holy shit! I've been hired to kill Albert Schweitzer, Erica thought, trying to hide her emotional response.

"In a small way, I guess. I'm not helping people directly like you do, though."

"What you do is very noble," Erica said as she hoped Jason would take the initiative and make the next move.

Jason wanted to ask this beautiful woman if she would have dinner with him some night soon, but sitting across the table from her, he felt a bit inferior, a bit unworthy of someone so in touch with the plight of the defenseless.

Jason had been more interested in the advancement of his career these days, winning a Pulitzer, fame, and fortune. He had lost his way, and telling his story over lunch, it had all returned to him. His quest for truth eventually replaced with a desire for glory. This woman made him feel ashamed—ashamed at how he used people to get information, ashamed that he had no compunction and could take Paulina to bed just to get information from her. Jason felt he had lost his scruples. In the end, the story became about him, about how he exposing the truth, and not for truth's sake, but for the adulation with which he would be showered.

The luncheon ended, and both parties seemed awkward in their attempts to close this chapter in their lives. Erica wondered just what troubled Jason and why he could not bring himself to suggest they see each other again. This would be a difficult play, not wanting to appear too aggressive and activate Jason's antenna. If he smelled a rat, she would be on the defensive from here on out. "I'll take that," Erica said to the waiter when he delivered the bill.

"I'm only letting you pay because of the car issue. I'm kind of old fashion. I think the man should pay." Jason cringed as he heard the words exit his mouth. Now she'll think I'm a chauvinist, he thought.

"I guess I'm old fashioned too. I kind of like it when a man takes the initiative. But I must say, I don't like when they think they're always right," Erica said, smiling. Did I go too far on that one? Erica thought.

The waiter, a chrome coffee pot in hand, returned to the table and poured coffee in both of his guests' cups, then picked up the bill, turned' and briskly walked away from the table.

"I would really like to do this again, if you're open to it," Jason said as he stirred his coffee.

"That sounds nice. I'd like that," Erica said, looking over the rim of her cup as she sipped.

"Good. I was a little worried that you might have been put off by my rambling."

"Actually, I've really enjoyed talking with you. For some reason—"

"You're comfortable talking to me," Jason interrupted.

"Yes," Erica replied, surprised. "That's just what I was going to say. Are you psychic?"

"No, not at all. I just feel the same way."

The waiter returned to the table with Erica's credit receipt and placed it on the table. Erica wrote in the tip and signed the copy.

"Would you like a liqueur?" Jason asked.

"Sure. Why not?"

"Two sherries," Jason said to the waiter.

The waiter returned with the sherries after a few moments, and the two continued to converse for the next forty-five minutes. Another round of drinks ordered, and the two talked and laughed at each other's stories. When Erica told Jason that she felt comfortable around him, she wasn't lying. Several times during the post-lunch conversation, Erica nearly gave herself away and told too much of the truth about her past. Erica had to keep on her toes. She had trouble trying to keep up. She had run out of cover story and had to improvise on the fly, always a dangerous proposition. Another cup of coffee, and the confab continued, both oblivious to the passage of time. Jason at one point took a quick look at his watch. Five forty-five, and the dinner crowd had just started to fill the restaurant.

"I was just wondering. Would you like to have dinner some evening?" Jason said clumsily.

"I would like that very much," Erica replied, smiling.

"How about tonight?" Jason asked with a smile. "Waiter," could we have menus please?"

The waiter nodded. For the next two hours, Erica let Jason do most of the talking—getting a real feel for this man, her target. The more he talked, the more she liked him, and the more apprehension crept into her psyche. The man across the table from her, not at all like the profile she had been given. Should she be concerned? Erica pondered as she laughed at Jason's stories. Should analyzing her target be part of the job? It wasn't. Her job, simply kill him.

Get Jason Brent to trust her enough that she could get close like she'd done dozens of times before—close enough to complete her task, collect her money, and move on to the next assignment.

The two rose from the table, and Erica led the way out of the restaurant. They stood side by side as the valet took Erica's ticket from her and ran off to retrieve her car.

Erica fiddled in her purse, looking for a few dollars of cash. Jason caught the movement of a vehicle as it approached the valet stand. The car stopped in front of them, and the valet jumped out of the car, held the door open for Erica. She stepped around the back of the vehicle with Jason right behind, placed several bills into the valet's palm as Jason stood by the car door. Erica slid into the driver seat and buckled her seat belt as Jason gently shut the door. He bent down his face even with the open car door window.

Jason cleared his throat. "Would you like to go out Saturday night?"

"I would like that very much. You still have my number when I called yesterday?" She nodded to Jason's phone in his pocket.

"Yes, I do. I know a great place with good food and live music," Jason responded, flushed with excitement.

"Sound's wonderful. I'll look forward to that," Erica said as she gave Jason a little wave and drove out of the parking lot.

"Very pretty lady,' commented the valet.

"You got that right," Jason proclaimed as he handed the valet his ticket.

Over the next several days, Jason tirelessly plugged along, putting in long hours following up every lead and going back over the old ones just to make sure he hadn't missed anything. Jason lived in his office, eating, sleeping, consumed by his obsession to find the person or persons behind the Global cover-up, but on Saturday night he shut it all down to spend the evening with Mary Jo.

Jason arrived at Mary Jo's Santa Monica apartment door at exactly six thirty in the evening. When she answered the door, Jason produced a single yellow rose from behind his back.

"It's customary in my family to bring flowers to a date," Jason said as she stared at the rose. "Well, flower anyway. I didn't want you to feel overwhelmed."

"It's very sweet of you, actually," Erica acknowledged as she opened the door wide and waved in Jason. Dressed in black, snug-fitted jeans and an un-tucked, light blue, shirt, Erica looked fetching. Anticipating his movements, Erica had left a few of her evenings makeup preparations to complete after Jason had arrived, giving him an opportunity to check out the apartment and make the rouse complete.

"I'll just need a couple of minutes to slip on my dress and finish putting my face on."

"It looks perfect just the way it is," Jason asserted as he stepped into the apartment.

"You're sweet. I'll be right back. Make yourself at home," Erica said as she turned and dashed into the bedroom.

Jason took a quick survey of the apartment. Neat and with a distinct woman's touch fresh flowers in a crystal vase accented the dining-room table.

The apartment had a vaulted, beamed ceiling that gave the illusion of a wide-open living space, with an area big enough to have a formal dining area and a compact but comfortable kitchen nook. Jason took several steps toward the overstuffed fabric couch and sat down on the comfortable cushions.

"You want a drink or something?" Erica yelled from the bedroom.

"No thanks. I'm fine, really," Jason yelled back. "I like your place. It has a nice feel to it."

"Thanks. I like it here," Erica said as she emerged from the bedroom.

Jason rose from the couch and watched, as the woman he knew as Mary walked into the living room. Jason stood for a moment, his mouth slightly open as she came to a stop just a few feet away from him, not saying a word.

"Is something wrong?" she asked as she quickly checked herself.

Undeniably a vision to behold, standing there before him. Jason had trouble finding words, mesmerized by the sheer beauty of this woman.

Her eyes were lined with dark liner that made them pop—drawing your attention to them in such a manner that the hairs on the back of Jason's neck bristled.

Ruby red lips and her dark hair that framed her face were almost too much for Jason to handle in one dose. An aqua blue, low-cut dress, hung magnificently on her body, showed just enough cleavage to give a hint of what beauty lay underneath the delicate fabric. The straps that rose up from her chest looped around her neck, exposing the heart-shaped birthmark, her back naked from shoulders to waist. The dress tight from just below the ribcage to her shapely hips, then flared out again as it formed a pleated skirt that hung just an inch above her knees. A simple silver, heart-shaped necklace, on a silver chain, hung just above her breastbone.

"No! No. Nothing's wrong," Jason assured, finally able to get his voice back. "You just look, amazing."

"It is a beautiful dress, isn't it?"

"It's 90 percent you, believe me. I wish I could paint, because I'd love to capture this on canvas."

Erica balked, taken aback by Jason's compliment.

"That's the nicest thing anyone has ever said to me in my entire life," Erica remarked flustered, forgetting again her agenda.

"Shall we go?" she said, trying to defuse the moment.

They dined, danced, and listened to good music for hours. Jason had finally relaxed and on his game, charming, jovial. Erica laughed as she had never laughed since her time with Ford. It felt good, and she felt truly sorry that the evening had to end.

Jason walked Erica to her apartment door, not leaving her at the building entrance, as he would have other women he had taken out for an evening on the town. The two stood at the door, Erica with her apartment keys in her hand.

"Thank you for a great time, Jason."

"I should be thanking you. I hope we can do this again, soon," Jason said coyly.

"I certainly hope so."

Jason placed his hands on her shoulders and gave her a kiss on the cheek. "Thanks again for letting me share this evening with you."

Jason took the keys from her hand, slipped the key into the lock, and opened the apartment door. He pushed it open and let Erica enter.

"I'll call you," he said as he watched Erica close the door.

Jason paused for a moment, then turned and walked jauntily down the hallway.

Once inside, Erica leaned her back against the door and took a deep breath.

"What am I doing? I'm letting this guy get to me. I wanted him to kiss me," Erica said to herself as she slid down the door to the floor. "You've got to get control of yourself."

Flushed with excitement, Jason went to his Santa Monica office after he left Mary Jo's apartment and worked into the wee hours of the morning. His cellphone announced an incoming call and awoke him from a deep sleep on the couch. It took a moment for Jason to get his bearings and track down his phone that he left somewhere buried under mounds of paperwork. Jason fumbled for the phone, scarcely able to depress the answer button before the call disconnected, and went to voice mail.

"Hello," a groggy Jason answered.

"You okay?" the female voice on the other end of the line said.

"Paulina! Yes, I'm fine. I just woke up."

"I got in early this morning so I could get a look at the vehicle log before anyone else came in," Paulina said anxiously.

"Good. Did you find anything?"

"Not really. Neither car signed out on the fifteenth, but there was something funny."

271 | Donna Tellum

"What's that?" Jason asked more awake now.

"The Lincoln had been logged out on the fourteenth and then again on the sixteenth. The problem is that the mileage in and out doesn't match. Sometime between the fourteenth and the sixteenth, the car logged nearly eighty unaccounted-for miles."

"Interesting. Who could have taken the car?"

"I can't be certain, but the only people who could just go to the garage and take those cars without permission are Zubin and David Edison."

"Good work 'P.' There's also something I wanted to tell you about when I see you."

"Sure, no worries. I'll check the security camera tapes for the fifteenth and see who drove the car out of the garage. It will take some doing, but I'll make it happen."

"Let me know as soon as you get an I.D. Then we can meet up, but be careful," Jason implored.

"I will. I'll call you tomorrow. I gotta go. Bye."

Jason hung up the phone then quickly dialed Mary Jo's number. His heart shuddered in his chest when he heard her sweet voice in his ear.

Free for dinner the subsequent evening, they set a date for seven o'clock. Jason had something pleasurable to look forward to as he went about his busy day.

The ensuing day dragged as Jason met with Jennifer, updating her on the progress of the Global story. He continued to follow up leads throughout the day, but each hour that passed, Jason grew more anxious as he waited for Paulina's call. By the end of the workday, the call never came. Jason forced himself not to call her, not wanting to expose Paulina to his nervousness.

He needed to let Paulina do what she needed to do by herself, and his constant phone calls weren't about to make it happen any faster; so many things could have held up her investigation into the security camera video. Jason looked at his watch, nearly seven o'clock. If he hurried, he could still be at Mary Jo's by seven for their dinner date.

Jason freshened up in his office bathroom, which become more frequent occurrence these days, then drove the few minutes to Mary Jo's. At five-minutes past seven he pressed the buzzer to the apartment.

20

SETTING THE TRAP

ERICA WAS READY for Jason's arrival when she heard the buzzer sound. Things were progressing nicely. Tonight she would attempt to advance their relationship to the next level, broach the intimacy subject, and see how Jason reacts.

Erica bounced to the door enthusiastically with a big smile on her face, opened the door, and swung it wide.

"Perfect timing. I'm ready to go."

"Good," Jason said flatly, as he entered the apartment. "You look great."

No mistaking Jason's mood; something bothered him, and it showed.

"You okay?" Erica questioned sympathetically. "You look troubled."

"It has to do with work."

"Anything I can help with."

"No, not really. What say we go for some sushi tonight?" Jason said with a slight smile, taking in her tight-fitting jeans and blue and white striped, hooded top.

"That's raw fish, isn't it?" Erica asked, furrowing her brow.

"You've never had sushi?"

"I've never had an appetite for bait."

"Oh, honey. You've been missing out. You have to try it. I know a place where the sushi melts in your mouth."

Erica frowned, gave her head a slight shake.

"Just try one. Trust me, you'll love it."

"And if I don't?"

"We go someplace else," Jason said smiling. "What do you say?"

"I guess."

Jason took Erica by the arm and led her out of the apartment.

Erica wearily stared at the raw fish that sat in front of her on her plate.

"So. What are you going to do? Look at it all night?" Jason asked as he shoved a piece of sushi in his mouth with chopsticks.

"I was all ready to eat it until it appeared in front of me."

"Close your eyes," Jason said as Erica looked back at him assiduously. "Go ahead, close them."

Erica closed her eyes.

"Now open your mouth."

Erica squeezed her eyes tightly shut as she slowly opened her mouth. Jason retrieved Erica's chopsticks off her plate and deftly picked up the piece of sushi, dipped it into a tiny saucer that contained a mixture of soy sauce and wasabi, and slipped it into her mouth. Erica bit down on the food and chewed several times before swallowing. Her face showed a sign of pleasure as she opened her eyes.

"Well?" Jason asked.

Erica didn't say a word. She just eyed the large plate in the middle of the table.

"Well, I'll get the check, and we'll go get a pizza."

"That won't be necessary. This actually tastes good."

"See, I told you," Jason said.

Erica plucked another piece of sushi with her fingers and downed it like a professional.

"I think I just created a monster," Jason quipped, causing Erica to let out a laugh.

The two ate sushi and laughed as the next hour and a half passed.

"You still seem a bit distant tonight," Erica said casually. "Is it that work thing?"

"I'm afraid so. I've been working on this story for months now, and things are not going well."

"Writer's block?"

"No, it's not that. I'm investigating this company."

"You're talking Global Energies?"

"Right."

"I've read several of your articles," said Erica.

"Then you know they've been involved in some serious matters. One of the people who had been talking to us has disappeared."

"Vanished?" Erica responded, startled.

"That's just it. People at the company tell me he had been terminated or took another job at another company." Jason paused, as he shook his head. "His wife tells me that Global sent him to work on a project out of the country, but she hasn't heard a word from him since he left. I made an inquiry, and she got an e-mail out of the blue from her husband. I don't know which is true."

"So your information source has dried up."

"I made contact with another employee, who tried to find out just what happened to our contact, and now she won't return my calls. It worries me. What I've been writing about has obviously hit a cord because they seem to want to get rid of anyone I talk to. I just hope that she wasn't hurt."

"They wouldn't hurt anyone, would they?" exclaimed Erica.

"My gut tells me that Mr. Walker, our first contact, was dealt with harshly."

"Aren't you afraid they might do something to you?"

"No, not really. The worst thing that could happen is that they may try to discredit me. If you murder a journalist, every reporter in the world is in your face, wanting answers. The code of the Fourth Estate. It would be a stupid move on their part."

Erica nodded her understanding as thoughts fired through her brain, the puzzle now became clear.

They finished their meal and left the restaurant. Jason took Erica to the Santa Monica Pier that was lit up like a Christmas tree and bustled with pedestrian traffic. Erica let her guard down, much to her dismay, unable to focus on the task at hand.

She felt a rush of pent-up emotions wash over her body as she let herself unwind for the first time in a long time. Jason seemed to have that effect on her. She once again felt comfortable and relaxed, and she wanted to enjoy it.

Erica found herself staring at Jason for long periods, wondering why the information she had been given didn't ringing true. Her intuition told a different story, and Erica had to put those thoughts out of her mind; thoughts that could cause a person in her profession to lose touch with reality. She could suddenly feel that she could be capable of loving again. Quickly, Erica pushed those thoughts out of her brain and waited for the right opportunity to spring the trap and snare her prey.

Jason bought tickets for the carousel and even convinced a reluctant Erica to ride the Ferris wheel. They ate cotton candy and played the carnival games along the pier. Jason shot basketball hoops and won her a very large stuffed tiger. They stopped at the end of the pier and watched the reflection of the bright moon bounce off the waves of the ocean. A cool, clear night, and Erica nestled herself under Jason's strong arm for warmth.

The night was indeed beautiful, and when Erica turned her head up towards Jason, he kissed her gently on the lips. The warmth of his lips on hers excited her. She couldn't help herself; she had to kiss him back. She turned to him, and they wrapped their arms around each other and kissed again.

Erica felt the strength in Jason's body as they embraced; the only sound the waves crashing against the pier. As she breathed in the scent of Jason's warm body, Erica's brain told her to spring the trap. The prey vulnerable and the time to take action was now. As if the voice emanated from somewhere out over the water, Erica heard herself say, "Take me home, Jason."

They rode in silence; Erica held Jason's hand as he guided his car through the dark streets for the next several minutes until they found themselves stopped in front of Erica's Santa Monica apartment.

Still holding hands, the two walked to Erica's apartment door. She slid the key into the lock, and the two entered the dimly lit apartment. As the door closed behind them, Erica folded into Jason's embrace, her lips pressed hard against Jason's, his arms tightly around her. When their lips separated, Jason smoothly swept Erica up into his arms and carried her to the bedroom. Jason stepped into the bedroom and kicked the door closed with his heel.

Only one small lamp on the rosewood dresser illuminated the room, it gave it a warm, golden glow. The bedroom simply decorated; a seven-foot, rosewood armoire dominated the room. No desk or any furniture indicated work took place in this room. A calming oil painting of the ocean hung on the wall at the head of the bed with nightstands on either side.

Jason gently set Erica onto the bed, kissed her as he grasped her arms, and slipped them from around his neck. Watching, almost trancelike, Erica lay on the bed as Jason took a step back, his eyes on her the entire time.

With his left foot, Jason pried off his right shoe and then did the same with his left. Then he slid onto the bed next to Erica, slipped his arm under her neck, and gathered her close to him, kissing her for what seemed an eternity.

The sound of kissing and moaning filled the room as the two groped and caressed each other for more than thirty minutes. Jason kissed her neck, lips, cheeks, eyes, and hair, gently touching her face, running his finger down her nose, outlining her lips. Feeling her breasts against his chest fully aroused him, and Jason could only imagine how incredible her naked body would feel pressed against his.

Erica clutched at Jason's body and pulled him as close as she could. Feeling his aroused body against hers, she wanted more, and the thoughts of what she hired on to do never had the chance of establishing a foothold in her consciousness. This man, this Jason Brent, awakened emotions that were buried for years, and once awakened these emotions could not be denied. Erica wanted Jason to make love to her. She wanted to be able to love someone again, but this someone was the someone, she had contracted to kill. Not a word spoken between them as Jason situated his body down towards the foot of the bed. He slid his hands down her shapely legs and, in one smooth motion, removed Erica's left shoe. Reaching over to her right, he slipped her right shoe off her foot. Her naked foot in his hand, Jason softly caressed her instep, sending a thrilling shiver up her leg.

Jason slowly slid his strong hands up her trembling legs. Erica reached down and began to unfasten her belt when Jason's hands took hold of hers and moved them to either side of her body. He then slipped the end of the leather belt out of the buckle and undid the button at the top of her jeans, then slowly pulled the zipper down. Erica raised her hips as Jason tightly grasped the lower legs of her pants and pulled them down until they were completely off; let them fall to the floor at the foot of the bed.

Jason took a long moment, taking time to appreciate how beautiful she looked in the soft, golden light. Erica watched with anticipation as Jason began to inch her knit-top up and over her head, and in a flash she lay on the bed in just her bra and silk panties. Jason's eyes drank in this vision of loveliness, committed it to memory, a memory he could count on to bring a smile to his face for years to come.

Jason reached out to her, and Erica took his hand and placed it on her toned abdomen. Jason delicately stroked her belly with his hand. Erica shut her eyes and let out a low, soft moan as Jason bent down and kissed her just below her navel. Blood rushed to her pelvic region, causing a sudden and intense throb. Opening her eyes, Erica saw Jason unbutton the top button of his shirt. She raised herself up, took his hands away, and unbuttoned his shirt. Her hands pressed against his hot flesh, crept up past his stomach, and lingered at his chest. Her fingers entwined in his chest hair then moved again upward until she wrapped her arms around his neck and pulled herself up close to his face. Her lips parted as Jason wrapped his arms around her and they kissed, tongues probed and tasted. Once their lips separated, Erica kissed his neck down to the space just below his sternum, tasting his salty sweat.

Erica pulled Jason's shirt off his shoulders and down his arms. Jason released her from his embrace, allowed Erica to slip the shirt off his arms, letting the garment drop to the floor.

Jason rolled off the bed and stood at its side, let his pants drop, stepped out of them, then bent over and pulled off his socks. He stood before her in just his underwear, giving Erica a glimpse of what she had felt pressed against her as she lay in bed. Jason's underwear showed an enormous bulge. Erica could not help herself; she reached out and rested her hand on his manhood then looked up at Jason, who had tilted his head back, his eyes closed, his legs shaking.

Erica reached around behind her and unclasped her bra then took Jason's hand in hers and gently pulled him back onto the bed.

Lying side by side, Jason ran his hand through Erica's hair, kissing her forehead, her lips, down her neck, until he stopped just below her throat. Jason slipped her bra straps down off her shoulders and slid them down her arms and off her body. As much as he could create the magnificence of her breast in his imagination, Jason discovered that his imagination hadn't gone nearly far enough in doing them justice. They were spectacular and all Jason could only stare do for the longest time. This must be the most beautiful woman he had ever seen. Jason watched as his hands moved up her body as if they had a mind of their own as they caressed her breasts.

Erica covered his hands with hers and directed his touch, Her temperature rising, she arched her back in reaction to that beautiful ache. That blazing desire she felt deep in her bones, torrid, white-hot passion, consumed her by the second.

Jason kissed her sweet flesh as he continued up her body, caressed her breasts with his lips, teased her nipples with his tongue, sucking, kissing, nuzzling. Erica drifted deeper into the ecstasy abyss. One by one, this man opened each of the locked emotions she had stored in safe places years ago, and those pent-up emotions gushed out in a torrent of swelling desire.

Erica felt Jason's hands slide down to her waist as she lifted her hips. He removed her silk panties in one smooth sensual swoop. Her entire body shivered with a deep yearning as she felt his warm breath taunting her love triangle. She arched her hips up and shuddered when she felt his tongue explore her moist labia. Erica's heart clenched. Her breath halted as the first orgasmic release washed over her body. Jason positioned himself directly over her as her pleasure spasms waned.

Erica's eyes opened and saw Jason's face hovering over her with a slight smile that creased the corner of his mouth, love deep in his eyes. Erica grasped Jason's hips with both hands and pulled him deep inside her. She wanted to surround him, engulf him; she wanted him to disappear inside her as she raised her legs and tightly circled them around his waist, causing her to experience another wave of pleasure.

Erica awoke early the next morning. She could feel Jason beside her, comfortably asleep. She raised herself up from the bed and looked down at him. It would be so easy to end this now, but their conversation the previous evening made perfect sense. This had to look like an accident so as to not arouse the ire of the Fourth Estate. Once the press got their teeth into you, they never let go. The first step now completed. She had Jason in the palm of her hand. He trusted her. The time had come to put the next part of the plan in motion.

At the office Jason worked on his next Global article most of the day, taking time to chat with Mary Jo when he could. He was smitten, and he knew it. He just had to keep himself from moving too fast and scaring this woman away.

Jason hadn't heard from Paulina all day so by ten o'clock that evening, he couldn't contain himself any longer. He called her cellphone.

"You've reached Paulina Gregory. I can't take your call at the moment, but leave me a message and I'll get back to you. Have a great day."

"'P,' call me back when you get this. I don't care what time it is; I need to talk to you," an anxious Jason said.

Jason disconnected the call and sat at his desk for a long time. Worry started to creep into his brain, and Jason tried to push those worries out of his thoughts, but the sinking feeling in his gut wouldn't go away. Jason closed up his office and went home for the evening.

Jason entered his dark house around ten thirty with a small, brown sandwich bag in his hand. He stepped into the narrow kitchen and selected one of the bottles of beer that were stored in the refrigerator, opened it, and tossed the cap on the cluttered counter.

Slogging to the comfortable couch in the living room, he dropped onto the soft cushions with a heavy sigh. Jason reached his hand into the bag, and when he brought it out, wrapped in white paper, a thick smoked turkey breast sandwich. Jason bit into it as though he hadn't eaten in days and washed it down with the cold brew. He looked at his watch, ten forty-five. Jason slipped his cellphone out of his pocket and saw that he had no word from Paulina. He dialed her number again.

"You've reached Paulina Gregory. I can't take your call at the moment, but leave me a message and I'll get back to you. Have a great day."

"Paulina, call me," Jason said and disconnected the call.

Jason awoke the following morning and found himself still on his couch, remnants of the turkey sandwich on the coffee table accompanied by three empty bottles of beer. Jason reached for his phone and checked for a call or a message he may have missed during the night and found nothing. At eight o'clock Jason dialed Paulina's number to no avail—just the same message he received the last time he called.

Something must be wrong. A foreboding feeling covered Jason like a blanket. He needed to get answers, and he needed those answers immediately.

Dialing his phone again, he called her office, hoping beyond hope that Paulina's lack of response could have been just an oversight and he had worked himself into a frenzy for nothing.

"Global Energies, how can I direct your call?" the friendly receptionist's voice purred into Jason's ear.

"Paulina Gregory, please," Jason said calmly.

"Who shall I say is calling?"

Jason thought for a moment, not wanting to give his real name, he had no idea who else knew about his investigations into Global's business practices.

"Pardon me?" Jason replied.

'Who's calling please?"

"Brent—Brent James."

"Hold please."

Jason listened to hold music for thirty seconds before another voice came on the line.

"Paulina Gregory's office. Can I help you?"

"Paulina?"

"No, this is Veronica, her assistant."

"I'd like to speak to Paulina. This is Brent. She knows me."

Veronica said, "I'm sorry, but Ms. Gregory is not in."

"When do you expect her?"

"Ms. Gregory has been called away on a family emergency, and I have no idea when she will return. I can take a message."

"No thanks," Jason said flatly and disconnected the call.

Jason bolted up from the couch and made a beeline for the bathroom. He showered and dressed as fast as humanly possible and jumped into his car and fought the morning rush of traffic toward Pasadena. His stomach twisted in a tight knot the whole way. Jason pulled onto Paulina's street and parked a blocked down from her building. He sat for several moments before getting out of his car. Parked a half a block from him sat the rented Prius with Erica taking photos.

The neighborhood was relatively quiet at this hour with only an occasional vehicle appearing on the street. Jason walked casually toward Paulina's building. Not a soul to be seen when he turned down the walkway to the foyer. Jason entered the building. Still with no one around, he took the elevator up to the fifth floor. The doors opened, and he found himself in front of Paulina's door. For reasons he could not understand, he pushed the buzzer for a long three seconds then waited. No sound came from behind the door. Jason reached down, grasped the doorknob, and gave it a twist. It didn't move; the door securely locked. Jason bent close to the door and peered at the deadbolt.

He pulled his wallet from his pants' pocket and slid out one of his credit cards. He jammed the card between the door and the doorjamb weather stripping, and saw that the bolt had not been set in the full locked position. Jason repositioned the card next to the doorknob and pushed. The card slid around the edge of the door, and with a couple of jiggles, the door swung open. He stepped in and quickly and silently closed the door behind him.

When Jason turned to the interior of the living space, he nearly dropped to the floor from the shock of what he saw.

21

'P'

JASON'S HEART SANK as his eyes surveyed the empty apartment. Not a chair, lamp, or pictures were to be found. The place had been stripped clean. Jason searched each room, each cupboard, each closet, and found nothing. It looked as though Paulina had never lived there. Jason made his way back to the apartment door and slowly opened it wide enough that he could get a view of the hallway.

Jason quietly slipped out into the vacant hall and closed the door behind him. Moments later, he was in his vehicle and driving back to his office.

* * * * *

Jason arrived at his office and immediately began researching county clerk real-estate files. He made phone calls to anyone he thought could help with his search. Jason needed to know who owned the building where Paulina had lived. By lunch, Jason had his answer. One of Global's holding companies owned the property.

No matter which way Jason turned, he faced Global at every corner. An extremely upset Jason placed a phone call to Jennifer, who had traveled to Chicago the previous evening.

"Jesus, Jason. Are you sure?" Jennifer questioned.

"As sure as I can be without any evidence. Two people have disappeared since I've been on this story," Jason said. "I'm responsible for two deaths. I don't think I can do this anymore."

"Calm down, Jason. We don't know anything of the kind yet. Paulina could've had an emergency."

"They cleaned out her apartment, Jen."

"Yes I agree, it's disturbing, but if you don't have any evidence . . ."

"What am I going to do? If I go to the authorities, that will just make whoever is behind this go deeper into hiding. It was never supposed to be like this."

"Jason, if you're right, they'll come after you next. There's no telling what they will do. You need to be careful," Jennifer pleaded.

"I've got to find out who took that limo out the night Walker disappeared. I just don't know how I'm going to get in there and check the tapes. I can't ask anyone else in the company to help me," a frustrated Jason insisted.

"You'll come up with something. I know it."

Just a few doors down from Jason's office, Erica sat in her vehicle, as she watched him pull out of the parking lot. Once Jason traveled a safe distance from her, Erica started her car and followed Jason along the surface streets until

291 I D o n n a   T e l l u m

he reached the on-ramp to U.S. 101. Jason entered the freeway and headed north.

"Just where are you taking us, Jason?" Erica said to herself. "What are you after today?"

Keeping Jason's car in view, Erica followed as the two cars sped north and continued in that direction for the next few minutes until he exited the freeway in the North Hollywood area. Jason finally stopped in front of an apartment building on Magnolia Avenue, exited his vehicle and walked up the walkway. Erica pulled up to the curb half a block away from Jason's vehicle and watched Jason disappear into the building.

Jason walked up three floors and meandered down the hall until he came to an apartment door with tarnished brass numbers nailed to it. At apartment 312, the number two cocked at a 45-degree angle. Jason pressed the buzzer mounted on the wall to the right of the door. After a moment, the door opened just a crack, and a pair of eyes behind corrective lenses peered around the door.

"Oh! Jason, it's you."

The door swung open, and Jason stepped into Franklin Eide's apartment. Franklin stood five foot nine with long, brown, matted-down hair. His eyes looked larger than normal, as his eyeglass lenses were as thick as the bottom of a popular soft drink bottle. Franklin a thin, frail-looking young man in his late twenties.

He wore a faded, yellow, button-down, short-sleeved shirt with vertical stripes—only one collar button fastened. His pants were faded, brown corduroy.

"Something wrong with the file I sent you?" Franklin asked as he took several steps across the living room and plopped down in the chair in front of his computer station.

Franklin's apartment displayed years of clutter with stacks and stacks of computer manuals and software boxes. Several flat screen computer monitors were against the wall to the right of the computer desk.

The tan couch also covered with computer magazines as well as the coffee table in front of it. A small counter separated the living room from the small kitchen. Dirty dinner plates rested on top of the counter, and the kitchen sink housed more dirty dishes and eating utensils. Jason collected several magazines from the couch to clear a space for him to take a seat, and dumped them on the cluttered table.

"You want a cup of coffee or something?" Franklin asked as he typed rapidly on the computer keyboard.

Jason took note of the soiled dinner plates. "No thanks, I'm good."

Franklin banged on the keyboard for another few seconds then spun around in his chair, facing Jason. "What can I do for you, Jason?"

"I need to get some information that is stored on a DVR device."

"That's pretty simple; you just need to get a—"

"It's not my DVR," Jason interrupted Franklin. "The DVR is connected to a video security system at a building downtown."

Franklin's eye opened wide.

"You mean a hard drive. Are you saying what I think you're saying?"

"I guess I am. I want to download what the system recorded on a certain day without anyone knowing that I did it."

"Cool!" Franklin exclaimed. "All I'll need to do is hack into the main frame, find the server that handles the security storage system, and download the data onto a remote device".

"So it can be done?" Jason asked.

"Sure. Piece-of-cake. Who are we hacking?"

Jason spent the next day in his office and tried to keep his thoughts on Global, but to no avail. Jason's thoughts kept drifting to Mary Jo. The touch of her hand, the sparkle in her eyes, the sound of her voice—Jason had trouble concentrating on his work for the first time in his life.

Sometime around noon, Jason picked up his phone and called Franklin to check on his progress.

"Hello," a weary voice said.

"It's Jason, Franklin. How's it coming?"

"Slow. I've been working on this most of the night, but these guys got some deep firewalls I have to get through. They know their stuff."

A worried Jason asked, "Can you get in?"

"I can get in. It's just going to take some time, but I'll get in."

"Okay. Get some rest, you need to keep alert."

"I know. As soon as I get something, I'll call."

"Sorry, man. I'm just a little impatient. Do what you need to do. I'll talk to you later," Jason said as he hung up his phone.

The day wore on as Jason worked on the Global story. He followed up on phone calls and answered e-mails. By the end of the day, hungry and wanting some company for dinner, Jason picked up his cellphone. Jennifer still in Chicago, Paulina still missing, and he couldn't inflict Mary Jo with his misery, so he decided picked up a sandwich on the way home and settled in for another lonely evening, like so many lonely evenings he had before, with only the sound of the television to keep him company. The life of a journalist was one of many weeks away from home chasing down a story. Most field reporters make it a point to settle in one place, developed a relationship with the community and hopefully find someone they can share their life with, once they get that desk job.

Jason, never one to sit still for very long, and the thought of a desk job just didn't interest him. The idea of finding that special someone who would be willing to put up with a man whose job made him travel the globe in search of the next big news story just wasn't in the cards.

Jason's past relationships all ended badly, usually with Jason ducking out of the way of some expensive knickknack thrown at him.

When Jason pushed the door open to his empty Hollywood Hills home, the thoughts of his past were rolling around in his mind. The house dark and deathly silent like a thousand times before—the only sound, the latch click, echoing in the foyer as the door closed.

The customary brown bag that housed the usual sandwich in his hand and his leather case slung over his shoulder, Jason noticed his footsteps echoing through the house as he walked across the hardwood floor into the living room.

He dropped the sandwich bag on the coffee table and his case on the couch before he shuffled into the kitchen to liberate a bottle of beer from the fridge.

As he traveled from the living room to the kitchen, the deep scar in the wall that separated the kitchen from the dining area caught his eye. A redhead he had seen over a year ago caused that damage. She had a pretty good arm, Jason remembered. A nice bottle of chardonnay went to waste. Couldn't make her understand that sometimes I had to entertain an attractive woman now and then to get the information I needed. Jason laughed.

"That lie was too ridiculous even for her to believe," Jason said to himself as he reached into the refrigerator and extracted his beverage.

Jason flopped onto the couch and took a long swallow of beer then set the bottle on the table and tore open the sandwich bag so that it lay flat on the coffee table, serving as a placemat.

Removing the sandwich from its wrapper, Jason brought the food up to his lips and took a generous bite. With his mouth full, he slumped into the couch, his back against the cushions. Maybe it's time that I look for that desk assignment, Jason thought to himself as he chewed. I could see myself now, settled in one place, coming home and finding someone waiting for me.

Erica, this woman that Jason knew only as Mary Jo, had struck a chord with him. He sailed in uncharted territory now. No one had ever made him think about his future before. Jason had only thought about the next assignment, the next big story, the next challenge. He had spent the last five years in Southern California, but that as much for convenience as for the aesthetics.

Jason could live just about anywhere. He had owned a home off the east coast, near Charlotte, North Carolina. He still had a small apartment he owned just outside of Paris. Jason would be open to anything but the person he would be sharing this with, the question he pondered now. This woman he just met . . . Could she be "the one?" Could something like meeting the right person you want to spend the rest of your life with happen this fast, this sudden?

Jason shook his head. All conjecture. The crazy thoughts Jason had were just that, crazy thoughts. It would be better off, for her anyway, if they never saw each other again. He still felt the guilt from Paulina's disappearance, which he had direct responsibility for, not to mention Walker's connection as well. He couldn't shake the idea that he was not worthy of someone like Mary Jo in his life after all he'd done.

By the time Jason finished his sandwich and beer dinner, he had come to the acceptance of the fact that he would never see this beautiful woman again. She would only be a memory of what might have been; just one of those chance meetings that you will remember on a quiet night many years from now. Jason put the thoughts of Mary Jo, what he would say to her the next time they met, out of his mind. Not one thought of her seeped into his consciousness after he had come to that conclusion, which made the shock all the more intense when his phone rang.

"Jason Brent."

"Jason, it's me, Mary Jo. Could you meet me for a drink?"

"Sure," he said, his heart nearly leapt out of his chest. "Where would you like to meet?"

"There's a little place on Wilshire—Max's Tavern."

"I know it. See you in twenty minutes."

Erica had seated herself at a corner booth to allow some quiet conversation. She had only been there a few minutes when Jason walked in and saw her. A big smile crossed his face as he walked towards her.

"I'm glad you called," Jason said as he slid into the booth and gave her a quick peck.

"I wanted to see you," Erica replied, showing no emotion.

"Is something wrong?" Jason asked. Thoughts of despair climbed back into his head.

"I thought we needed to talk . . . after the other night."

"That was an amazing night."

"I kind of need to know where we are going from here. I don't want to assume."

"I hoped we could take this to the next level, see where this could go. I think we might have something special," Jason's thoughts of despair vaporized instantly.

Erica gave Jason a smile, and he reached across the table and took her hand in his.

As the evening progressed, Erica paid critical attention to Jason's drinking habits and discovered that the myth that journalists were heavy drinkers was not a myth at all;

they did indeed drink. Her plan would be simple and deadly. Over a few glasses of wine, Erica would slip Jason a drug that would increase his blood alcohol to nearly toxic levels. A blow to the head and a push into the pool would be all it would take to complete her contract. She just needed Jason to take her to his home.

At the end of the evening, Jason walked Erica to her car, and they kissed. Jason wanted her in his life, and he wasn't about to let her get away from him.

"Why don't you come over to my house tomorrow night? I'll make you a dinner you'll never forget," a proud Jason said. "Bring your swimsuit; I got a pool.' His mind immediately composed a picture of her in a bikini.

"It's a date," Erica replied and then kissed him again, long and hard.

Jason returned to his home with thoughts of Mary Jo invading his mind. He had never felt like this before, and this feeling much more than just the physical attraction; it was something deeper.

This is my soul mate, Jason thought to himself as he flopped down on his couch.

He became aware that he smiled for no apparent reason except that he thought words that he had found humorous when spoken by other people he had known. Soul mate? Is that what this feels like? When you find that person that you dare think you want to spend the rest of your life with? Was this the feeling that his parents felt when they first met? His parents showed Jason a deep love between them, a devoted love.

Jason lost his mother shortly after his father had died, and it wasn't until now that it dawned on him. It wasn't the cancer that took her from this earth; half of her soul died when his father passed.

Jason's life had suddenly changed, and as far as he was concerned, it had changed for the better. Energized from the thought of sharing his life with this woman, Jason dove back into his work with a new exuberance. He had a future more than just his profession, more than just the next story. The next story—the next story, what happened to Paulina Gregory? Unable to quell his adrenalin rush, Jason sat down at the desk in his den and started writing his next article.

As soon as she entered her apartment, Erica immediately started to implement her plan. She retrieved a locked metal box from the closet in the bedroom. Opened it and removed two file folders. Each folder contained photographs.

One held the photos she had taken personally, and the other contained photos she copied from satellite images of the Hollywood Hills. She spread the photos that she took of Jason and the area around his office on the floor of the living room. Then, to the left of those photos, she spread out the satellite photos of Jason Brent's home.

Erica selected one photo from the Hollywood Hills group and set it aside. The photo showed an aerial view of Jason's property.

The home, built on a steep incline, dropped off fifty feet at the edge of the property, where an infinity pool looked out to an incredible view of Santa Monica. In the United States, nine people die in swimming pool accidents each day. She knew the statistic—she had researched it.

The most common cause of swimming pool drowning among adults is injuries suffered when diving into a pool under the influence of alcohol. Erica now had the 'way;' she just needed Jason to provide the 'means.'

Erica just finishing her breakfast the next morning when her contact cellphone began to buzz. This the first call on that phone since she had accepted the contract to kill Jason Brent. Erica rose from the table ad quickly darted to her leather bag that rested on the kitchen counter. She reached in and pressed the answer button.

"What is it?" Erica said into the phone.

"Have you seen the morning papers?" the voice chided on the other end.

"I don't get the newspaper, Mr. Edison. Why don't you just say why you called me?"

"Brent published another article. He needs to be taken care of now."

"You want this to look like an accident? Well, it takes time. You need to be patient," Erica said calmly.

"We can't wait any longer," Edison snapped.

"Look. I'll do it my way. If that's not good enough for you, I'll give you your money back. Just tell me what account number to transfer the funds."

"Let's not get all crazy. I just need you to know that time is of the essence."

"Rest assured, Mr. Edison. The job is set for tonight, so you can relax," Erica said sternly as she disconnected the call.

22

Springing the Trap

JASON WORKED in his office for several hours on his next article when his office phone beeped, and alerted him to an incoming call. He stopped typing and reached for the phone.

"Jason Brent."

"It's Franklin. I hacked into Global's system."

Jason sat straight up in his chair his hand gripped the receiver tight—tight enough to make his knuckles turn white.

"Jason? You there?" Franklin said.

"Yeah! I'm here, I'm here. What did you find?" Jason said, trying to keep his anxiety in check.

"I'm running through the recording from the garage camera for the fifteenth and haven't found either of the limo's leaving the building on that day, so I'm checking again to see if I missed anything."

"Okay," Jason said, somewhat deflated.

"It's interesting the way they have this system set up. The executive floor has no cameras at all. There is no way to get any images of that floor. No camera in the executive elevator either. Anyone who worked on that floor can come into and out of the building without anyone noticing," Franklin said.

"That's good to know."

"I'll let you know as soon as I've got something concrete."

"Great, Franklin. Good work. I'll talk to you soon." Jason put the phone back in its cradle and sat back in his chair, on the scent once again.

Erica scanned the photos of Jason's home laid out across the kitchen table. She reached for the photo showing the image of the swimming pool and picked it up. As long as she stuck to the plan, everything would work out perfectly, echoed the thought that ran through her mind until a sudden cloud of doubt wormed its way into her consciousness. Where were these doubts coming from? Just another contract, another job, but something nagged at her gut, something that told her that things were not as they appeared to be. Again, she shoved those thoughts aside. Just another job she hired on to do, and she needed to stay focused on the task at hand. Jason Brent would have a fatal accident, and he would have it soon—the sooner the better. Erica didn't like getting phone calls from complaining clients.

Jason prepared dinner for Erica when the chirping of his cellphone interrupted him.

305 | D o n n a   T e l l u m

"Hello," Jason said.

"It's Franklin. I got the image you're looking for. It turns out that the car hadn't been out on the fifteenth. It went out on the night of the fourteenth. I got a grainy image for you."

"Great. Send it along. Good work, Franklin. I owe you big time."

Jason trudged into his home office. He plopped down at his desk and fired up his laptop. He opened the e-mail attachment sent by Franklin. The picture grainy and had a shadow across the windshield. The face of the man behind the wheel completely blurred, and his features were difficult to see clearly. Jason printed a copy of the photo and inspected it with a magnifying glass. There wasn't much to look at so he shoved it in the desk drawer.

Erica assembled her plan to deal with Mr. Brent once and for all. Jason Brent, her target, just didn't fit the profile of a man who could cause destruction and the deaths of innocent people to further his career. A respectful man, she thought, a man who had principles, which again caused her to pause. Something just didn't add up, but Erica wasn't hired to solve math problems.

I don't care if it doesn't add up. I'm hired to do a job, and I'm going to do it. I don't care if he's a great guy with principles. Not my problem, Erica thought to herself. She needed to eliminate a thorn in the side of a corporation. It was not in her interest to get involved in the background of the target.

She needed to do the job and move on, on to what she had vowed to do years ago, but had put it on the back burner: finding the persons responsible for the deaths of her parents. Once this is over, Erica would make that mission her priority. She rose from the couch and walked into the bedroom, slid open the closet door, and retrieved the leather case she had stored there. She set the case on the bed and spun the combination lock wheels with her thumbs, then opened the latches. The bottom of the case filled with a foam base with holes bored into it. In each of the holes a small, glass bottle. She selected one of the bottles filled with a clear liquid and set it on the dresser.

On the shelf in the closet, Erica slid out a cardboard box. Opening the box, she selected a small, plastic bottle with a black, screw-on lid. She unscrewed the lid and transferred a portion of the clear liquid from the glass bottle into the plastic one. Screwed on the lid, Erica then held it up to the light. All looked good. Erica replaced the glass bottle in the case, re-locked it, and returned it to the closet. Erica took the plastic bottle and slid it into a small pocket located inside her purse. With all in order for tonight, Erica took a deep breath then went into the bathroom to get ready for her dinner date with Jason.

* * * * *

Jason had just looked at the digital clock on the stove when his doorbell rang. Seven o'clock exactly, another thing that Jason loved about Mary Jo, her punctuality, Jason thought as he tossed the dishtowel he had draped over his shoulder onto the kitchen counter and trotted to the door. He thought to himself that this would be an unforgettable night—a night of magical surprises.

Erica heard Jason's footsteps echo over the wood floor as he came to the door. The door opened, and Jason greeted her with a generous smile.

"Come in. You're right on time," Jason said.

Erica, dressed in denim jeans, a white knitted top, covered by a matching jacket, looked fetching as she stepped into the foyer. Her eyes immediately drawn to the original artwork that hung on the wall to her right impressed her—a local artist with a great deal of talent, Erica surmised. Jason's home exquisitely detailed, obviously professionally decorated, but done in a very masculine way, almost rustic. A brown leather couch dominated the living-room area with an oak coffee table that rested on a colorful Persian rug. Jason had furnished his home in an eclectic style of modern furniture accented with antique accessories.

"I love your house," Erica exclaimed.

"Thank you. Come into the kitchen. I'll pour you some wine, and I can check on our dinner. It's just about ready."

Jason led Erica into the kitchen. On the counter, chilled in a bucket of ice, a bottle of chardonnay, two wine glasses rested next to the bucket.

Jason filled one of the glasses and handed it to Erica, then poured himself a drink. Erica looked around the kitchen—noticed the gourmet equipment.

"You have some nice stuff here."

"Cooking is one of my hobbies, but I don't get to use them that often. It hardly seems worth going to all the trouble when you're only cooking for yourself. It's much more fun when there's someone to share it with," Jason said.

"So what are we having?"

"I thought we'd start with some imported cheeses as an appetizer. Then we'll sit down for some grilled Pacific Salmon with a mango salsa, asparagus, and parsley Yukon Gold potatoes," Jason said proudly.

"Mmmm. That sounds wonderful."

They drank wine and sampled the selection of imported cheeses in between Jason jumping up to check on the dinner from time to time. With everything ready, Jason led Erica to the dining table and served dinner.

Erica found herself enjoying Jason's company so much that once again she forgot her mission. She didn't need to fake her pleasure in his company or the meal; she was indeed having a good time, and her face registered her delight.

With dinner concluded, Jason picked up the plates and arranged them in the dishwasher, ordering Erica to relax and finish her wine. Jason still had dessert to serve, vanilla bean ice cream with a raspberry cognac sauce.

Erica relaxed at the table, sipping her wine, when Jason appeared with a tray in his hands, which held stemmed crystal glasses that contained the ice cream dessert and two cups of coffee. The two sat across from each other, enjoyed their coffees without saying much. The entire meal sumptuous, and Erica had no trouble letting Jason know that she enjoyed every moment of this wonderful evening.

"I think you missed your calling, Jason. You should've been a chef. This was magnificent, right down to the last detail," she said as she sipped her coffee. If only he had been a chef, she thought. I would be sitting here just enjoying this time together instead of waiting for the opportunity to end his life. What a waste.

As Erica drifted back into the present moment, she noticed Jason looked at her over his cup of coffee as he sipped the rich brew. She could only see his eyes, and it hit her like a cold slap in the face—those smiling eyes. As Jason brought the cup down from his lips, she saw that smile move to his mouth ever so slightly.

Erica wanted to say something, change the subject— break the tension of the moment, something to get him to stop looking at her like that. Try as she might, Erica couldn't get her brain to form a sentence. She just stared back, mesmerized by his smiling eyes, eyes that she had known from her past . . . eyes that were full of love.

"You went someplace there for a while," Jason said in almost a whisper.

"Yes I did," Erica said quietly. "I was thinking, you know? Sometimes you don't want things to end; you just want them to go on and on, just the way they are."

"I do know," Jason said as he reached across the table and touched the back of Erica's hand with his fingers.

Erica felt her breath shudder in her chest; her heart flip-flopped like a freshly caught fish jumping around in the bottom of a boat. Concentrate. Don't lose you composure, the voice in Erica's head told her, but her heart just kept beating wildly.

"How about a cognac?" Jason said as he gave her hand a gentle squeeze.

"Love one. Thanks. I just need to use the powder room."

"On your right. Just down the hall."

Erica rose from the table, scooped up her purse, and in only a moment stood in front of the bathroom mirror looking at her reflection. Her face drawn and tense.

She needed to relax and put the thoughts of how much Jason reminded her of Ford out of her head. She had to get this over with, and now the time to take action.

Erica turned on the cold water and soaked a washcloth under the tap. She wrung it out and held the cold cloth to the back of her neck, taking deep breaths, trying to calm her nerves. She soaked the cloth again and pressed it against her forehead. The coolness felt good to her. The tension eased. Her mind began to come around again. She regained her focus.

Erica quickly retouched her makeup and emerged from the bathroom with renewed confidence. "I can't remember when I've eaten so much and enjoyed it so . . ." Erica stopped in mid-sentence as she strolled into the dining room, straightening her top.

Jason had disappeared. On the table were two brandy glasses, each containing a measure of the golden-brown liquid. Erica set her purse down on her chair.

"Jason?" Erica called.

Erica walked into the living room, but found no one. She quickly and silently glided to the rear of the house and caught site of Jason standing out on his terrace, beyond the pool, leaning forward on the fence at the edge of his property. Erica slipped back to the dining table, opened her purse, and extracted the small, plastic bottle from its hiding place. In a second, the top came off, and Erica poured the clear liquid into one of the brandy glasses.

She picked up the glass and swirled the liquid around to mix the contents. Holding the treated brandy glass in her left hand, Erica picked up the other glass in her right.

Jason didn't hear the sliding door leading to the terrace open and close, followed by footsteps coming toward him. Erica stopped just a few steps behind Jason; he just stood there staring off into space. She carefully placed the two brandies on a small glass-top table just two feet to the right of her. Erica stood there for a moment then sidled up abreast Jason as he continued to stare off.

"Is there something wrong?" Erica said.

Jason blinked and after a moment came back to earth.

"No. I was just taking a moment. You know, no matter how crazy the world can be sometimes, you can always take time to see the beauty that's around you and take time just to enjoy it," Jason said. "Just look at that moonrise."

Erica didn't hear Jason say anything past, "take time to enjoy it." She flashed back in Romania again with her father. She felt Jason's arm slide around her waist. Without thinking, Erica nestled her head onto Jason's strong shoulder. She felt safe and protected, a feeling she hadn't felt in years. Jason turned his head toward her, his arm tight around her waist, as he pushed his face into Erica's hair, breathing in its gentle scent. Erica raised her head from Jason's shoulder and turned to him, and he to her. He took his left hand and with his index finger, traced the outline of her luscious lips. Jason explored the features of Erica's face with his eyes, his hand brushing gently across her cheek. Erica's pulse quickened. She could feel Jason's chest rise and fall as he held her close to him.

Kiss me, Jason. Kiss me, please, the voice in Erica's head said. I want you to kiss me, now.

Jason bent his head down, and his lips gently caressed her mouth. His lips moved to her chin, her cheek, and gently onto her lips again. Erica neared the threshold of ecstasy; this teasing driving her toward insanity.

"Kiss me, Jason," Erica whispered as she pressed her lips hard against his, her knees nearly buckling.

Jason slowly pulled away and looked at her long and hard. His mouth wanted to say, "I love you," but he couldn't form the words. The words screamed in his brain, but the neurons refused to fire, refused to transfer the information to his audio cortex, activating his vocal cords, mouth, and tongue. His lips parted slightly, but no sound came out. Jason could only do the next best thing, kiss her again more passionately than before. The two separated after nearly a minute of Jason's lips exploring Erica's idyllic mouth as both of their tongues had blended in orchestral harmony. Erica, light headed and off balance, stepped back unsteadily, bumped into the small table behind her that held the brandy glasses. As if the sound of the fallen glasses rolling off the table came from another universe light years away, Erica heard a voice echoing in her ears.

"You okay?" Jason asked.

"What?" Erica heard her voice say, as if it too were coming from another universe.

"I think you had too much to drink, Mary."

"Drink?" said Erica, still in a fog. "I knocked over the drinks."

"Don't worry; nothing broke. They just fell on the grass," Jason said as he wrapped his arms around her, pulling her close to him.

Erica buried her face in Jason's chest. The smell of his clean, starched shirt mixed with his sweat replicated an exotic fragrant bouquet. It excited her, and she breathed it in, increasing her arousal.

Erica looked up, her eyes searching, taking in every feature of Jason's face. He smiled, and Erica felt herself gently falling into a deep, black hole, tumbling, weightless, falling down and down, she wanted it to stop. She needed it to stop. This couldn't be happening to her.

"I . . . I . . .," she stammered.

Putting his fingers up to her lips, Jason said, "Don't talk. Just let me hold you."

There was no hope for Erica now, in full free-fall, unable to stop the momentum and regain her senses. I don't want this to happen, she thought as Jason bent down and scooped her up in his arms. I don't want to fall in love with this man. I need to run. I need to get out of here. I need to, but I don't want to. Erica thought. I want him to make love to me. I want to lose myself in him. I want to love him.

Her arms around his neck, Jason carried Erica into the house and down the hall until they came to Jason's bedroom. At the threshold, he stopped, pulled her up to him with his strong arms, and kissed her deeply, then allowed her body to settle back into the cradle position they were in before he kissed her. Jason stepped into the bedroom and glided to the bed, where he gently deposited her. She loosened her hands from around his neck. The moonlight illuminated the room with a bluish hue. Jason moved to the mahogany dresser, set against the wall, without stumbling over the chair along the side of the bed. On the top of the dresser a glass jar contained a single candle. Jason picked up a book of matches, lit the candle and placed it in front of the large mirror that hung on the wall. The candlelight reflecting off the mirror gave the room a warm glow.

Jason slid into the bed next to Erica and slipped his arm around her neck, pulled her toward him, and kissed her deeply. Erica let go her emotional chains and released herself into Jason's arms.

Erica awoke from a deep sleep entangled in Jason's arms. Just the green glow of the digital clock resting on the nightstand illuminated the room. 3:35 a.m., the clock face read as Erica carefully wiggled out from under Jason's warm body. She put her feet on the thick, carpeted, bedroom floor and stood up, she nearly fell back onto the bed; her legs wouldn't cooperate. After an unsteady moment, she regained her equilibrium and felt with her foot by the bed, finding her jeans. Cautiously bending over, she picked up her pants and felt the pocket for her cellphone. She slipped it out and pressed the activation button that caused the phone's face to give off a dim glow. Using her phone as a flashlight, she found her top, picked it up, and quietly left the room.

Erica shuffled into the living room, slipped the top over her head. The bright moonlight illuminated the room just enough that she could see the clear outlines of the furniture. Sliding into her pants, Erica made her way onto the patio and to the small table that once held the brandy glasses. Erica found the glasses in the grass, empty and now dry. She picked them up and returned them to the kitchen, then rinsed the glasses off and left them in the sink. Placing both of her hands on the edge of the sink, Erica lowered her head. This was not how this supposed to happen. This man had opened up her heart. No denying it, he loved her. He said it to her last night, and as much as she would like to believe it wasn't true, she loved him too.

How could this be true? Erica thought to herself. It was true, and now she had a serious dilemma. How could she even think about killing the man she loved? Erica turned around and sunk down onto the floor, her hand rubbed her forehead, unable to stop the tears forming in her eyes.

Jason wobbled out of his bedroom in his bathrobe and wearily strolled into the kitchen, following the scent of coffee brewing. Attached to a coffee mug on the counter a bright yellow post-it note, on it a message in Erica's hand that read:

'Had to make an early meeting. I'll talk to you later. Enjoy. MJ'

Jason read the note and smiled to himself. "And I was going to cook you a delicious breakfast," Jason said then poured his mug full of coffee.

With his mug in hand, Jason sat down at his home office desk and fired up his laptop, checking for messages. He worked at his desk for more than an hour before he showered and dressed to venture out into the world a different man than just ten short hours earlier.

Jason arrived at his Santa Monica office late in the morning. All quiet, and he had just sat down at his desk when the phone rang, disturbing the silence. Jason eagerly picked it up.

"Jason Brent!"

"Hey, Jason. It's Franklin."

"What's up?" Jason asked.

"I found something interesting you should know about."

"Talk to me."

"Since I was able to hack into the Global system, I checked on Walker's account for you. It is still active, but what I just found out is, the e-mails sent to Mrs. Walker's account are coming from the Global I.P. address. Those messages are not coming from South America like you thought."

"You never cease to amaze me, Franklin. Good job."

"They've hacked into your e-mail too. You want me to—"

"No! Don't do anything. Let them read my story before it hits the wire."

"I put a worm into the Global server, so I can get in anytime I want, until they find it. So if you need anything else, let me know," Franklin proudly said.

"You got it, bud. Talk to you later. And thanks," Jason said and hung up the phone.

Jason closed the screen he had worked on and opened up a blank page. He stared at the screen for several moments then began typing.

'What is Global Energies Covering Up?'

Jason's fingers flew over the keyboard as he banged out an article exposing the irregularities in Global's business practices. Jason deftly alluded to the disappearance of a Global employee who had been helping him research his story. Jason mixed fact with innuendo in his attempt to draw someone from Global out into the open.

Erica paced her Santa Monica apartment and attempted to make sense of what happened to her. She yearned for Jason to wrap his arms around her and hold her as he did the night before, but the entire time, her brain reminded her of the job—her job, her contract. She hired on to kill Jason Brent, not fall in love with him.

Erica gritted her teeth and stomped into the bedroom, flung open the closet door, nearly knocking it off its tracks, and yanked the leather briefcase from its hiding place. She turned and tossed the case on the bed, then took a step towards it and spun the combination wheels, clicking the locks open. Grasping the top of the bottle from the previous day, she lifted it out of the case and brought it up to eye level, staring intently at the colorless liquid. Squeezing the bottle in the palm of her hand, Erica returned to the living room and placed the bottle in her purse, determined to finish the job she contracted to do.

Erica jumped about two feet off the floor when her contact cellphone rang. Edison, she thought. Erica had to let the phone ring several times before she could compose herself enough to answer it. Her nerves on edge, she took a deep breath and picked it up.

"Yes," Erica said sternly.

"I'm hoping you have good news for me."

"Things didn't go as planned. I'll need a little more time."

"How much more time?" Edison asked.

"A few more days," Erica responded curtly.

"You've got two," Edison said then clicked off the line.

Erica looked at her phone for several seconds. "Bastard!"

Jason worked tirelessly for most of the day, and when satisfied with the completed article, he scheduled a meeting with Jennifer, for late that afternoon. She had conveniently returned to L.A. for the week.

Jason had just parked his car at the hotel and walked through the lobby as he dialed Mary Jo, and after a few rings, he heard her voice come through the phone.

"Hey, Jason. How is it going?"

"Good. It's good. Listen, I've got some important business to take care of, and we can't have dinner tonight. I'm sorry."

"What about tomorrow?" Erica said cheerfully.

"Is that okay with you?"

"That's fine. How about I come by your place after I finish work?" Erica said, disguising her disappointment.

"Perfect. I should be home by six," Jason said, clicking off the line.

Jason rode the elevator of the Sophia Hotel in Beverly Hills to the tenth floor. Just a short walk from the elevator, Jason found himself standing at Jennifer's hotel-room door. He took a deep breath and rapped on the door. This is going to be a hard sell, he thought to himself. Jason heard the lock click, and the door opened.

"Come in." Jennifer said, "You want a drink?"

"No. I'm good."

Jennifer stood in the center of the room with several sheets of paper in her hand.

"You really went to town on these guys. A lot of this is just speculation!" Jennifer said adamantly.

"I indicated that. I'm not saying that everything in there is fact, just conjecture."

"What do you hope to accomplish?"

"Get someone mad at Global," Jason said with a slight smile.

"And that will do what?" Jennifer said angrily.

"I hope they'll come out and rebut the story. They will have to expose themselves to questions from the press."

"Are you sure you want to do it this way?"

"I think it's the only way," Jason said emphatically.

"Okay, but you better be sure about what you're doing because this could get all of us in a lot of trouble."

"Thanks," Jason said, not knowing what kind of trouble he had let himself in for, he cleared his throat.

Moments later, Jason left Jennifer's suite and made his way down to the parking structure, got into his car, and back onto the streets of Los Angeles. He rolled down the windows of the car. Even though the evening turned overcast and cool, Jason needed the air conditioner on to compensate for the rise in his body temperature as excitement coursed through his body.

23

It's a shit storm out there

JASON, BACK at his desk in his Santa Monica office hammering away on his computer the subsequent morning, suddenly stopped typing when his cellphone buzzed in his jacket pocket. Jason retrieved the device, glanced at the display, and pressed the speaker button.

"Hey, Jen. How are you?"

"I don't know yet. I need to see you to discuss your exposé before it hits the wire tomorrow morning," Jennifer said wearily.

"I can be at your hotel in an hour."

"Good. See you then."

Jason clicked off his phone and returned to his laptop, unable to keep a smile from coming over his face.

Jason made it to Jennifer's hotel in less than forty-five minutes blowing through yellow lights at every opportunity whistling like a happy carefree kid.

He briskly walked down the hotel corridor to Jennifer's room and stopped in front of her door. He rapped several times, bouncing joyfully on the balls of his feet. The door swung open, and Jennifer greeted the still whistling Jason with a broad smile.

"You sound awfully cheerful?"

"I'm in a good mood," said Jason as he stepped into the room.

"Well good. Then you won't mind me telling you that I made a couple of minor changes to your article. Legal reasons."

"That's fine."

"Wow! Is this the Jason Brent, renowned journalist who has a cow when you change even one comma?"

"Yeah, it's me. I trust you."

"I like it when you're in a good mood. It excites me." Jennifer took the few steps necessary to place herself in front of him. She slid both arms around his neck and kissed him hard on the lips. Jason put his hands on her hips and gently pushed her away from him until the force broke their embrace.

"What's wrong, Jason. I've got my needs, you know."

"I have to tell you something."

She looked him straight in the eyes.

"Oh shit. You've met someone," Jennifer said.

"I'm in love, and I want to settle down with her."

"I've heard that before," Jennifer said, laughing.

"I mean it. It's for real this time."

Jennifer studied Jason for several moments. His tone of voice and his demeanor indicated sincerity.

"Isn't this rather sudden?"

"When it happens, it happens. You know what I mean?"

"Well, I'm happy for you. I'll miss our sleepovers, so I guess I'll just have to wait until this one—"

"It won't. This is the one, Jen. I know it."

"Okay," an unbelieving Jennifer said.

"About this article. Thanks for sticking your neck out for me."

"Okay, I don't know who you are anymore. I just hope she knows she's getting quite a man," Jennifer said. "So . . . let's get to work. I want to go over a few more things with you."

The following morning, Erica read the article Jason wrote after it hit the news wire. Papers and broadcast networks picked up the story, and the buzz attracted a lot attention. Reporters from as far as New York were jumping on any flight available to Los Angeles to try and get an exclusive with a Global executive and get their reaction to the scathing report.

After spending a sleepless night mentally rehearsing every detail of her plan, Erica knew time had run out. Within the next twenty-four hours, this would be over, and she could move on to her next challenge. Nothing about this job had gone according to plan.

Jason awoke early that morning despite his lack of sleep, and he brimmed with energy. The first thing on his agenda, to check the news services for the responses to his article. As expected, the media had descended on the Global Energies building. Jason showered, dressed and set out for what he anticipated would be an interesting day. Within twenty-four hours, a gaggle of reporters had descended on Global Energies, causing them one massive headache—a headache that could give Jason the edge he needed to find the last piece of the puzzle that would complete the picture. He would put an end to Global's illegal activities or produce a headache that would get him fired, and he'd become a pariah in the journalistic society. Either way, a lot was at stake for Jason Brent.

By mid-afternoon, Jason stopped responding to e-mails that were coming in by the thousands. He had to busy-the-lines coming into his office; the phone virtually glowed red hot from the relentless barrage of calls. The office, quiet no more than five minutes, when another call came to his cellphone, the screen displayed the name, 'Jennifer'.

"Hey, boss. How're things?" Jason said facetiously.

"It's a shit storm out there. The Global people started calling about twenty minutes ago wanting a retraction. They're threatening to sue for libel," Jennifer said excitedly.

"So what are we going to do?"

"I gave the information to the legal department. That will give us some time. Worst-case scenario, we'll have to print an apology and beg forgiveness. I want to know as soon as you find out anything, okay?"

"You'll be the first I call," Jason said, letting out a deep sigh.

After a late lunch, Jason went downtown to the Global Energies building. He only had to get within two blocks of the structure before he saw broadcast media trucks with their microwave dishes high into the air, choking off the side streets and uploading video images of the surrounding area. Jason found a parking lot that wasn't completely full about six blocks from Global, as close as he or anyone would get on this busy day.

He parked his car and then trekked the long city blocks until he found himself standing across the street from the Global Energies International headquarters. Exactly what Jason had expected; the building under siege from reporters of every shape and size, from every form of media outlet. Global couldn't ignore this kind of scrutiny for very long. They would need to answer questions and that time would come soon.

Jason pressed closer and stopped from time to time to question bystanders and reporters who were not interviewing passersby. From what he could gather, the phone calls into Global from the media started at nine o'clock in the morning, jamming their switchboard. No one at Global had been aware of the article until one of the P.R. Managers downloaded it from the internet. At that point, without Paulina Gregory to handle the crisis, the

Public Relations Department had shut down, no longer taking calls or giving out any statements.

The article had blind-sided them, and Jason, content to let things simmer for a few hours, sat back to enjoy his success before he would make his next move.

The press pounced on Global employees leaving the building like vultures throughout the day, with every exit staked-out by dozens of reporters hungry for a scoop. Jason spent most of his day at his office searching all the stories that came across the wire that had to do with Global. Around four o'clock in the afternoon, he headed back downtown, playing a hunch.

David Edison stormed out of his office, his teeth clinched tightly. As he marched down the hall, he dialed Erica's contact number. After only one ring, he heard her voice in his ear.

"Yes."

"Just listen. This better be finished tonight. Brent has caused us too much trouble for this to go on any longer. Get it done," Edison demanded as he jammed the phone into his pocket.

Jason positioned himself at the end of the bar at the Oak Room Grill, giving him a perfect view of the entrance to the establishment without being conspicuous. At 5:35 PM his hunch paid dividends.

In walked Kathy Lewis, the co-worker, whom he met that night he first approached Paulina. A bit overwrought from the affairs of the day, Kathy grabbed the first empty booth just off to the right of the entrance. Jason signaled the waitress over to him.

"Can I get you something?" she said politely.

"See that woman sitting in the booth by the door?" Jason said as he pointed his thumb in the direction of the booth.

"Yeah, sure."

"Get her whatever she wants to drink and give her this card." Jason handed the waitress a business card.

"Sure thing."

Jason watched as the girl glided across the room and stopped at Kathy's booth. She spoke to Kathy for a moment, nodded then set the card Jason had given her on the table. Kathy stared at it for a moment, then picked it up and read the front of the card.

She turned the card over and read the written message on the back, then slipped the card under the drink coaster that rested on the table in front of her.

She shifted in her seat and turned her head just enough so that she could get a look at Jason seated at the end of the bar. Jason made eye contact with her and motioned to her to walk to the back of the bar where the restrooms were located. Kathy nodded and about to rise when two males entered and called to her, moving to her booth.

One of the men slid into the booth opposite Kathy, but before the other man could slide in next to her, she stopped him and spoke to him for a moment. He then let her out of the booth and sat in her place.

Jason slid off his bar stool and walked down the small hallway leading to the restrooms. Jason found a dark place by the rear entrance and called to Kathy when he observed no one would hear him but her.

"You remember me?" Jason asked.

"Now I do," Kathy said. "Your name has been bounced around all day today. I read the article. Is it true?"

"I think it is," Jason said somberly. "I want to show you something."

Jason produced a piece of paper from his jacket pocket. "Do you recognize him?" Jason said as he handed the photo of the man behind the wheel of the Global limo.

"That's David—David Edison," Kathy said through her teeth. "That bastard."

"What do you know about him?"

"He's one of the executives, but no one knows what he does," she said defiantly.

"How do you know him?"

"He and Paulina were an item once, but it was all hush, hush. He treated her like shit; pushed her around," Kathy said angrily. "Paulina told me David had always involved himself in something shady. I warned her not to trust him."

"Thanks. You've been a great help," Jason said.

"Are you going to find out what happened to Paulina?"

"If it's the last thing I do," Jason said, giving Kathy a little smile as he disappeared though the back door.

Jason had just turned up the street from his home, when his cellphone rang.

"Hello, its Jason."

"Hey dude, how they hangin'?" the voice on the other end of the line said.

"Greg. You got something for me?"

"Come on. What, do you think I'd let my old buddy down? No way, Jose. It took a little bit of doing, and I had to grease several palms, if you know what I mean, but I finally got access to some security camera video of the Global office in Dubai."

"And?" Jason said anxiously.

"I got a photo of the guy who comes once a year," Greg said proudly.

"Good work. Listen. Can you fax it to me? My e-mail has been compromised."

"You bet. The only thing is I wasn't able to get a name on the guy."

"That's fine. I'll be home in a couple of minutes. I'll call you back," Jason said as he disconnected the call.

When Jason walked into his home office, the photo Greg had sent him sat in the fax machine's basket. He turned on the desk lamp and laid the photo on the desk under the bright light, then retrieved the photo of David Edison behind the wheel of the limo and placed it next to the Dubai photo. Greg's security camera photo showed a clear image of David Edison as he entered the Dubai office building. It looked as though Edison could be the man behind Global's operation. As Jason stared at the photos, his cellphone rang.

"Hello?"

"It's Greg. Did you get the fax?"

"Yeah. I'm looking at it right now. This guy is David Edison. He's responsible for possibly two deaths that I'm aware of."

"You know this guy?" Greg said, shocked.

"Only by photograph. Thanks for the help, Greg. I owe you."

"You got it, buddy," Greg said.

The lights burned late into the night in the Global executive offices as David Edison met with his boss, Zubin Ratko. David's brow registered extreme concern as Zubin paced his spacious office.

"This should've been taken care of by now," Zubin shouted. "For two million dollars, I expect some results."

Edison sat motionless in his chair, seething with rage.

"I've got assurance that it will be done by tonight," Edison said flatly.

"I don't need assurances. I need action," Zubin said, slamming his fist on his desk. "This Brent son of a bitch is getting close. He contacted another one of our managers today. Those damn news trucks are all around the building. I've got reporter's crawling up my ass, for Christ's sake."

"I know, I know. I'll take care of it," Edison said, displeased with the verbal abuse. "I want to make sure it looks like an accident."

"No mistakes, David. Your life depends on it," Ratko barked.

24

A Shocking Discovery

JUST AFTER six o'clock Erica stood at Jason's front door with a pizza box in one hand and a bottle of wine under her arm. She breathed in deeply, pushed the doorbell, and heard it chime inside the house. It couldn't have been more than ten seconds before Jason swung the door open and greeted Erica with a big smile.

"Hey, Mary Jo. Right on time," Jason said jovially before his eyes spied the pizza box in Erica's hand. "Pizza?"

"I thought we'd eat in, and I didn't want you to go to all that work cooking, so I brought my old stand-by dinner, with dessert," she said as she pulled the bottle out from under her arm.

"Well don't just stand there; come in."

Erica stepped across the threshold, and before she spoke another word, Jason kissed her and slid his arms around her waist. Erica nearly dropped the bottle of wine. She felt that black hole open up again in front of her, and without putting up an ounce of resistance, she just stepped in it and fell. Her entire nervous system came alive; sparks erupted everywhere, tumbling out of control. The sound of the front door slamming shut behind her that brought her back to reality.

It approached eight o'clock and the pizza consumed, and the first bottle of wine already empty when Erica suggested that they take a dip in the pool.

"Did you bring your suit?" Jason asked.

"Why? I don't think your neighbors can see into the pool."

"You're right," Jason said, smiling. "What do we need suits for anyway."

Erica and Jason stripped off their clothes in the living room. Jason could not hide his excitement once he saw Erica naked again.

"I'll get us some towels," Jason said sheepishly as he darted off to the bathroom.

"I'll pour us some brandies; it's a bit chilly out."

"Good idea," Jason yelled from the bathroom.

Erica reached into her purse next to the coffee table and slipped the vial out of its hiding place. She dashed to the kitchen and grabbed two brandy glasses from the cupboard. In one, she poured a portion of the clear liquid. She held both the glasses in her left hand as she trotted to the liquor cabinet in the dining room, found the bottle of Napoleon. She just finished pouring brandy into the glass with the clear liquid in it as Jason entered the living room with two large bath towels in his hand, covering his embarrassment.

"I've poured you a drink," Erica said as she held out the glass containing the tainted brandy.

Jason took the drink from her hand as Erica poured brandy into her glass. Jason held his glass up to her, in the form of a toast.

"Here's to us," he said.

The two touched their glasses together and then both sipped the warm liquid. Erica's eyes never left Jason's face, as she looked for any registration that indicated something was amiss.

"Let's swim," Jason said eagerly.

Erica gave him a nod, and the two strolled through the house out onto the deck and next to the pool, where they set their brandies on a small table between two chaise lounge chairs. The water warm enough that both walked in the shallow end without much discomfort.

They swam to the deep end of the pool, where Jason took Erica in his arms and held her close to him, kissing her. Jason's hands caressed Erica's smooth, creamy flesh, each touch excited him more. Erica decided then and there that she wanted him. She wanted him now, just one more time. They floated together back to the shallow end of the pool, where the water just reached their chests when they stood. There in the pool, Erica mounted him; felt him deep inside her, the weightless effect of the water only heightened their pleasure.

It didn't take long for Erica to reach the peak of her pleasure, the blissful rhythmic spasms compelled her to let out a muffled scream and dig her fingers deep into the flesh of Jason's back. The thought of bringing her to the height of ecstasy brought Jason to his. Holding her tightly, her legs wrapped around his waist, Jason carried her out of the pool and to the padded chaise lounge chairs that were just a few feet from the side of the pool.

Erica let her legs drop, and the two lovers separated, Jason scooped her up into his arms and then laying her onto the chaise lounge covered her with the bath towel. Kneeling down beside her, Jason leaned over and kissed her.

"I love you so much," Jason whispered, then sat down in the lounge chair next to hers and wrapped his towel around himself. Erica sat up, reached over to the table holding the brandy glasses, picked up Jason's glass, and handed it to him. She picked up hers and held it out toward Jason.

"Here's to love," she said, smiling.

They touched glasses, and as Erica watched, Jason downed his brandy in one gulp.

"Look at those stars," Jason said as he lay on his back, his brandy glass on his chest. "You could almost reach out and touch them."

No more than five minutes later that Erica noticed Jason's breathing become slow and easy. The drug taking effect, as Jason became extremely inebriated.

Erica rose from her chair and trotted into the house. In twenty minutes, she had the place cleaned and everything put away that would indicate that she had been there. Satisfied, she made her way back to the pool where Jason lay in a drunken stupor. Erica knelt down next to Jason's head and stroked his hair. It would be simple. Just tip over the chair, and roll him into the pool.

"Simple, as easy as falling off a . . .," Erica whispered as she kissed Jason on the mouth.

It wasn't easy. She couldn't do it. Erica had broken the first rule of her profession. Never get emotionally involved with your target. Emotionally involved an understatement, for Erica had fallen in love with this man. This man had touched her heart, and Erica couldn't fathom how she let this happen. That nagging feeling had returned as she discovered that Jason could not the man she had been led to believe.

Erica dashed into the house and went directly to Jason's office. On his desk lay his laptop. Erica sat down at the desk and powered up the computer. When the screen came to life, a blank space labeled "password" stared back at her, the cursor blinking rhythmically.

Erica pulled on the desk drawer just at her right hand, and found it securely locked. Erica bolted off the chair and into the living room in seconds. She scooped her purse off the coffee table and returned to the office.

Opening her purse, Erica retrieved a small, rectangular, leather case containing her lock-picking tools. She slid out a thin, wire-like tool and a small, flat, metal screwdriver. Erica went to work on the lock and had it open in less than thirty seconds. Inside the drawer, she found a black binder the size of a personal diary. Thumbing through the binder, Erica found what she looked for, the password page. She typed the password that corresponded to the laptop and logged onto the computer.

Erica scanned the files for nearly three-quarters of an hour and found nothing that could implicate Jason Brent in any illegal activity. As she continued to search, she discovered that Jason assignments had him out of the state on the day of the oilrig explosion. His files indicated that he had received a tip that the company used old and worn-out equipment replacement parts, sold as new. Erica now convinced that she had been hired to kill one of the good guys. Erica closed the computer and sat back in the chair.

"Fuck me," Erica uttered aloud.

Erica rushed back outside.

"Jason!" "Jason, wake up," Erica said as she shook him.

"Wha . . .," a groggy Jason said.

"You had too much to drink. Come on. I'll help you to bed."

Erica put her arm under Jason's back to help him sit up. Once up, Jason tried to lie back down.

"Come on. You can do it," Erica said as she got Jason to sit up and then stand on rubbery legs.

Slowly, one-step at a time, Erica guided an unstable Jason to his bedroom and deposited him into his bed without much difficulty. Once Jason hit the mattress, he passed out cold. Erica covered him, kissed him on the lips, and closed the bedroom door as she left Jason comfortably asleep.

Erica trudged into the living room and flopped onto the couch. Her life, officially a complete and utter mess and she needed to get out of this, but how. As she sat and thought she heard Jason's cellphone going off in the office. Erica rose from the couch and went to the liquor cabinet. There, she poured herself another brandy. As she took a sip, Jason's cellphone rang again. Whoever the caller, they were persistent. Erica sat in silence. Then the phone rang again. Erica followed the sound to the office. On his desk, Erica could see the phone screen glow as the caller called again. Another minute passed before the fax machine came to life. This must be urgent; Erica thought as she turned on the light and stepped to the fax machine.

As the machine started to spit out paper, Erica noticed the two photos on Jason's desk, one with the driver circled in red ink and scrawled beneath the name, 'David Edison.' The other had the words 'Edison in Dubai' written across the bottom.

The fax machine suddenly stopped. Two sheets of paper rested in its basket. Erica turned and started to leave the office, but decided to go back and find out what could be so important for Jason to see tonight. Erica lifted the papers from the basket.

FROM: GREG BAKER: DUBAI FIELD OFFICE

TO: Jason Brent; Los Angeles USA

Jason: I sent the Dubai pic to everyone I knew looking for ID. Don't know who this David Edison guy is, but the guy in this pic is a match. A Major in the Serbian army. Disappeared UNTIL now.

You're welcome.

Greg.

Erica felt the blood in her body drop into her feet. Her hands shaking, she looked at the faxed photo Greg had sent to Jason of four men in Serbian uniforms, smiling. In the photo Erica saw her father, twenty some years ago, and standing next to him with an arrow drawn, pointing to his head, a young David Edison. Written underneath the image the name, Mikael Vukuvic, the man who murdered her parents and the man she had been hunting all these years.

Erica's mind raced at the speed of light as she tried to process what in god's name she had just discovered. David Edison is Mikael Vukuvic, the man who murdered her mother and directly responsible for the death of her father.

She had hunted this man since the day she saw the smoke rising from their chimney ten years ago. Erica's blood slowly began to course through her body again, but this time her blood was at a boil. "If Vukuvic worked for Skoffski, then he has to still be working for him. But who is Skoffski now?" Erica mused.

"What did you say?" Jason said from the door of the office.

"Ja—Jason!" Erica stammered, and she turned with a start.

A bleary-eyed Jason leaned against the doorframe, hair tousled, cotton robe wrapped around him. He rubbed his hands on his face in an attempt to brush the cobwebs out of his brain. Erica folded the papers in her hand and shoved them in her pocket.

"You said something. Sounded like a foreign language or something."

"You better sit down on the couch. I'll make us some coffee," Erica said as she assisted him to the living-room couch.

Once Erica had Jason comfortably on the couch, she darted into the kitchen and filled the coffee-maker to capacity. She would need every strong ounce of the dark liquid before the morning sun filled the house with its bright, warm light.

"God, my head is pounding. I've never had a hangover like this before," Jason said as he rested on the couch. "I don't even remember drinking that much."

"Can I make you something to eat?" Erica called to Jason from the kitchen.

"I'm not hungry."

As the coffee maker delivered its stream of hot brew, Erica slid a mug under the machine, filled it nearly to the brim, and brought it to Jason.

"Here, this should help wake you up," Erica said.

"What's going on, Mare?"

"I've got a lot to tell you, so drink up."

Erica dashed back into the kitchen to fix herself a cup.

"It's really important that you listen to what I'm going to tell you, okay?" Erica said, losing her southern twang.

"Sure. Then can we go back to bed?" Jason said, not aware her voice had changed.

Erica took a long swallow of coffee. This wasn't going to be easy, but it had to be done.

By the third cup of coffee, Jason, more alert began speaking coherently. Erica had made some toast and set a bowl of fresh fruit on the coffee table, which Jason ate heartily as Erica sipped coffee and paced the living room.

"You feeling better?" Erica asked.

"Much. I think I'll jump into the shower."

"We need to talk, and we need to talk now," Erica said sternly.

Jason's face registered alarm. "Mary, what's wrong? What happened?" he said, startled.

"First of all, my name is not Mary Jo Sommerson. I haven't been truthful with you. My real name is Erica Drago," Erica said as she nervously stood before Jason. "Actually, that's not true either; it's Adrijana Erica Sekulic."

"What is this all about Mary . . . Erica? What are you saying?"

"I was hired by the man you know as David Edison to kill you. I'm a hired assassin."

Jason sat for a moment, motionless, and then let out a laugh. A smile took over his face as he shook his head.

"Okay, enough with the jokes. I've been broken up with in many ways, but I've got to say this is the best yet. If you don't want to see me anymore, just tell me."

"Jason, listen to me. I was hired to kill you because of what you're working on. If I don't do it, someone else will. Your life is in danger," Erica said earnestly.

"This is ridiculous," Jason said with a great deal of disdain. "When I told you I loved you, I meant it. If you don't love me, you don't have to make up some fantastic story. Just tell me."

"Don't move," Erica said, and she rushed out the front door of the house.

Jason sat glumly on the couch for the next several minutes when Erica bounded through the door with a briefcase in her hand.

She stopped at the coffee table and opened the case, then spun it around so Jason could look inside.

"Go ahead. Take everything out," Erica said curtly.

Jason began to remove items from the case. First, the 9 mm semi-automatic pistol with a silencer attached. He held it in his hand for a moment, carefully looked at it then set it down on the table. He pulled out a manila folder and set it down next to the gun. Next came out two passports. One Canadian, the other German.

"Open the folder," Erica ordered.

Jason opened the folder, and inside were photos of him. Photos taken by Erica surreptitiously—at his office, shopping, even at his favorite coffee shop. The comprehensive photo gallery of Jason's activities taken over the last few weeks left him dumbfounded. He looked up at Erica with a disbelieving expression on his face.

"I've been stalking you for weeks, Jason; documenting your daily habits, looking for an opportunity to get close to you. Then something happened." Her tone softened. "I fell in love with you. I tried not to, but . . . ."

"This is crazy. How do I know you're telling me the truth now?"

"Because you're not dead. You must trust me. Listen to me. I'm not talking with that silly accent anymore," Erica said, sitting down next to Jason.

"Yeah, your accent is gone," Jason said, confused.

"That's because I'm not who I said I was," Erica said vehemently. "My life has been a life of lies. That's how I made my living. But you have to believe me, you are in extreme danger."

"How were you going to kill me?" Jason asked, his eyes focused on the photos.

"That's irrelevant."

"No, it's not. If you want me to believe you, you'll tell me how you were going to do it."

"I gave you a drug that made you drunk enough to pass out so I could drown you in the pool. It was supposed to look like an accident."

"Jesus Christ!" Jason blurted. "Just like that?"

"Listen, I had been informed that were a shit and were responsible for the deaths of innocent people just so you could sell newspapers."

Jason stared at the photos, the gun, and then at Erica.

"So, none of this was real. You were just manipulating me."

"I love you, Jason; you have got to believe me," Erica pleaded, enunciating every word.

"I love someone named Mary Jo, not Erica . . . whatever your real name is."

"You fell in love with me, Jason. And I fell in love with you. I am the same person. Those feelings you feel and I feel are real, but it won't mean anything if you don't trust me. You won't survive the weekend without me."

"How do I know that? You lied to me once; why wouldn't you do it again?"

"Because, if I wanted to kill you, you'd be floating in the pool facedown right now."

Jason sat in thought for a few minutes, periodically looking at Erica, then back at the hardwood floor, while Erica rose from the couch and paced in front of the coffee table.

"You got a fax this morning," Erica said, removing the folded papers from her pocket.

Jason looked up from the couch. Erica unfolded the papers and placed them in front of him.

"Your friend Greg stumbled onto David Edison's real identity. He's Mikael Vukuvic. The man standing next to him! That's my father, Goran Sekulic. Mikael murdered my mother when I was ten years old, and he was responsible for my father's death," Erica said with an outpouring of emotion as she sat down on the couch next to Jason. "I vowed to find him and make him pay for what he did. This man is responsible for many deaths, including the two you wrote about in your article."

Jason looked directly at Erica with a great deal of mournfulness in his eyes.

"There is not a doubt in my mind that Mikael had them killed if he didn't do it himself. He's evil, and the man he worked for, Andrus Skoffski, is worse."

"So, now what?" Jason scoffed.

"I'm going to call Edison and tell him the job is done, but I will need to talk to him about . . . I don't know, something."

"Shouldn't we call the police?" Jason asked a bit unnerved.

"No police. There is no evidence of any crime being committed," she said emphatically. "The minute these guys smell cops, they're gone, and if that happens, it will take me another ten years to find them."

Jason opened his mouth to object.

"You're going to my place to stay safe while I take care of this." Erica leaned over and gave Jason a kiss on the cheek. "Get dressed, and pack some clothes."

As they drove to her Mount Washington residence, Erica told Jason her life story, going back to her tenth birthday. Erica convinced that Skoffski still pulled Vukuvic's strings, not smart enough to run an organization on his own.

"Do you think that the other man in the photo with your father is Skoffski?" Jason asked.

"I don't know. If I ever met the man, I was a very little girl."

"Well, the guy pulling Edison's strings now is a man named Zubin Ratko. He could be Skoffski."

"That would make sense."

"Listen, I don't need to be put away for safe keeping, waiting for someone to come and kill me. I can help you. You could use me," Jason said, pleading.

Erica thought for a moment. "You ever used a gun before?" she said condescendingly.

"Does paintball count?" Jason asked, giving her a half smile. Although he still seemed somewhat lost in thought, his humor could never be stifled for long.

Erica stared at Jason. "This isn't a game, Jason. It's for real, and they want you dead. I need to handle this myself."

"But I've got a guy who's hacked into Global's mainframe, and if this guy Skoffski is who I think he is, then you need me to get you in that building."

"Or you can just tell your contact to help me."

"Right. The story of the century that directly affects me, and I'm sitting on the sidelines. Not gonna happen," Jason said emphatically.

Erica drove on, looking straight ahead, as her mind processed the information. "You do exactly what I tell you and nothing more. Is that clear?"

"Yes, ma'am," Jason said with a wry smile.

Jason sat in the sparse Mount Washington house's living room looking the place over, trying to get a feel for who lived there. Erica came out of the bedroom with a large, metal case. She plopped it on the floor next to the couch and opened it up. Inside were several weapons of different sizes. She pulled out a small-caliber automatic pistol, cleared the chamber, and then inserted a loaded clip and handed it to Jason.

"Here. Try not to shoot me, or yourself."

Then she retrieved a 9 mm Beretta and attached a silencer to it. She slammed a clip in and put three more clips in her back pocket.

"Are you expecting an army?"

"Let's hope we don't need any more than this," Erica said coldly. "Last chance to change your mind."

"It's show time," Jason said with as much bravado as he could muster under the circumstances.

"You did not just say that," Erica said with a smirk. "I'm making the call."

Erica picked up her cellphone and dialed Edison. After two rings, Erica heard Edison's voice in her ear.

"Edison."

"It's done," Erica said flatly.

"About time. I'll transfer the rest of your fee as soon as I have confirmation."

"Listen, eliminating Jason Brent is the least of your worries."

"What do you mean by that?" David said, confounded.

"Does the name Zubin Ratko have any meaning to you?"

"Why?"

"I found out he's put a contract on you for two million dollars."

"Fuck! That bastard! He turned on me!"

"Anyway, you've been so patient with me on this job — thought I'd give you the heads up. Call it professional courtesy. Be careful."

The line went quite for several seconds. "Wait, you still there? I want to hire you to kill Ratko," a nervous David said.

"I really don't work that way," Erica responded.

"Listen, I'm calling Fogarty and requesting you anyway, so let's save time and get the deal done now!" Edison said, extremely agitated.

"Okay. Meet me at the The Buzz Cafe on Santa Monica at four thirty. I'll get a table in front on the sidewalk. I'll be in a blue jacket, white blouse, a Bloomingdale's shopping bag on the table."

"Okay. I'll be there," a relieved Edison said as Erica hung up the phone.

"Wow! You are an excellent liar," Jason said, impressed but a little disturbed.

"I know," Erica said with a sigh. "So here's the plan: I meet Edison at the cafe, get the details on Ratko and when he leaves you follow him to wherever he goes. Don't lose him!"

Erica reached into one of the pockets of the briefcase and extracted what looked like a four-inch, black tube. She held the device up to Jason.

"This is a battery-operated drill," Erica said as she pushed the 'On' button with her thumb, the drill whirred to life.

"It will be dark enough by the time I finish my meeting with Edison that he'll have to turn on his car lights. While he's with me, you take this and drill a single hole in his left taillight cover.

"The hole will be small enough that it won't be seen very well in the day, but when he turns on his lights, it will be like a beacon. You'll be able to see it for blocks," Erica said as she handed the drill to Jason.

"I can do that," Jason said confidently as he slid the drill into his pocket.

"Next. Call this hacker friend of yours. I want to talk to him."

25

Holy Shit! I just killed him!

ERICA, HER EYES hidden behind dark sunglasses, wore black, leather gloves and sat at a sidewalk table in front of The Buzz Cafe. The cafe situated on the corner, gave Jason a panoramic view of the entire corner from his vantage point, parked across the street. The area bustled with foot traffic as passersby went about their business in the trendy neighborhood of chic boutiques and eclectic eateries. Erica sat patiently at the table when she heard Jason's soft voice in her earpiece.

"He just parked his car about half a block west of you. He's walking toward you now."

Erica smoothly removed the earpiece, stuffed it down her shirt collar, and remained motionless as she waited for David Edison to approach. Erica had to wait less than a minute when David Edison sat himself at Erica's table. He maneuvered his chair so that the back pressed against the building's wall, preventing any approach from the rear.

"Mr. Edison," Erica said.

"Yes. So how do we do this?"

"Half up front," Erica said flatly as she slid a small slip of paper across the table to Edison. "That's the new account number."

With Edison safely occupied with Erica, Jason got out of his car and walked the half block to where Edison had parked. Pedestrian traffic flowed along the sidewalk in both directions, with no one paying any attention to the man standing beside the black, parked car. Jason stepped to the rear of the vehicle and stood next to the left taillight. Holding the drill against his thigh, he pressed the button, and as the drill engaged, he casually leaned toward the vehicle—the drill took only a few seconds to cut through the red plastic covering the taillight. Jason casually sauntered away from the vehicle and crossed the street, returning to his car.

"When can you get this done?" Edison asked nervously." I don't have much time; Ratko will act fast."

"That depends on how much information you can give me."

"What kind of information?"

"Who is this guy? Where can I find him? How can I get close enough to him without him suspecting anything? The more you can give me, the better. If I'm doing my own research, it will take longer."

David Edison let out a sigh.

"Zubin Ratko is the head of Global Energies. He's a dangerous man—believe me."

"How so?" Erica said without any emotion.

"He had people eliminated to get to where he is today, specifically Abar Mohommed Kalil, a prominent banker for the world's largest oil conglomerate. He embezzled millions from government funds to gain leverage in the oil business. He'll stop at nothing to get what he wants," Edison said fearfully.

"Why is he after you?"

"I know things . . . lots of things?"

"I see. Anything you can tell me?"

"Just this: he was once secretary to the Serbian minister of defense. His real name is Andrus Skoffski."

"Now he wants you out of the picture?"

"The trouble Global is in right now is partially my fault. He's going to make me take the fall."

"How do I get to him?"

"He's at the Global building right now, but getting into the building is next to impossible without being seen. Security monitors the cameras all the time. He has an apartment on the top floor. He usually leaves around nine o'clock every evening. He has a girlfriend who lives up in the hills, off Mulholland."

"You don't care how I do it?"

"No. Just get it done, and fast," Edison said excitedly.

"When can you transfer the money?"

"I'll do it now," Edison said as he pulled his cellphone from his jacket pocket.

356

356

"Good. I'll call you this evening. Don't worry. Mr. Ratko will not make it to his girlfriend's tonight."

"I could use someone like you," Edison said as he punched numbers into his cellphone. "Once you've taken care of Ratko, I'm taking over the operation. I pay well."

"We'll talk after this is done," Erica said in a manner that dispelled any doubts of her prowess to complete the job. David Edison let out a relieved sigh as Erica rose from her chair, picked up her shopping bag, and strolled down the boulevard to disappear, mixing in with the crowd. Edison looked up and down the street then rose and walked quickly to his car, got in, and pulled away from the curb as Jason followed a safe distance behind.

Erica got into her car and put her earpiece back in her ear, slipped her cellphone out of her jacket pocket, and pressed a button.

"You still with him?" she said into the phone.

"I can see the bright light coming from his car a mile away," Jason replied. "Everything go okay?"

"Ratko is Skoffski. Edison told me that he had a Dubai financier killed so he could take over his business."

"Wow! This is huge," Jason exclaimed. "What do we do now?"

"Call me as soon as he gets to his destination," Erica ordered, then pressed a button ending the call. Erica quickly scrolled through her phone directory and dialed another number.

"Franklin, it's Erica."

"Hey. Where are you?" Franklin asked.

"I'm on the other side of town right now. I'll need you to send me the floor plan for the apartment at the top of the Global building."

"Okay. I'm accessing the system right now. It will take me a few minutes."

"Just send it to this number when you've got it. I'll get back to you when I'm ready." Erica disconnected the call. For the next forty-five minutes, Erica sat in her car. Her thoughts were about her relationship, or lack thereof, with Jason. Could there be a chance for them, or had that opportunity gone by the boards. Erica's cellphone buzzed suddenly disturbing the silence.

"Where are you now?" Erica said.

"At Edison's place. It's in Rancho Palos Verdes."

With Edison's address plugged into her GPS, Erica drove, keeping within the speed limit; the trip would take an hour in the late evening traffic. When she arrived, she parked just behind Jason's vehicle and signaled him to come to her.

Jason opened the passenger door and slid into the seat. "He came straight here after he met with you. Two guys showed up about ten minutes ago. I know one for sure is in the front of the house," Jason said.

"Two men?"

"Yeah, two. The house is just about twenty yards up the road," Jason said pointing. "Tall hedges are on either side of the driveway. The house is maybe fifty feet from the hedges. The garage is detached and sets all the way back."

"Good work," Erica said as she got out of the car.

Jason followed Erica to the rear of her vehicle. She opened the trunk, removed a long canvas bag from it, and then took out a pair of night vision goggles. She closed the trunk lid, placed the bag on the closed trunk, and unzipped it, to reveal the parts of a crossbow.

"A crossbow?"

Within a minute Erica had the bow assembled and cranked the winch to arm her weapon.

"A gun will give off a flash. One of those guys or Edison could see it, and we're up shit creek," Erica said prudently.

"What do you want me to do?"

"Stay by the car until I come for you. I mean it," Erica said firmly. "I can't be worrying about you and do this at the same time."

"Okay," Jason said as she hurriedly crept up the quiet street.

Erica peered through the goggles and saw a beefy man with a shaved head dressed completely in black. He stood at the edge of the driveway a few feet from the main entrance of the house. Erica stealthily maneuvered around the hedge to get a clear shot at the man.

She took aim with the crossbow and held for a moment. In the distance, a dog could be heard barking, and as the man turned his head to the direction of the noise, a soft, almost musical note sang as the taught bowstring released, sending the deadly projectile on its lethal course. The beefy man had no opportunity to cry out as the bolt hit him in the neck, in the region of his vocal cords; he went to the ground in a heap, gasping for air. Before Erica could make her way to him, he was dead.

With the man in front down and her crossbow armed again, she quietly moved to the rear of the house, she kept herself pressed against the building to avoid detection. When she reached the end of the house structure there before her sitting in a lawn chair twenty feet from her position a young man with long, greasy hair and a close-cropped beard. Erica took careful aim, and once again, the delicate song of the taut bowstring sang out; the projectile hit the man in his chest and pierced his heart, killing him instantly.

Erica quickly made her way back to her car, where Jason patiently waited.

"It's clear now," Erica said as she opened the car door and tossed the crossbow onto the back seat. "You still have the gun I gave you?"

Jason nodded and reached into his inside jacket pocket and produced the small caliber weapon. She took the gun from him and attached a silencer to it.

"Let's go," Erica said.

The two stood at the rear entrance to the house. Jason could just make out the form of a man seated in the lawn chair and abruptly stopped.

"Don't worry. He's asleep," Erica whispered.

Jason apprehensively nodded.

"Keep on my left side," she said as she tried the door.

Locked, but it only took her thirty seconds and the lock picked and the door open. The two slipped inside without a sound. They stepped from the rear entrance into the kitchen of the house and found no one. The two had just crept into the living room when they heard a toilet flush on the other side of the house, where Erica suspected the bedrooms were located. Edison, taken by surprise as he entered the living room and found Erica and Jason standing there, abruptly stopped.

"What the fuck!" exclaimed Edison. "You told me he was dead."

"I told you that I had taken care of him. I never said he was dead."

Edison's eyes darted around the room as he became extremely agitated, "Why are you here? I paid you millions! You're supposed to be eliminating Skoffski!

"Oh, don't worry about your boss, he'll get his."

"What the fuck does that mean, Drago?" Edison said, puzzled. "You think this is a game here? You going to call the cops now and have me arrested?"

Edison laughed and moved to the phone.

"I've got cops on my payroll, bitch. Politicians and judges are my country club buddies. I'll never see the inside of the police station! Now, get the fuck out of my house and go do what I paid you to do, Drago."

"It's not Drago. I'm Adrijana Sekulic."

Edison's jaw dropped to the floor. His eyes looked Erica up and down as the realization came over him.

"But you're supposed to be . . ."

He composed himself and smiled with a sense of bravado.

"Your father . . . clever to the end," Edison said admiringly. "It's uncanny how much you look like your mother. Can't believe I didn't notice at the coffee shop. Such a shame to kill your mother; a beautiful woman, in my defense, I was aiming for your father. Then he cheated me that day in Romania, taking poison before I had a chance to kill him," Edison quipped, trying to push the issue.

"What? You think this is some kind of movie? You think I'm going to lose my cool and scream at you, all emotional and shit, to get me off my game?"

Jason turned to Erica, noticing the cold, unemotional demeanor and her steely stare fixed on Edison.

"Jason, any questions you'd like to ask Mr. Edison, or do you prefer Vukuvic?" she said boldly.

"Did you order the killings of Walker and Gregory?" Jason asked.

"No. Ratko did."

"But why did you have to kill them?"

"Walker was on to what we were doing."

"Because Walker had found duplicate serial numbers when he did a personal inspection after the rig explosion," Jason said, his eyes boring into Edison's.

"Yeah, pretty much. He stuck his nose where it didn't belong."

"What happened to Paulina?" Jason asked impatiently.

"She was talking to you, so she had to be dealt with," Edison said smugly. "You should blame yourself."

Jason got riled up.

"I took her out to a site in Lancaster, where I buried her right after I finished raping her," he said with glee.

Jason, about to explode into a rage turned bright red.

"But there's something else you don't know —" Edison smirked.

"You filthy son-of-a-bitch!"

Before Edison could speak another word, the gun rose from Jason's side. Erica reached out her arm to stop him, but it was too late. Jason squeezed off a round that hit Edison in the shoulder. The next several shots came in rapid succession as Jason repeatedly pulled the trigger. The rounds slammed into Edison, sending him backward from the impact until he crashed into a table and knocked a crystal vase to the floor. The vase smashed into thousands of shards as Edison slowly rocked forward and impacted the floor with a resounding thud—his eyes open in a blank stare.

Erica went to Jason, who stood rigid, the gun in his hand, his finger tight around the trigger.

"Jason?" Erica said, quietly. "It's okay. Let me have the gun."

Erica reached out and placed her hand on the weapon. Jason held it with a vice-like grip. She strained to pry the gun loose from his hand, and after several attempts, Jason relaxed enough that she pried the weapon from him.

"Holy shit! I just killed him," Jason said, shaken. "My life's over. I'm going to fucking jail."

"Jason, calm down."

"We gotta call the police," Jason said frightened.

"Jason, listen to me. Focus. Take a deep breath."

Jason took several deep breaths.

"Don't worry." Erica said calmly, "The cops will bag the brass casings for evidence, and when they check with the FBI, they'll find that it's the same type of ammo used by the Serbian Secret Police."

Erica shoved Jason towards the back door of the house. "You should've just let me kill him."

Erica stored her equipment in her car as Jason watched, still on an adrenaline rush.

"I've never shot anyone before," Jason said blandly. "I think I'm going to be sick."

"We don't have time for that," Erica replied.

"What do we do now?" a confused Jason asked.

"We've got to get out of here, first. I suggest you get a hotel room for the night. There could be someone watching your house."

"Do you think?" Jason said, his head turned to look for anything that might indicate he was in danger.

"I don't know. I'm just thinking you should be careful," Erica said, closing her car trunk. "You better get a move on before someone sees you. You got what you wanted. You know what happened to Walker and Gregory. I've still got a job to do. I made a mistake by letting you get involved with this.

"Listen, Jason. I'm a hired killer. Assassins and journalist don't mix. I'm a necessary evil, but an evil none-the-less. This will never work out. Just go write your prize-winning story. I'm only going to bring you trouble," Erica said as she turned to get into her car.

Jason stood for a moment looking at Erica.

"So . . . that's it?" Jason said, shrugging his shoulders. "Just like that, we're done?"

"Just like that—short and sweet. It's for the best."

"But I just killed a man!" Jason exclaimed.

Erica opened her car door and slid in behind the wheel.

"Yeah! I know. If you hadn't, I would have. We'll always have that."

The engine started, and Erica immediately pulled away from the curb, leaving Jason standing by the side of the road as he watched her taillights disappear into the night.

26

I'm sorry it had to be this way

THE CLOCK on the dashboard showed seven thirty when Erica parked her car just a few blocks from the Global Energies building. Erica exited her car and with purpose walked toward the Global building. She reached into her pocket, pulled out her cellphone and dialed.

"Hello," Franklin said.

"Franklin."

"You ready?"

"Just a block away."

"Hold on," Franklin said.

Erica hung on the line for nearly a minute before Franklin's voice sounded in her ear.

"I'm in. Go to the service entrance in the rear of the building. You can get to it by taking the alley on the left side of the building."

"Got it. Stay on the line. I'll tell you when I'm there," Erica said as she walked briskly down the street.

She made her way to the left of the building entrance and found the alley that led to the service entrance. The security camera had not been replaced and still inoperative.

"I'm at the service entrance," Erica whispered into her phone.

"Give me a sec. You'll hear a buzz, and the lock will open," Franklin said into Erica's ear.

Erica waited only a moment before the door buzzed and she slid in without making a sound.

"I'm in."

Erica briskly slipped down the corridor, and in just moments, she stood in front of the elevator door. "I'm there."

"I'm sending the elevator down," Franklin said. "When the door opens, I'm going to take out the camera. When I say now, get in and take the elevator to the lobby."

"Got it."

Erica quietly inched along the corridor of the lobby after the service elevator delivered her there. Her body, pressed tightly against the wall, kept her unobserved by the security cameras. "I'm at the main lobby elevators," Erica said.

"I'm going to cut out the cameras. The executive elevator is by itself across from the lobby elevators. Move now!"

Erica dashed across the floor to the executive elevator. The doors opened just as she stopped in front. She slipped in just a split second before the lobby security cameras came back on line and pressed herself against the back elevator wall as the doors took an eternity to close.

"I'm in the elevator, Franklin."

"Give me a minute; I need to run a program to find a code for you to punch in."

Erica's back leaned against the elevator as she waited for Franklin to come back with the code. One minute passed, then two minutes. Erica glanced at her watch; nearly three minutes had gone by with no word from Franklin.

Stuck in the elevator, Erica had not a clue as to what awaited her outside the elevator doors, in case she had to open them and try another route. Erica took a deep breath, in an attempt to calm herself.

"Come on Franklin . . . Franklin! Can you hear me? You still there?" Erica said as she tapped her earpiece.

Erica softly banged her head against the elevator wall. I love you too much, Jason—too much to put you in that situation again. So I need to let you go, Erica told herself as she glanced at her watch again.

"Franklin? Can you hear me?" Erica whispered into her phone. Only static echoed in her ear.

"I'm sorry it had to be this way, Jason, but it was for your own good," Erica said, as she felt the operation about to go south.

27

The Ultimate Betrayal

ERICA REACHED TO PRESS the 'Open Door' button and make her escape when Franklin's voice crackled in her ear.

"You still with me?"

"Yes, I'm here. Jesus, Franklin, what happened to you?"

"I guess there's a bad signal there. You didn't respond to my first call.

"Make this quick."

"Try this code; six, three, nine, three, seven. The two floor buttons will light up."

Erica pressed the code into the keypad next to the elevator door. The two buttons above the keypad lit up. The top button corresponded to the penthouse and the lower to the executive offices. Erica pressed the lower one. The elevator sprang to life and began ascending.

"I'm on my way to the executive offices."

"There are stairs up to the suite just down the hall to your left. The elevator code will open the doors that are located in the stairwell."

"Good. I'll call you when I'm ready to get out of here," Erica said as she disconnected the call from Franklin. The elevator doors opened, and directly in front of Erica were two closed doors to the executive suite and mounted on the wall next to them a keypad to gain entry.

Erica leaned out, looked in either direction, and to her surprise, found an empty hallway with another set of office doors with a key entry pad.

Erica stepped out of the elevator and silently moved to the stairwell and as quietly as possible opened the door and slipped out onto the executive office landing. Slowly, she took one step at a time; Erica climbed the flight of stairs without making a sound on the metal staircase until she found herself standing at the door to the penthouse.

Erica entered the security code, and the door lock clicked open. Erica gently pushed the door open and peeked around the corner. The hall clear of anyone, Erica stepped into the penthouse. Thick-cut pile carpet covered the floor, allowing Erica to move silently down the hall to the first room she came to, a bedroom. Small and sparsely decorated, it gave the appearance of a guest room. As she moved further down the hall, she came to a larger bedroom. This one looked lived in; the dresser top held several personal items, and the walls decorated with expensive artwork.

Across the hall from the bedroom a spacious living area with a large entertainment center covering the far wall. The furniture in the room top quality, a thick, plush couch with four sitting chairs squared off the room. An antique coffee table with matching end tables held porcelain antique vases. Original artwork hung from the walls, depicting outdoor scenes. Just beyond the living area a dining room and off to the left of the dining area a kitchen. Erica surveyed the area and found no one. She continued cautiously down the hall, where she could see a room closed off by large double doors, the door to the right partially open. Erica headed in that direction and could hear a male voice come from inside. The man spoke with a perceptible Serbian accent to someone on the phone.

Erica crept up to the door and listened at the opening. The person inside responded with, "yes," "ahs," and "hmmms" to the unheard caller. Erica peeked around the door and peered into the room. The office, spacious with large windows, overlooked the city on three sides of the room.

A large liquor cabinet with a sink to the left of the entrance, stocked with at least fifty bottles of various beverages and a small refrigerator at the end of the cabinet. Along the windows directly across from the entrance to the office sat a large glass conference table surrounded with leather chairs. To the right of the doors, along the wall, a large mahogany credenza, which held a cut crystal bowl filled with fresh fruit.

On either side of the bowl were fine china coffee cups and dessert plates. An original oil painting of a seventeenth-century aristocrat dressed in a red silk outfit complete with white, powdered wig, hung over the credenza. At the far end of the office stood an excessively large mahogany desk with a massive leather office chair behind it and standing next to the chair, gazing out the window, Zubin Ratko, aka, Andrus Skoffski. Erica oozed into the room without a sound. Skoffski finished his call, and before he turned to replace his desk phone on its cradle, the metallic sound of the office door clicking shut startled him. Skoffski turned with a lurch to the sound and nearly dropped the phone when he saw Erica standing next to the door.

"Who the hell are you, and how did you get in here?" a frightened Skoffski demanded.

"I've been looking for you for a long time," Erica evenly said.

"I'm calling security," Skoffski threatened, as his hand reached for the phone console.

In a microsecond, Erica had her pistol up and fired a single round that hit the phone console and sent it flying off the desk and slamming into the window behind it. Skoffski stood frozen in fear with the phone receiver still in his hand, the cord swinging loosely.

"What do you want?" Skoffski questioned as he dropped the receiver from his hand.

Erica slowly and deliberately stalked Skoffski, her pistol in her gloved hand held steadily at his belly.

"Who are you?" he asked as he backed up against the window, still unsettled.

Erica stopped at the edge of the desk, directly in front of Skoffski.

"You don't recognize me?" she asked.

Skoffski's eyes explored Erica's face intently, stopping at her eyes.

"Something about you is familiar, but I don't know who you are?"

"Does this help?" Erica said, as she unbuttoned the top two buttons of her blouse and pulled the collar off her neck to reveal her heart-shaped birthmark.

Skoffski's forehead tightened, formed a deep, vertical crease above his nose. "I remember that birthmark. But I thought . . ."

"No, I'm not dead. I am Adrijana Sekulic. Today is judgment day. You will pay for what you did to my parents, you piece of shit."

"You kill me now, and you'll never know who was really behind the killing of your parents," Skoffski pleaded.

"Then who was it? Vukuvic?"

"No. He's nothing."

"Who is it?" demanded Erica.

"Milosevic. He's behind everything."

"President Milosevic?" a shocked Erica asked. "I don't believe it."

"Your father getting close to the truth. He told Milosevic everything he had uncovered. Money being funneled out of programs for the schools and hospitals and being put into foreign banks," Skoffski said.

Erica lowered her gun, as the information seeped into her brain—the ultimate betrayal. Her father's most trusted friend set him up.

"Milosevic knew that time was short, so we had to move fast. The assassination attempt? Just a ruse to get your father to let his guard down," a placid Skoffski stated. "Do you think I would have been able to escape if Milosevic wasn't helping me?"

"So, that's how you knew of my father's movements?"

"All except where you and your father disappeared to. He told no one that location. Milosevic knew that as long as your father was alive, we were all in danger."

"Where is he now?" Erica asked firmly.

Skoffski turned his desk chair, sat down, his movements slow and exaggerated so as not to startle Erica.

"I asked you a question."

Skoffski rocked back in his chair and brought his hands up, fingertips together, and rested his forefingers against his upper lip.

"He's in hiding. This is where we make a deal," Skoffski bargained. "His current contact information is in the wall safe, inside the liquor cabinet."

"Open it," Erica ordered.

"The deal is, I give you the information, and you let me leave here, unharmed."

Erica, conflicted by the change of events, thought for a moment. Skoffski wasn't the person who directly betrayed her father. Milosevic now became her prime objective. Milosevic was the key. Skoffski could wait for another day, but Erica knew that day would eventually come.

"You have my word," Erica relented. "Now get me the information."

Skoffski eased himself from his chair and stepped to the liquor cabinet with Erica just four steps behind him. He opened the double doors and removed a silver ice bucket from the center shelf, then slid open the panel the bucket had been covering. Behind the panel the black metal door of a wall safe. Skoffski spun the combination dial to the left and then to the right. Grasped the chrome handle on the door and twisted the lever down. The door swung open. As Erica watched closely, Skoffski withdrew a four-inch by six-inch, black leather book.

"The information is in here," Skoffski said as he turned to Erica.

With a flick of his wrist, Skoffski tossed the book at Erica's face. The book came towards Erica in a flash, and her natural reflex action caused her to turn her head away as the book flew by her. In that instant, Skoffski had his hand inside the safe, his fingers wrapped around a small pistol.

Erica saw the motion of Skoffski's hand as it emerged from the dark space inside the safe. Erica fired, hitting Skoffski in the upper right thigh, where the bullet smashed into his femur, causing him to double over in agony, unable to level his gun to fire. In the blink of an eye, Erica stood next to Skoffski. Her left hand grasped his gun as she backhanded him with her pistol across his face. Skoffski fell to the floor. Erica twisted the gun in his hand until he could no longer hold onto it. She ripped the gun from him and hit him again across the face with her pistol.

"You're a fool," Erica claimed. "I'm a person of my word, and I would have let you go unharmed."

Skoffski put his hand on his bleeding cheekbone.

"Now you're going to tell me where Milosevic is hiding."

"Why would I do that?" Skoffski asked, grunting the words through agonizing pain.

"By the time I get through with you, you'll be begging me to kill you, or you can tell me what I want to know and maybe you'll get to a doctor before you bleed out."

Skoffski looked at the wound on his thigh. It hurt, but not bleeding that badly.

"I'll give you one more chance to tell me where to find Milosevic," Erica warned, punctuating each word.

Skoffski didn't look up. He just lay on the floor, his eyes focused on his wound. Erica pointed her pistol and fired one round, hitting Skoffski in the left thigh. Skoffski screamed out in pain.

"Tell me, or I'll keep putting bullets in you," demanded Erica as Skoffski rolled on the floor in agony.

Erica slammed her booted foot down on Skoffski's left ankle, stopping his rolling motion. She bent over and with the hot barrel of the silencer; she probed the gaping wound in Skoffski's left thigh. Skoffski let out another excruciating scream. Erica let up on the pressure before Skoffski passed out from the pain. Erica didn't repeat her question; she just squeezed off another round just below Skoffski's knee.

"Stop!" Skoffski screamed. "I'll tell you what you want to know."

"Where is Milosevic?" Erica yelled.

"Dubai. He's in Dubai," Skoffski moaned.

"Dubai?" Erica asked.

"The Secret Service had been looking for him since he stepped down from the government and they discovered what he had done."

Erica stood for a long moment, processing all the information she had just discovered.

"What are you going to do to me?" a shaking Skoffski asked, as he looked up at her.

Erica pointed her pistol at the center of his forehead then dropped her arm down to her side.

"You're not worth another bullet," Erica said as she turned and walked out of the door. "You'll be dead before I get to the lobby."

Skoffski struggled to get to his feet, but he had lost too much blood and just collapsed to the floor, passed out cold from the pain.

Erica made her way back to the stairs and to the elevators. Once inside the elevator, she called Franklin.

"Everything okay?" Franklin asked.

"It's all good. I'm in the elevator going down to the lobby."

"Stay with me. I'll knock out the cameras as soon as you're ready."

The elevator stopped at the lobby floor.

"I'm ready."

"Hold on" Franklin said. "Three, two, one. Go now!"

Erica waited for the elevator door to open then silently traveled along the corridor and to the service elevator unnoticed. Once in the service elevator it was less than a minute when she emerged onto the loading dock. Erica walked in a normal manner to her car and was on her way home, for the first time she could breathe easy after the tense ordeal.

28

Tell Me You Don't Love Me

JASON STOPPED at a neighborhood bar in West Hollywood for a drink. All Jason could think about, Erica. All that had transpired over the last two days, his feelings for her imbedded deep into his soul. He wanted and needed her—that apparent, but did he know which Erica he need and wanted. After several cocktails, Jason decided to summon the nerve to confront her and find out just who is the real Erica. The woman that touched his heart, the woman he met that first night when she scratched his car—somewhere, under all the lies, under all the deception, was that woman, the woman he fell in love with.

As Jason drove up into the Mount Washington area, he tried to think of the right words to say, but none would make themselves available.

He stopped in front of Erica's home and sat in the car for a moment; his nerve had waned during the long drive, and now he felt apprehensive.

Lights were seen burning from inside the house as he sat with the motor running for more than five minutes, unable to get out of the car and walk up to Erica's front door. Finally giving in to his fears, Jason put the car in gear and started back down the hill, to return home with the possibly of never seeing Erica again. The word "never" echoed in his brain. If it was "never," it would be on his terms. Jason turned the car around and drove back up the hill with renewed determination.

The doorbell chimed as Erica sat at her small kitchen table staring at the frozen dinner she had just taken out of the freezer.

Wearily, she turned and went to the door. Through the peephole, she saw Jason, as he stood demoralized at her threshold.

"What do you want?" Erica quipped as she opened the door.

"I'd like to talk to you."

"Not now, Jason. It's not a good time,"

"I just don't know what to do about you."

"You don't have to do anything." Erica answered.

"I'm not sure what to think," a confused Jason said.

"Then stop thinking,"

"I don't know how I feel about you anymore. All these lies."

"I explained that. You need to accept that it's over. You should just go and forget about this. It will only get you into trouble. You should go home and write your story. You've got a scoop."

Jason couldn't find words to say that conveyed what he felt. He turned to walk away then stopped.

"What are you going to do?" Jason asked.

"That's none of your business," Erica replied as she started to close the door.

Jason looked at her for a long moment then turned and walked away again. Erica watched for a moment then shut the door.

Erica walked back to the couch and crumbled onto it, exhausted. As hard as she tried, she couldn't keep the tears from flowing. Erica's emotions erupted like a volcano as she sobbed uncontrollably.

The news of Zubin Ratko, alias Andrus Skoffski, hit the wire services the subsequent morning. According to the news, police suspected a professional assassination. Information, already coming out, that Skoffski was a man wanted by the Serbian Secret Service, killed by a Serbian team.

Jason wrote all night composing his story, which news outlets picked up all over the world. Jason's report had the most comprehensive facts regarding the murder of David Edison and his bodyguards. It read as though he actually could have been present during the crime.

The state department now up in arms, furious with Serbia for conducting an operation on U.S. soil without notifying them sent a scathing memo to the ambassador. The Serbian government although pleased with Skoffski's demise, denied it had any responsibility in the operation but that considered business-as-usual for Serbia.

Jason's piece included the practice of Global Energies shipping old, defective equipment to drilling sites and claiming that the equipment new. This prompted federal inspectors to set up an emergency inspection tour of all drilling sites owned or associated with Global Energies to insure that all equipment used was in good, working condition.

Jason's information led police to the Global facility in Lancaster where Paulina Gregory and Peter Walker's bodies were recovered. Jason spend most of his time on the phone day and night talking with reporters and filing follow-up articles for three days straight, but through it all, his mind on Erica.

The doorbell rang as Erica packed her bags. She had already cleared out her Santa Monica apartment and in the process of doing the same at her house. Erica's heart sank to the pit of her stomach when she saw Jason on her doorstep.

"Jason! What are you doing here?"

"You've been on my mind every minute. This can't end like this," Jason pleaded.

"We've been over this, Jason. You need to leave me alone."

"Just give me five minutes, please."

Erica stepped back and allowed Jason to enter. The first thing to catch Jason's eyes the state of the interior of the home.

"It looks like you're moving."

"Yes, I'm moving. There's nothing here for me anymore," Erica said indignantly.

"I've thought about this for days now. I've gotten everything I ever thought I wanted. I've broken a huge story that will probably win me a Pulitzer. I can write my own ticket."

"I'm happy for you. Thanks for coming by to share," Erica quipped sarcastically.

"What I'm trying to say is that none of that matters anymore. You matter. I love you, and I don't want you to go," Jason pleaded passionately. "I want to be with you."

"It won't work, Jason. I thought about it too. We come from two different worlds."

"It doesn't matter anymore, Erica. I understand what it must have been like for you. I felt it too, when Edison told me what he did to Paulina. I wanted to kill him. I'm glad I killed him."

"It just won't work. Our relationship started with a lie. You will always be wondering if I'm telling you the truth or not."

"That's not true, Erica," Jason cautioned, as he moved to her. "I put myself in your shoes. You weren't given the facts. You were manipulated and lied to by Edison. The person you thought you were after was some self-absorbed journalist who would let innocent people die just to further his career."

Erica looked Jason straight in the eye.

"From what they told you, I was some kind of worthless asshole who deserved what he got," Jason said as he waited for Erica to give some kind of response. "Am I right?"

"Yes, you're right, but—"

"There are no 'buts,' Erica. That's what you thought. I can understand that. Now you know who I really am, and I know who you really are. You're not evil. You exact justice when the system can't. The real evils are corporations who murder and mistreat the innocent, who are supposed to be protected by the politicians and our courts. You are necessary but you're not evil."

"You can put aside all the lies?" Erica asked, wishing this could all be true.

Is he really capable to put all this aside? Can he no longer feel betrayed? Erica thought to herself.

"I've already forgotten those lies. I don't think it matters how we met; it's just that we did meet. What matters to me is that I fell in love with you from the first. If you can tell me that you don't love me, then I'll go. If all this was just part of the act, the role you played, then I will leave here now and won't bother you ever again."

Jason and Erica stood staring at each other—neither said a word. Erica knew that he told her the cold, hard truth. Once he walked out that door, she knew that she would never see this man again, this man that brought meaning to her life again, this man who stood before her professing his love for her, this man whom she fell desperately in love with.

"Say you don't love me, Erica," Jason demanded. "Say it, and I'm out of your life forever."

Erica knew that telling the truth at this moment in time could be the worst thing to happen to Jason Brent. "You don't know what you're asking Jason," Erica warned.

"I do know what I'm asking," Jason assured, as he put his hands on her shoulders. "Tell me you don't love me."

"I can't," Erica replied, as she stared at her shoes. "If I told you I didn't love you, I'd be lying."

A slight smile appeared at the corner of her mouth. "I know how much you hate it when I lie to you."

"Then you do love me," Jason exclaimed as he took her into his arms.

"Yes, I love you, Jason Brent. I love you."

Jason slid his arms around her and kissed her hard on the lips. Erica kissed him back. They separated, and she looked him directly in the eye.

"Are you sure, Jason?' she asked. "I have to tell you; this won't be easy."

"Are you getting all melodramatic on me now? I'm more sure than I've ever been about anything," Jason professed as he kissed her again.

He picked her up and Erica wrapped her legs around his waist as she tore at his shirt; their lips locked together as Jason's hands groped her underneath her blouse. The touch of his hot hands on her flesh excited her as they backed into the bedroom, her hands clutching fists full of Jason's shirt. Their lips separated, and Erica looked at Jason like a hungry tigress eyeing a wounded gazelle. She bit his lower lip, hard, just hard enough to induce a low, guttural moan.

Erica ripped open the top of his shirt, exposing his chest. She explored the top of his left pectoral muscle with her tongue, tantalizing him as he ran his hand up to her luscious breasts, enticing, arousing—Erica sank her teeth into Jason's nipple.

Jason, experienced an arousal like none he had ever experienced before, threw himself and Erica onto the bed, he on top of her.

Jason straddled her, tore at Erica's blouse, ripped it off, and threw it across the room. Erica stared up at Jason, breathing deeply. Her breasts heaved up and down as she watched him grasp her bra from the front and rip it in two, her glorious mounds released into his hot hands.

"I want you now, Jason," Erica said lustily.

"You already got me," replied Jason as his warm, wet mouth covered her nipple.

Erica dug her fingers into Jason's hair, holding his head tightly against her as he kissed her body then moved down, tracing her pelvic bone with his tongue, enticing Erica to unleash a scream of exquisite pleasure.

They clawed and scratched each other in magnificent ecstasy as Erica reached the peak of sexual delight several times before she rolled Jason on his back and aggressively mounted him.

The sexual gymnastics continued for two hours, each of the lovers taking turns in pleasuring the other until they entangled themselves in the final throws of passion, each collapsing in blissful exhaustion.

* * * * *

Erica awoke wrapped in Jason's arms. The bedroom dark, as the sun had set nearly an hour earlier. Jason stirred then rolled over and kissed Erica on the lips as he caressed her face with his hand.

"Hungry?" Erica asked.

"Starving. I haven't eaten in days."

"I'll make us some eggs," Erica said as she slipped out of bed.

They ate hardily and held hands across the table. Jason felt as though he became himself again, strong and confident, ready to take on the world.

"How do you like Paris?" Jason asked.

"Paris is nice. I like Paris."

"I've got a little apartment I own there. I can take a position at the Paris office. We can settle down there. My job pays well."

"We don't need money, Jason," Erica said. "I've got plenty."

"How much is plenty?" Jason asked mockingly.

"Millions."

Jason stopped mid-bite.

"Did you say millions?"

"About ten, I think."

Jason choked on his food.

"What?"

"I've got more work to do."

"Work?" Jason inquired.

"Milosevic's the man behind it all. He's somewhere in Dubai. With your contacts and my skills, we can track him down. He's the last link in the chain."

Erica set her fork down, leaned back in her chair and brought her hands up fingertip to fingertip in the steeple position. She looked straight into Jason's eyes. "I want you to come with me. What do you say?"

Jason stared at Erica, his mouth half-open, unable to process the latest development in his relationship with Erica. Jason repeated her words in his head to make sure he understood. She, about to embark on another manhunt, and he would be her accomplice. How could he even think of such a thing? He was no spy. He had no training in this kind of work. This is nothing less than insane, Jason thought. It's totally out of the question.

His mother had always warned him to never eat spicy foods after eight o'clock, saying, "It will give you bad dreams." Jason started to chew again, wondering if he would awake from this bad dream.

29

Another Day To Die

ERICA DROVE the dark streets of Dubai after a long day of running down leads. Three months had passed since she left Los Angeles under the name of Leonora Kashan, a photojournalist documenting the boon in tourism in and around the United Arab Emirates city. Her credentials allowed her access to all areas without suspicion.

Erica had hit several walls in the search for Branislav Milosevic. The Serbian Secret Service trail had gone cold for years, but her old friend Dimitri had made some inquiries. The Serbs were tight-lipped on any information that concerned the former president, so this would be a long and hard investigation, nothing new for Erica. She was in this for the duration. Erica turned her car into the parking structure of the Sand Castles Properties complex, a modern assembly of elegantly appointed condominiums that overlooked the Dubai Sailing Club Marina.

Erica parked her car, took the elevator to the residential level, and meandered along the walkway to the two-bedroom condo that served as her headquarters.

She inserted her key into the lock, and opened the door to the dark, quiet apartment. She turned on the small lamp that rested on a table just inside the door, in the spacious foyer. The foyer decorated with a colorful tile floor, had a narrow rug running along the length of the hallway.

To the right of the entrance stood an oak hall tree with a beveled mirror in the center. Erica slipped off her leather jacket and hung it on the only free wood dowel. She rubbed her back with her hands to relieve the stiffness, then walked through the living room, passed the large, brown leather couch, stepping between it and the beautifully restored steamer trunk that served as a coffee table, and into the kitchen.

She stopped suddenly when movement caught her eye. The sheer drapes that hung over the balcony doors fluttered in the breeze. Erica went to the doors to discover that they were open just about four inches. She closed the door and locked it then strolled through the kitchen, passed by the dark guest bedroom, its door wide open. Erica paused and stepped out of her shoes; her feet sunk deep into the plush carpeting. Then she carefully stepped up to the master bedroom.

The door, slightly ajar, enabled Erica to stick her head in by just moving the door open a few inches. The blinds were open, and enough ambient light gave the room a gray feel, just enough light to see the shapes of the furniture that decorated the room. Erica could just make out a form on the bed. She slowly bent down and set her shoes on the carpeted floor then rose again, stopping with her knees bent in a 30-degree angle. With a swift springing leap, Erica came down on the bed with such force, the form bounced into the air.

"Jesus, Erica. What the hell was that?"

"It's Leonora, remember?"

"Yeah, I remember," Jason responded, still a bit groggy. "I'm starting to get the hang of it."

"Good," Erica responded as she kissed him on the lips.

"How did it go today?" Jason asked, yawning.

"Nothing panned out—all dead ends."

"I made you dinner. It's in the oven. I'll set the table." Jason rolled out of bed and turned on the light in the bedroom. "Wash up. Then you can eat," Jason said as he headed for the kitchen.

"Didn't you eat already?" Erica yelled.

"No. I wanted to wait for you," he called back.

Erica slid her hands behind her head and stared at the ceiling. A smile crossed her face as she heard Jason bang plates together setting the table. A warm feeling came over her as she lay there. This was something she'd gotten used to and something she liked. For the first time in a long time, her obsession to avenge her parents' death no longer paramount in her mind.

"Let's eat!" Jason yelled from the dining room.

"I'm coming, my love!" Erica hollered as she looked at the huge diamond ring on her finger then rolled off the bed.

The aroma of chicken marsala wafted through the apartment as Erica strode into the kitchen and came up behind Jason, wrapped her arms around him as he heaped portions onto the plates on the counter.

"I love you," she said, squeezing Jason as hard as she could. Erica released her hug, and Jason turned to face her.

"I love you, too," he whispered as he kissed her passionately on her lips.

Erica smiled that special smile when the two separated from the kiss and backed away, raised her left hand and waved her index finger in a 'follow me' fashion as she continued to back out of the kitchen. Jason, a huge smile across his face, followed her to the bedroom.

"Chicken marsala tastes better cold anyway," Jason muttered as he unbuttoned his shirt.

As Erica backed her way into the bedroom, she thought to herself, As long as I have Jason, I'll be happy. Happy? That word never a part of her vocabulary before. But she was happy—happy that Jason was her husband and loved her, happy to be alive. Milosevic would have to wait another day to die.

THE END

www.ingramcontent.com/pod-product-compliance
Lightning Source LLC
Chambersburg PA
CBHW071223250626
47163CB00001B/77